Rarely does a story carry itself while teaching eternal truths, but such is the case with author Jim Norman's first published work. Set in Central Oregon, although believable anywhere, the truths of God's Word are fully taught and the reader is drawn into the lives of the characters. These faithful of the local church begin to notice something: God is alive and well and waiting to commune with those who diligently seek Him. They find the answer to the question: What does it mean to have Christ in us, the hope of Glory? The characters take us through the mysteries that have been lost to the church for many centuries but that God has kept until such a time as now. The story may be fictional, but when the truths expressed within are grasped, even by a remnant of today's churchgoers, this story could be a narrative right out of the Book of Acts, happening in your own local church.

~ Drew Anker

BEFORE THE *Trumpet Blows*

JIM NORMAN

Belleville, Ontario, Canada

Library and Archives Canada Cataloguing in Publication

Norman, Jim, 1960-
     Before the trumpet blows : the rising of the glorious church / Jim Norman.

Includes bibliographical references.
ISBN 1-55306-977-3

     1. Christian fiction, American. I. Title.

PS3614.O736B43 2005   813'.6   C2005-903932-9

For more information or
to order additional copies, please contact:

Jim Norman
jnorman@bendcable.com

Guardian Books is an imprint of *Essence Publishing,* a Christian Book Publisher dedicated to furthering the work of Christ through the written word.. For more information, contact:
20 Hanna Court, Belleville, Ontario, Canada K8P 5J2
Phone: 1-800-238-6376 • Fax: (613) 962-3055
E-mail: publishing@essencegroup.com
Internet: www.essencegroup.com

WORD OF PROPHECY

*For there are new days about to come upon the earth.
And it will be, as you're sitting and observing My
return, as if I pulled the veil back, and the curtain
shall be removed. And you shall see the intention I
have for the earth that you live upon, and you shall see
grand and glorious things—things that men have only
been able to guess about; things that men have only
been able to dream about. But behold, when I pull
back the curtain, you shall behold Me, and you shall
see Me face to face and shall say, "It's above what I
thought; it's beyond what I dreamed; it's above what I
could have imagined." For the Glory of the Lord is
greater in the latter days than ever former considered
in the early days. For the Glory of the Lord will be
manifestation of Me in the place where you live; you'll
see. And the Glory of the Lord will be an overpowering, overabundant thing not suspected and not
expected. For today I say it would be as a thief in the
night, and even though you know the times and the*

seasons, you know the whereabouts and the openings of the Lord, this shall be beyond those splendid things that you've imagined. This shall be above the glorious things that you've thought of. For it shall be a revealing of Me, says the Lord.

Word of the Lord delivered by Pastor Trudy Roberts
Sunday morning service, October 5, 2003

There are a few people that I want to express appreciation
for, the first being my Lord Jesus,
who is full of love and goodness.

I also thank my loving wife, without whose love and
encouragement I never would have started this project or
even finished it.

Two others who were always encouraging me to continue
were Steve and his wife Karen,
and I thank them for their support.

The last two that I want to acknowledge are my pastors,
Jerry and Trudy.
Without them and their love and commitment to Jesus,
I wouldn't have had in me all the things necessary
to write this story.

I love you all and thank you for being there for me.

INTRODUCTION

Before I started writing this story, I felt that there was a need for the Body of Christ as a whole to be made aware of the goodness of God—the goodness of God that Jesus revealed and walked in. There are many Christians who are already aware of what I'm writing in this story, but there are even more who are not. In these days, there are many Christians who have no hope that God will intervene on their behalf in their trials and hardships. My deepest desire was to write a story that would instill in them a new and living hope to believe for God's help, with all of the appropriate Scriptures to nurture and cultivate that hope. Jesus revealed the heart of God toward people and what God would be willing to do to help them out of their troubles. I know that God's people will go through many trials and hardships in their walks with Him, but the Bible is abundantly clear about where God stands when it comes to sickness, disease, poverty, and lack for His people. Although we may go through these situations, Jesus revealed that there is victory to be found as we believe in God's divine help.

Jesus never turned anyone away who came to Him for healing, and He trained His disciples to be just like Him. He said in Luke 6:40, *"A disciple is not above his teacher, but everyone who is perfectly trained will be like his teacher."* He also said to them, in Matthew 10:7-8, *"And as you go, preach, saying, 'The kingdom of heaven is at hand.' Heal the sick, cleanse the lepers, raise the dead, cast out demons. Freely you have received, freely give."* Also, in Mark 9:23, *"If you can believe, all things are possible to him who believes."* And again, in Matthew 19:26, He said, *"With men this is impossible, but with God all things are possible."* This story was written to reveal what is possible to those who believe and who will take God at His word.

Although the doctrines of God's goodness are ever-lasting, I chose to use the setting of the last-days' Church and its Holy-Spirit-led rise to power to present all of God's goodness in all of its glory. I've set forth in the story, along with His goodness, the belief of the Glorious Church, which He will present to Himself, without spot or wrinkle, on that day He calls us heavenward (Ephesians 5:27). As the Glorious Church comes to completion, His manifold wisdom will be *"made known by the church to the principalities and powers in the heavenly places, according to the eternal purpose which He accomplished in Christ Jesus our Lord"* (Ephesians 3:10-11). Before the end, all of the spiritual hosts will see and know that God is able to overcome all the schemes and tactics of Satan.

But I also want to say this: these things will only come to pass as all of us do our own part, seeking God with all of our hearts so that we will know His voice when He speaks to us and gives our directions. We must all step up and take our places in the Body to strengthen the whole, and then God's

Glory will be manifested to all. The greater our unity, the more we will be able to be used by God to accomplish His goals in these last days. You can read about this in Ephesians 4:11-24. When you read that text, pray about it and meditate on those Scriptures. You will begin to see the basis for this story.

There are enough Scripture references throughout the book to back up all of the doctrines that are set forth in the story, so open up your Bible and read them for yourself, asking God to open the eyes of your understanding that you may be encouraged to believe in His goodness and His willingness to help you. So, dear reader, read the story and enjoy.

In Christ,
Jim Norman

CHAPTER ONE

"What was that, Lord?"

"Take five thousand dollars out of your account today."

What do you want me to do with it?"

"Wait."

After prayer and over breakfast, he told his wife, Linda, what the Lord wanted him to do. She became excited over the prospect of helping someone again in a very special way. There was a time when they couldn't help people as much as they had wanted to, but now it was pure joy. Because of God's blessing in their life, they were now able to help others in ways they had never dreamed about. It was one thing to see that someone had a need and to help them out, but it was entirely different when the Lord told them to help someone, even total strangers, and actually gave them the details of the situation. It added the aspect of the supernatural, or divine intervention, not for her or Mac's sake but for the sake of the recipient.

So after his Bible study time and some phone calls, Mac went to the bank and withdrew the specified amount. He was excited about it, for that amount of money would be quite a blessing for whoever received it. He knew God well enough to know that whatever He wanted him to do, it was for the best. When he obeyed, everything always worked out, and he received such satisfaction from it that it was always worth it. Trusting and obeying God's commands always brought blessing to somebody, but for himself it was an overwhelming joy just to see others getting a blessing. There was such a special blessing in helping others to see God working on their behalf that Mac would never disobey the Lord's commands to do so.

"Keep it with you today."

After the bank visit, he drove over to the church to talk to his pastor. He was the godliest man Mac had ever met, always seeking God's heart on everything he did. Mac wanted to talk over a few things with him, about the Lord and the way things were changing during his prayer time. God's Presence was becoming so strong while he was in prayer the last couple of weeks that he wanted to see if the pastor had any insight on why it was happening.

The two of them had become close friends twelve years earlier, and Pastor John was the one who had led Mac into the deeper things of God: to press into the Spirit of God, to seek the God of all creation diligently, and to know His voice above all others. God said that those who seek Him diligently would find Him and that He would reward them for it. Because of Pastor John, Mac and Linda had found out how true that was.

Pulling into the parking lot, he saw that the pastor was in, and also the maintenance man and the secretary. There were also several other cars in the lot, two of which he didn't recognize.

The pastor was in counseling with a couple that was going to be married soon. All of the couples that received his counseling and applied it to their marriages stayed married, and happily so. Of course there would be problems, but it always came down to applying God's wisdom to their everyday living. That would see them through the tough days as well as the good ones. A few couples had eventually divorced, but most of those weren't even serving God now. If they had only applied the pastor's counseling and maintained a strong relationship with Jesus, they would still be married and serving God.

"Good morning, Mac," greeted the secretary, Julie.

"Good morning, Julie. Will the pastor be done soon?"

"Maybe another half hour. Are you going to wait?"

"No, that's all right. I just stopped in for a visit. I've got some errands to do this morning, so I'll just check in later, but you could let him know I stopped by."

"Okay, I'll do that. Have a blessed day."

"Thank you, and you also."

Stepping through the door, Mac saw the maintenance man, Joe, coming around the corner of the building. "Lord, is Joe the one today?"

"*No. Kevin.*"

"Hi, Joe. How are you today?"

"Good. Real good. The Lord just keeps on blessing me every day. I just don't know what He sees in me."

"A good heart, for one thing. He sees someone who loves Him and wants to please Him. In God's eyes, that is a precious thing," replied Mac.

Joe looked at Mac, searching his eyes. He saw what he always saw in Mac's eyes: sincerity.

"Thank you, Mac, I really appreciate that. Especially coming from you."

"You are certainly welcome, Joe. If you need anything, don't hesitate to ask."

"Time for me to go to work. Have a good day, Mac."

"I will." And I am looking forward to it, he thought. "You also."

He drove away, remembering how Joe came to be working at the church. He had walked into a morning service one Sunday, looking a little anxious, not sure of what to expect. It had been a long time since he had been in a church. But in the first five minutes he had been greeted by at least ten people giving him a very warm smile and handshake. The odd thing was, it felt like they were welcoming him as a loved one just returning from a long absence. There was sincerity in their voices and on their faces that he had not seen in a long time. When the singing service started, he looked around at the way the people were raising their hands and singing with joy and happiness. He had never seen anyone doing anything like that in churches he had attended when he was younger, but it brought a sense of knowing that these people knew God. They knew God in a way he had never dreamed about, and by the end of the praise portion of the singing, he was glad that he had come in. He began to feel like a weight was being lifted from him, and he started to enjoy singing the words about a loving and caring God.

When the music turned to worship, Joe felt an overwhelming Presence of something come into the sanctuary. He found himself weeping, not knowing why, except that that Presence seemed to be taking notice of him. Then the song leader asked anyone needing prayer to come forward to the altar. Joe found himself walking down the aisle, not really knowing why, but he felt that Presence pulling him forward. He knew he was not alone; there were others walking down all the aisles. In his entire life, Joe had never felt anything like that. He sensed that something very important, very profound, was about to take place in his life. As he neared the front of the sanctuary, he felt that Presence becoming stronger and stronger, and an overpowering fear began to rise in him, demanding that he turn around and run from the building.

He reached the altar, and as he was about to turn around to flee, a hand reached out and touched his arm. He froze in place as he felt an electric-like warmth coming from the hand and it began to spread throughout his body. The fear was suddenly gone, and he knew that the Spirit of the living God had touched him.

Joe's eyes were closed, tears streaming down his face, and he heard a voice speaking to him. *"You knew Me when you were a young boy, but as you became older you drifted away from Me. I made a promise to your grandmother that I would bring you back. Now I ask you, do you want to know Me again?"*

"Yes. Yes, Lord. I want you back in my life. Please forgive me.

"'You came here because I drew you by My Spirit. In a moment of desperation, you called to Me and asked, 'Where are You, God? There are so many churches.' You did not know why you came to this place, but I wanted to tell you something. It had to be told here so that you would know that I am here. This is not the only place that I am, but this is where I wanted you to meet My people, for I have a plan for your life and this is where you will get your training. My servants here have proven themselves faithful, and they will take you under their wing as a cherished son of Mine. When you are ready I will send you out,

but for now remember that I have called you by name, that you are My son, and that I love you.' Thus saith your God."

As Joe opened his eyes, he found himself looking into the face of Pastor John. It was the pastor's hand that was on his arm, and as he realized that this man was a total stranger, he knew that God had indeed spoken to him through this man. For he had spoken of things that no one else knew about him. As he looked into his eyes, he saw the love of God there, and he knew that this would be his home.

For two years Joe had been coming faithfully to the house of God, day by day drawing closer to God and learning His Word and His ways. He had left behind the drugs and alcohol, the womanizing and running to every party. The Spirit of God miraculously set him free from all of his vices on the day of his reconciliation. In the church he had met a good and godly woman and now had been married to her for nearly six months. They were very much in love, and both had the same heartbeat for God.

Recently, Joe had turned thirty-four. His bride, Peggy, was close behind at thirty-two. The day Joe went forward and gave his life to the Lord, God spoke to Peggy and told her, *"That man will serve Me wholeheartedly, and he will be your husband."* She never told a soul about what God had said to her concerning Joe until two months had gone by. One day Peggy was visiting with the pastor's wife, Kathy, when the subject turned to Peg's dating and trying to find a suitable man for a husband.

Kathy asked, "Have you had any leads on a husband yet? Whatever happened with that Stan you went out with?"

"Well, he just didn't work out. I found out that his walk with the Lord wasn't what he made it out to be. I had one marriage to a guy who was a heathen—I still have a few scars to prove it—and once is enough. But to tell you the truth, I have had a lead on another guy. The Spirit of God pointed him out one day and said that he will serve Him whole-heartedly. He also said that he would be my husband."

Kathy looked at Peggy, smiled, and asked, "Is it Joe?"

Peggy, slightly surprised, replied, "I should have known you would know that. But I have hardly spoken twenty words to him since he came to us. I've been praying about it but haven't had any direction yet on how to approach him."

"Have patience, Peggy. If the Lord told you, then He will guide you into it. Just don't rush it; Joe has some growing to do for now, and watching him learn about Jesus is really sweet," Kathy replied.

And so several months went by, with only minimal contact with Joe. Peggy made small talk with him and recommended books in the church library for him to read. Slowly, Peggy was able to help Joe with his understanding of the Bible, the principles of God, His attributes, and His character.

As Joe was learning of God from people, he was also praying and seeking God diligently in his private time. God promised in His Word that if His people would seek Him diligently, they would find Him. Thus Joe found God and developed a relationship with Him in the Spirit. Joe grew spiritually by leaps and bounds by applying himself to do so with all sincerity.

For years he had shared in all that the world had to offer and found himself empty, devoid of life, not even caring what happened. It was then that he had begun thinking of his grandmother, of her Christian faith, her continual reading of the Bible and praying. He remembered how strong she was when his grandpa died, how she helped his mother and his uncle with the grief of the loss of their dad.

She knew God. That was easy to tell. He remembered that as a boy he had walked in on his grandmother while she was praying one time, and although she was alone, it had seemed like there was someone in the room with her. He knew that there was more to life than just the things that you can see, but as time went by, turning into years, he was sidetracked from thinking about God. He went the way of the world and left God in his past, seeking only to fulfill his own desires.

An early marriage at age twenty-one lasted only two years, for he had turned into a selfish, cynical young man. He was more concerned about what his wife did wrong than what she did right, and soon she became very bitter towards him. When someone came along who began to compliment her, to encourage her, and to build up her self-esteem, it was a small step to falling in love with him and leaving Joe behind.

After the divorce, Joe's cynical side became dominant, and he never found a loving relationship again, although he did go through several short-term girlfriends. The last relationship ended in a drunken argument and the throwing of dishes and furniture. When the police showed up, he was taken to jail to cool off for the night. When Joe returned home the next day, his girlfriend and most of their stuff were gone. Joe spent the next several weekends getting drunk and then getting reprimands at work for showing up with a hangover. That last day on the job, a Monday, he showed up very late and with a terrible hangover. It was the last straw for the boss, and Joe was promptly fired. Joe couldn't remember the next five days because of the alcoholic blur he was living in, but on Saturday when he awoke, he began to take stock of his life. He didn't like what he saw.

Breaking down and sobbing, he began to pray. "God, where are You? There are so many churches, and I don't know where to go. I have made such a mess of my life, and I don't know what to do." It was then that Joe remembered his coworker Collice.

"*Yes.*"

Joe looked around to see if someone was behind him, but there was no one. What was that voice? he wondered.

Collice had tried to get him to go to a church over on Twelfth Street several times, but he had just blown her off. She had told him that the Presence of God was in the church services, but he just figured that she was a religious nut. But now that he was at the bottom, he was ready to try anything. Thinking back about his grandmother, he knew that it would be in the church that he would find what he was looking for.

That very afternoon was the turning point for the direction of Joe's life. He decided that, no matter what, he was going to be in that church service the following day. And now look at Joe—serving God wholeheartedly and enjoying it, married to a wonderful woman of God, working at a steady job at the church, living a life full of peace and joy. Joe had never been this happy in his entire life.

Mac was driving down the highway toward Bend, heading for the local home improvement store to pick up a few odds and ends to build a bookshelf. Thinking about Joe always brought a smile to his face. He had shared many dinners with Joe and attended Bible studies with him, so Mac had come to know much about him. Joe's was only one more success story in the Kingdom of God.

Mac walked into the store, looking at the overhead banners to find the aisle with the wood pieces he wanted. Meandering along, he noticed that the store was very busy. There were lots of people, and Mac liked to watch people.

Sometimes the Lord would point out someone and tell Mac something about him or her. On some occasions the Lord would even have Mac go up to them and speak to them, to tell them certain things about themselves that a stranger would have no way of knowing. Sometimes it would be a word of advice; at other times it would be a word of encouragement; still other times it would be a word of correction. Mac had been accepted and rejected numerous times, but mostly the people that the Lord would have him minister to would receive what he had to say.

Mac walked down the aisle of lumber and continued across the way to the finished oak section. As he looked over the different sizes, he noticed a man coming up the aisle in his direction. The man stopped and began looking over the hemlock moldings, then looked up and caught Mac's eyes on him. Mac noticed that the man looked a little weary and depressed; there was a look of worry about him.

Mac asked the Lord, "Is there something we can do for him, Lord?"

"Yes."

"What would you like me to do?"

"That is Kevin. He has been seeking Me for help. He is about to lose his house and his wife's car. The enemy has been attacking him to get him to go back on his faith, but he has held steadfast to Me. Go to him."

Two and a half weeks earlier, Kevin had come to his wits' end. It seemed like he couldn't even buy a job. He had just hung up the phone with his last prospective customer.

"I needed that job," he spoke aloud. He had been counting on that job to get himself caught up. In the last two months he had lost every job that he had bid on. His bills were long overdue, and now he just saw his last hope disappear. He hadn't wanted to sell any of his equipment, but maybe he had better start considering it, for he was running out of time. But, in his spirit, he just felt that he shouldn't sell anything, that God would provide for them.

"I am your hope." A still whisper nudged its way into his thinking.

"Yes. There is still the Lord. I will not give up. But how?"

Kevin walked into his office and closed the door. He had to pray right now; the despair was already growing, and he had to fight it before it had the chance to overtake his mind. He knelt down in the middle of the room and bent his head to the floor.

"God, I thank You that You are my God and that You call me son. I thank You and praise You for the salvation that I have in Jesus. Lord, I thank You that all my sins are forgiven and that You have cleansed my heart from all impurities. I ask now, Lord, for forgiveness for the despair that I have allowed in, and I ask for Your help in getting rid of it."

Kevin remained quiet for a while, thinking of how to pray about his situation. "Don't start praying religiously; be honest. God already knows what I need, so just ask for it."

"Lord," he began, "I need your help. I am out of money, and the bank is going to take our house and car if I don't come up with some money for the back payments I owe. I don't know how you can help me, but I believe You have a way. Lord, tell me if there is anything that I can do to solve this. Am I doing anything wrong? Lord, have I forgotten to do something? Lord, I need some wisdom. Your word says that if anyone lacks wisdom, let him ask of God, who gives to all liberally and without reproach. Well Lord, I am asking for wisdom. I need to know how to resolve this problem of not having any money to make my payments. I ask for mercy, Lord, with the bill collectors, and for grace in this time of need. In Jesus' name I ask. Amen."

As Kevin prayed, the despair began to dissipate, until all that was left was the peace of God.

Out of that newfound peace drifted another whisper. "*I Am the Lord Your Provider.*"

Two weeks went by, and nothing happened. No money came in, no new jobs, no inheritance from a long lost aunt. Kevin's wife was beginning to show the worry and fear of losing the house and the car. They were praying together daily, but it just seemed like they were getting nowhere. The deadline for the payments was coming up in three days, and he didn't see anything that looked promising. Except the Word. There was always a promise in the Word of God. "God said that He is my Provider. He said that He gives us the power to get wealth that He may establish His covenant in the earth. Let's see. Where is that Scripture verse? Isn't that in Deuteronomy? Is it chapter eight and verse eighteen?" He opened his Bible and looked it up. "Yes, there it is. And also God doesn't change; He is the same yesterday, today, and forever. If He said that He gives His people the power to get wealth, then He must want us to be able to get it, even today."

"Lord God, my time is running out. I only have three more days, so could You please hurry? You are my Provider," prayed Kevin.

With two days left, Kevin was reading about the unjust judge who helped out the persistent widow. So he knew that he had to be persistent to get his breakthrough. Sooner or later God would see to it that he would receive it, as long as he kept at it and believed for God's best. For God cared more about Kevin than the unjust judge cared for the widow. Persistence obtained good results, even from a judge who could care less about the one he helped, so how much more would the righteous judge, Jesus, help those He loves who are persistent in their seeking Him for a breakthrough?

Later in the afternoon, Kevin carried a large cardboard box filled with files from his office to stack in the garage. He opened the garage door and walked through, carrying the heavy box. He turned to step around his son's bicycle, and as he did so, the box pushed against a plank that was leaning against the wall. Before he knew it, the plank was sliding down the wall, and when it made contact with the window trim it broke right through it.

"Oh no! Just what I needed. The enemy likes to add insult to injury. Well, I praise You, God, for You are a firm foundation, and You will not fall or break apart."

Kevin and his wife prayed together that night, and both of them felt that God had heard their prayer. They thanked Him for the answer that was on the way. The following morning, they prayed together again and gave thanks to the Lord for their payments being made. Later in the morning the bank called, asking for payment on the house. Kevin told them he would be in later in the day, that the money was on the way. Kevin didn't know what to do, so he decided to run to the Home Depot before lunch and look for a piece of molding for the garage window.

On his drive over to the store, Kevin tried to pray along the way. He only had until the end of the business day to make his payments. He began to worry, and doubt began to take over his thinking. What was he going to do if he lost his house?

At that very moment, the Holy Spirit spoke to Kevin's wife, Sue, and told her to pray, right now, for Kevin's faith.

"Take authority over doubt and fear, for I am with you." For the next fifteen minutes she prayed as fervently as she knew how.

Kevin entered the store, still thinking about having to start over in a rental. He was beginning to feel guilty for bringing this onto his family; it must all be his fault for not doing something right. As he kept walking along, looking for the molding section, the blame just kept building and was about to overwhelm him.

Out of nowhere a whisper came. *"I have provided for you."*

At that moment it felt as though a great cloud was lifting from around him, and he started to feel better immediately. He knew that God had someone praying for him right then, and he began to praise God for deliverance just as he turned up the molding aisle.

He saw a man looking at the oak boards. He looked away, and then for some reason his attention was brought back to the man. There was something about him, a sense of something…godly. Kevin could feel the love of God emanating from this man, a very rare occurrence in his life. Something was going on. He could feel it. Looking again at the wood pieces, he tried not to look at the stranger. Only a few seconds had gone by when Kevin noticed the man coming toward him. As he got closer, Kevin could sense the Presence of God. When the stranger stopped in front of him, Kevin looked up and into his eyes.

CHAPTER TWO

"Hello. You have a little project too, huh?" Mac began.

"Yes. I have to replace a piece of molding on a window," answered Kevin.

"Yes, I know. You were carrying a heavy box into your garage and knocked over a plank leaning against the wall. The plank hit the molding on the window and broke it in two."

The man was now looking at Mac with astonishment all over his countenance. "Do I know you?" the man asked.

"No. We have never met. But you were asking God for help, and this morning while I was praying God told me what you needed, Kevin," answered Mac.

"How do you know my name?"

Mac looked into Kevin's eyes and replied, "The Spirit of God told me your name. He also told me you were close to losing your house and your wife Sue's car. You have been seeking your God for help, and because you have held onto your faith through all of those attacks of the enemy, I am now here to bring the help that you asked for."

There was a tear starting to run from Kevin's eye. He reached up and wiped it away. Kevin felt a little awkward starting to cry before a stranger. Mac placed a hand on Kevin's shoulder and took one of his hands in his other.

"God would say to you, '*My son, I have called you by name and you are Mine. I have watched over you, and I have listened to your prayers. You have done well in holding to your faith through trials and hardships, and I am proud of you. I have sent My messenger with your answer, for I love you with an everlasting love.*'"

When Mac started speaking, there were tears starting to flow down Kevin's cheeks. By the time Mac had finished, Kevin was sobbing, tears falling to the floor.

"Kevin," Mac said, "I have something for you." Mac reached into his jacket pocket and pulled out a thick envelope. Kevin pulled a handkerchief out of his pocket and began drying his eyes and wiping his nose. When he could see clearly, he saw Mac holding out an envelope with a big smile on his face.

"Pay your three house payments and the two on the car. There will be enough left over for your insurance and your tithe. There is one other thing. You will receive a call tomorrow concerning a big job that you were told was given to someone else. They ran into problems, so now you will get the job."

Kevin, his eyes red and moist, looked into Mac's face. He could see the love of God there and a simple sincerity that overwhelmed him. "How can I ever thank you for this? I don't even know your name."

"My name's Mac, and the look on your face is thanks enough for me. But really, God is the one to thank. He has blessed me in such a way that I can bless others in need. And I wouldn't have even known about you unless the Lord had told me Himself. Just keep on seeking God, and be obedient to what He tells you. He will lead you into success if you will follow where He leads."

"Mac, your generosity and obedience to God overwhelm me. There is something about you that is hard for me to put my finger on, but I can see that you know so much more about God than I do. I'd like to get together again some-time. I can see that there are a lot of things that you can teach me to make my walk with Jesus better," stated Kevin. He almost held his breath in anticipation of Mac's answer. He could already think of a whole range of questions that he would ask if they had the time.

It was several seconds before Mac gave his answer. "Kevin, that is something you need to pray about first. But here is my card. Call me some time. Right now I would think that you need to get home and let your wife know about your blessing."

Kevin looked at Mac and smiled. "Yes, you're right. Thank you, and God bless you, Mac." A tear began to escape again, and Mac stepped up to Kevin and wrapped his arms around him and held him tight for a moment in a fatherly embrace.

"This is from God and me." Mac stepped away. "Good-bye, and God bless you."

As Mac turned away, Kevin was wiping his eyes again. When he reached the oak section, he looked back at where Kevin had been, but he had already disappeared from the aisle.

"Thank You, Father, for using me to bless Kevin. I really like him, and I think I'll be hearing from him again. Lord, do you mind that I gave Kevin my name and number?" asked Mac.

"No. You will be speaking much into his life, and when they come to My house of prayer and teaching they will begin to learn more fully what I have called them to do."

Kevin hurried from the store, so excited to get home to tell Sue about this whole experience that he forgot about the molding he was going to buy. When he got into his truck, he opened the envelope to see exactly what was in it. He knew it was cash by how thick it was. He pulled out the money and counted it: fifty one-hundred-dollar bills! Five thousand dollars!

"Thank You, Father. You are so good," choked out Kevin. The money was an absolute blessing, for sure, but what really excited him was the way that the Lord had brought it about. To really know, by experiential knowledge, that God is watching over you day by day, listening to every prayer that you make and formulating a plan to take care of you, was life changing. Tears started flowing again as he thought about Mac. The man was almost unreal, to be able to hear God's voice in such a clear manner that he knew names and situations, to know what happened yesterday with the broken trim, and to know about his spiritual life, even as private as that was, and to know about that big job he was counting on. There was a whole lot more to walking with Jesus than he had ever been told.

His pastor, just the other day, talked about trials coming from God to teach us a lesson about something. But according to Mac, these trials came straight from the enemy and not from God. Could it be that the trials come not to teach us something but rather to push us away from God? And yet God uses the trials to get us to press more into Him. If we would not falter in our time of trial, we would emerge out of them the stronger and more dedicated Christian, knowing God better and more able to trust Him in our everyday living, no matter what comes about.

"To have God reach into time at this very moment, to take care of my own personal problem in a supernatural way, making it known that He takes a personal interest in my welfare, it just blows my mind." Kevin's thoughts kept racing, thinking over everything that Mac had to say. Never in his life had he experienced anything like this. By the time that Kevin reached his house, he had the tears under control but wasn't sure if he could tell the story to Sue without breaking down.

As he pulled into his driveway, his throat started to tighten, and he couldn't swallow. When he saw his wife come hurrying out of the front door, the small gasps for air began, those sobbing gasps that come when you are trying not to cry. He opened the door and stood up, and when Sue saw him beginning to sob with the tears flowing profusely, she hugged him to her. She began to weep herself as she felt his body wracked with the deep sobs of someone who is under great stress or grief. After a moment, when she was finally able to get her voice to work, she leaned back from Kevin to look into his face.

"Honey," Sue asked, "what happened? Right after you left, God told me to start praying for you, to bind doubt and fear, so I prayed for about fifteen minutes, and then it was like everything was fine. But now here you are sobbing. Tell me what happened." There was care and worry in her voice as she sought to find out what troubled her beloved.

Kevin tried to answer, but he couldn't get anything out; his throat was just too tight to work. After a moment he was able to slow the sobs and started to speak. It took three times starting, but finally he was able to tell the story.

With his voice still breaking and scratchy, Kevin said, "I was getting worried on the way over to the store, and it just kept getting worse and worse. It actually got out of control, and by the time I entered the store I was really dragging my feet. As I was walking toward the lumber, it was like I heard a whisper that said, '*I have provided for you.*' And then that cloud of fear began to disappear, and it wasn't until then that I realized where my thoughts had been. When I stopped at the molding section, I noticed a man down the aisle looking at me. God's Presence was so strong on him that I could feel it; I could hardly look away from him. After a moment the man walked up to me and asked about my project, and when I told him that I was replacing a broken piece of molding, he told me how it got broke. And then he called me by my name and mentioned your name and the payments that we owe. He said that he was praying just this morning and the Lord told him about me and how to help. Can you believe this?"

Excitedly, Kevin reached into his coat pocket and pulled out the envelope with the money in it. "Then he gave me this. Look in here and tell me that you see what I see," said Kevin.

Sue took the envelope and opened it. As she pulled out the cash and counted it, tears started to run down her cheeks.

"There is five thousand dollars here," whispered Sue. "God has provided for us."

They both went to their knees in the front yard, not caring who might be watching, and began to pray. As the tears fell they both gave thanks to the Lord, the God of all creation, for stepping into their lives in a personal way, bringing them help when He was their only hope.

They both went to the bank and made all their payments together. The loan officer, Mike, asked how they got together the money; did they borrow it from a relative? Of course that was a door unknowingly opened wide by the banker for their testimony to be told, and they took full advantage of it.

Kevin told the story from first to last, down to the smallest detail. By the time he was finished, Mike was astounded at the story. The loan officer was a Christian also, but he had never heard anything like this before.

"So," asked Mike, "how do you propose to pay this guy back?"

"We don't have to," replied Kevin. "It was a gift. The guy didn't say anything about wanting to be paid back. I'm sure that if he did, he would have said something about it being only a loan."

"Oh, there was something else that he said. You know that big job that I had been counting on but it was given to another company?" Mike nodded his head. "Well, he said that I am going to get a call tomorrow from the owner of the project to tell me that the job is mine. He said the other bidder ran into some trouble, so I am next in line."

"Well," Mike started, "that sounds good, but call me as soon as you find out if you get the job. I'd be real interested to see if this guy really hears from God. Did you get his name?"

"Yes, as a matter of fact I did. He gave me his card and said to call him sometime and we could talk," answered Kevin.

"When you find out tomorrow about the job, give him a call. I think that if this guy is for real I would like to know where he goes to church. I believe that would be worth checking out myself," said Mike.

Kevin and Sue stood up to go. Kevin held out his hand and said, "Thanks, Mike, for working with us on this. We really appreciate what you've done for us." They shook hands and said good-bye.

When Kevin and Sue arrived back at home after they had stopped by the insurance agency, they made a few calls to their closest friends to tell them about their blessing. They were all astounded and very happy to hear the story. Of course it was a surprise to most of them that Kevin and Sue were hurting financially, because they just never talked about it. All the more reason to believe that Mac was for real. How else could he have known so much detail about them if no one else knew what they were going through? That Mac had a relationship with the Lord that every one of them envied and desired was very evident. They all knew that the early church disciples in the Bible had a relationship with Jesus close enough that they had two way conversations with the Lord, but nothing like that had ever happened to any of them, nor to anyone that they had ever heard of. They had wondered what it would be like, but since it wasn't taught or talked about in their church, it seemed an impossibility.

Kevin began to think about how many people actually hear from God. There are a lot of people who talk about the Lord telling them something, but it usually boils down to just a feeling or an impression. If it seems godly or lines up with the Bible, then it gets tagged with that "I heard from God." Sometimes it is from God, but many times it may only be our flesh talking to us, telling us what we want to hear; other times it is actually the enemy leading us astray in our doctrines, our thinking, and our actions. The only way to combat the deceiver is to truly know the voice of the Lord.

Look at Mac, for instance. Look at what can be accomplished by knowing God's voice. But without having the guidance and insight of God, we will not know the plans and schemes that the enemy has devised for us, and we certainly will not know how to avoid or defeat them. But knowing God, of course, is going to be based on what we find revealed about Him in the Bible: His attributes, His character, His ways, His power, His relationship to us, and His love and desire for us. We can easily know God with our mind and our thinking process, but to know Him with our heart will only come through much prayer and seeking—which is what Mac seems to have accomplished.

As it says in Jeremiah 29, 12-13, *"Then you will call upon Me and go and pray to Me, and I will listen to you. And you will seek Me and find Me, when you search for me with all your heart."* God was speaking to the Jewish people with these words, but the principle of seeking Him and finding Him applies to all people and to all generations. God wants to be found by people; if He did not, then He would not have had it recorded in His Word. The revealed things of God belong to all of us; that is why they have been revealed for us to know and to live by. Kevin could hardly wait to be able to meet with Mac again.

CHAPTER THREE

When Mac arrived home, he went straight to his wife and told her about Kevin and everything that had happened. Chills rolled up and down her spine while listening to the details. It always impressed her how the Lord could bless someone so mightily. She was glad that the Lord had found them faithful enough for Him to use to fulfill such great blessings for others.

Linda began thinking about how people are and what they want. They are looking for the real deal, but if we don't step up and take our place as the sons and daughters of God, walking as Jesus walked and manifesting God's goodness and grace to people, then we are only so much dead religion and theory that no one wants to believe in. We must seek our God and be led of His Spirit in all that we do, so that we have maximum impact on those around us.

And that's just where Linda and Mac were finding themselves. They weren't perfect of course, but they had found

God and come to terms with who the boss should be and why. God's ways are best, and as long as they continued to seek Him and stay obedient to His instructions, they would be successful in advancing the Kingdom of God.

But there are those in the world, even as in Jesus' day, who don't want anything to do with God. No matter what you say to them, they will not believe. If they were to accept the fact that there is an Almighty God, they would have to face the facts: they are wrong and have been for a long time; they have sin in their life; they are not the boss; and they won't have the last word. All of these are based in pride, which is why it is so hard to break through them. Jesus had the same problem with the Pharisees; their prideful hearts kept them from receiving the truth about God and His Kingdom.

Mac remembered back when pride was a problem in his life. Pride didn't keep him from accepting God but kept him from giving his all to God. Mac always liked being the boss of his life, and it was hard to relinquish control to God. Because of this, God let Mac run his own life until he made such a mess of it that he had to turn to God fully, in his heart and mind, to get the mess cleaned up. Everything that Mac tried to do never worked out to satisfaction, and when he finally turned to the Lord wholeheartedly and with sincerity, he was behind in all of his bills, he had been turned in to collections numerous times, and even the tax man was after him.

But God, in His great mercy, gave Mac and Linda a plan and the ability to get caught up on everything. Jobs started coming in. Not just jobs, but jobs that paid well. Mac asked God where and when to spend his money, and God answered him. Mac no longer bought stuff that had a hidden defect in it, and he never had to pay top dollar for anything, for God always led him to the best deal. Mac was even content when he had to wait to buy something he wanted or needed until the Lord gave him the direction to do it, because he knew he would get the best deal around. Mac learned to hear God's voice in the little things, and because he was obedient to that voice, God began to talk to him of greater and more important things. Even as it says in Jeremiah, 33:3, *"Call to Me, and I will answer you, and show you great and mighty things, which you do not know,"* Mac began receiving revelation knowledge from God's Spirit. He learned that if God's people would continue to seek Him diligently and be obedient and faithful to what He tells them, then they would be promoted in the Kingdom of God. Salvation is not based on works, but people's advancement in the Kingdom of God is based on what they do with what God tells them. Even as the servants of the ruler who distributed his money among them, the ones who are faithful in what they have will be given more.

As Mac and Linda sought God and obeyed His voice when He spoke to them, they were led into the deeper things of God. They did not learn anything that is not in the Bible, but rather they received revelation knowledge of what is there, and, by God's Spirit, they learned how to walk it out. Many Christians have a superficial walk with the Lord, and if they stay that way, they will never enter their true calling or truly walk as Jesus did. There are no secret things in the Kingdom; there is the Word of God, and all Christians can learn and walk in everything they are supposed to by what they find in it. The revelation of God and all that He is about is in His Word. To be successful in the Kingdom of God, Christians must be seeking God daily and sincerely. They must not let themselves get into a religious mode of praying, studying the Word, and going to church. For God is a living God and desires His people to know Him as their closest friend.

One day at work, Mac was just working away and meditating on God and His goodness when an idea came to him about a new invention. He thought about the idea awhile, all the different angles of it, and decided that it was a good idea. Mac became more excited over it as the afternoon passed, and when he reached home, he told his wife about it and asked for her input. The following day they checked the stores to see if anything like it was for sale. There wasn't any product like it in the market place, and it seemed like a very sellable idea. Through an acquaintance they found a lawyer to help them patent the idea to protect it. In the church, there was a man who was well off financially, and they went to him with their idea. He liked it so well that he became their financial partner in the manufacturing and marketing of their new product.

One year after the product emerged on the market, Mac and Linda were new millionaires. Since they had been devoted tithers to their church for several years, they were ready to tithe and more on their new wealth. They sought the Lord on what to do with their newfound wealth, and because they had already learned to hear His voice in the small things, they could hear Him clearly on the big things. For themselves, they upgraded some of their belongings and also found out what a real vacation is. But they always kept their eyes and hearts open for those that they could help financially, seeking God in all things.

Mac and Linda knew there were some people who thought they were wrong in spending money on themselves, that it was self-gratification. But they believed that came out of jealousy and a false humility about being poor. Mac and

Linda had learned that God wants His people to be blessed and it pleases Him to do so. He gives them all things richly to enjoy, as it says in First Timothy. And in Deuteronomy it says that God gives His people the power to get wealth that He may establish His covenant in the earth. It is God's will that they are the head and not the tail, above and not beneath, and that they are blessed in their families, their storage barns (bank accounts in today's culture), and all that they set their hand to. His people must understand that the blessing, both spiritually and financially, are part of God's goodness and grace toward them, so that they will get past having a false humility about being poor. Mac and Linda had come to grips with this subject and had received the victory over it.

Mac and Linda knew that God is a God of blessing, as it is shown throughout the Bible, in both the Old Testament and the New Testament. Why the mainstream church doesn't want to see it in the Word of God or teach it from the pulpit is a mystery, even to this day, and they had a hard time understanding that fact.

Pastor John had taught on the blessing of God so many times that Mac and Linda knew the Scripture text by heart. Along with their personal study time on the subject, they had a certainty in their heart about God's goodness. God lays out the blessing and the curse before Israel in the book of Deuteronomy 28. God says that if His people would diligently obey the voice of the Lord their God and observe carefully all of His commandments, then the Lord their God would set them high above all nations of the earth.

"And all these blessings shall come upon you and overtake you, because you obey the voice of the LORD your God. Blessed shall you be in the city, and blessed shall you

be in the country. Blessed shall be the fruit of your body [our children], *the produce of your ground and the increase of your herds, the increase of your cattle and the offspring of your flocks. Blessed shall be your basket and your kneading bowl. Blessed shall you be when you come in, and blessed shall you be when you go out.*

"*The* LORD *will cause your enemies who rise against you to be defeated before your face; they shall come out against you one way and flee before you seven ways. The* LORD *will command the blessing on you in your storehouses and in all to which you set your hand, and He will bless you in the land which the* LORD *your God is giving you. The* LORD *will establish you as a holy people to Himself, just as He has sworn to you, if you keep the commandments of the* LORD *your God and walk in His ways. Then all peoples of the earth shall see that you are called by the name of the* LORD, *and they shall be afraid of you.*

"*And the Lord will grant you plenty of goods, in the fruit of your body, in the increase of your livestock, and in the produce of your ground, in the land of which the* LORD *swore to your fathers to give you. The* LORD *will open to you His good treasure, the heavens, to give the rain to your land in its season, and to bless all the work of your hand. You shall lend to many nations, but you shall not borrow. And the* LORD *will make you the head and not the tail; you shall be above only, and not be beneath, if you heed the commandments of the* LORD *your God, which I command you today, and are careful to observe them. So you shall not turn aside from any of the words which I command you this day, to the right or the left, to go after other gods to serve them.*"

In Mac's mind, the teaching on God's goodness being expressed in blessing His people was as clear-cut and understandable as two plus two equals four. But because of the blinders that the enemy has placed over so many people, this teaching has gone unnoticed and untaught to the majority of Christians.

Mac had meditated on this subject a lot. The pastor had taught on it quite in depth and also went back to it frequently to support other teachings. They had discussed it between them and had come up with some of these conclusions. It was interesting to note that as the United States Constitution and Bill of Rights were written and fashioned from God's principles and His ways, as set forth in the Bible, many of God's promises that were made to the nation Israel have apparently come to pass for the United States as a nation. As our nation was founded on God and His principles by faithful men and women who believed in Jesus with their whole hearts, they did their best to promote righteousness in our laws and also to protect their religious freedom from a corrupt or godless government in the future. From their dedication to God and forming our foundation on Him, our whole nation has been blessed over the years and has become in a short time period, as far as nations go, the most powerful and richest nation on earth. But of course, non-Christians will never admit to anything like that. That conclusion would be too supportive of Christianity.

But as you come to know God's character, His attributes, and His goodness, it becomes clear that this is God's heart toward His people, whether the Israelites of the Old Testament or the Christian believers of today who have been grafted into the vine and now share in all the blessings and the promises of the Lord to Israel (Ephesians 2; 2

Corinthians 1). In 2 Corinthians 1:20, the apostle Paul writes, *"For all the promises of God in Him* [Jesus] *are Yes, and in Him Amen, to the glory of God through us."*

Mac remembered a conversation that he had with Pastor John, a few months back, about God's blessings in Deuteronomy and why they aren't being taught to most believers.

"One of the reasons this is not being taught and embraced in the mainstream Christ-believing churches may be that the words 'obey His commandments,' in chapter 28 of Deuteronomy, are used too often for comfort. Most people don't want to have to follow a set of rules, so the preacher doesn't want to have to say that you do, and so cause a riot in his church. You know the saying, 'We are not under the law but under grace.' A lot of people don't want to have to obey anything, and how dare the preacher tell them that they do. It's not that we are under the law, but if the Spirit of God controls us then we will not be transgressing the law of God either," explained Pastor John. He paused for a moment and then continued.

"Do you recall the text where the lawyer asked Jesus what he should do to inherit eternal life, and Jesus answered by asking him what was written in the law, what was his reading of it?"

"Yes."

"The lawyer answered him, '"You shall love the Lord your God with all your heart, with all your soul, with all your strength, and with all your mind," and 'Your neighbor as yourself.' Jesus said, 'You have answered rightly; do this and you will live.'

"In the same manner in another text, a lawyer asked Jesus which is the greatest commandment. 'Jesus answered,

"'You shall love the Lord your God with all your heart, with all your soul, and with all your mind.' This is the first and greatest commandment. And the second is like it: 'You shall love your neighbor as yourself.' On these two commandments hang all the Law and the Prophets."

"Christians know they are to love the Lord their God with all their heart, but they don't seek Him often enough to get to know Him in such a way that they can love Him with all of their heart. If the majority of Christians don't love God with their whole heart, then they won't love their neighbor as themselves. They can't. If we truly loved God as we ought to, then it would be a lot easier to love our neighbor, and we would not be transgressing the law of God every time we turn around. Most of man's sin is against his neighbor, but if we truly loved our neighbor we would not sin against him. Of course the question was raised, and still is today, 'Who is my neighbor?'"

Mac was following closely, and when Pastor John paused, he jumped in with the answer. "Jesus answered that question in the parable of the Good Samaritan in Luke, chapter 10. Our neighbor is the person who needs help. Plain and simple."

"Yes, Mac, that is the short and simple truth—the person who needs help. Now, if Christians would obey these two commandments, loving God and their neighbor also, the rest of the commandments would not even be an issue. That is not to say that we can go out and kill someone, or steal, or lie, or cheat, or dishonor our parents just so long as we love the Lord our God with our whole heart. But rather, if we love the Lord our God with all of our heart, and mind, and strength, and soul, we will not be thinking about killing, stealing, lying, coveting, or any other sin. Occasionally we may have a small slipup, but for the most part, we would be walking sin free and not be concerned in any way about all of the other commandments. The Law of Moses was set forth as a standard for the people to live by. The people at that time did not have the indwelling Spirit of God within them, and so they needed a written standard to know all of the details of the dos and don'ts, what is right and what is wrong.

"Even today, people who do not live by the Spirit of God need a written standard of law to live by. The majority of Jesus-believing people do not love the Lord their God with all their heart, mind, soul, and strength, so they try to live according to all the law rather than to the two greatest commandments. But because they try to do it in the flesh, rather than by the Spirit of God, they will only fail at keeping the whole law, and condemnation will result. And we all know that people who are walking in condemnation, which the law always brings when you fail, will seek to condemn others who transgress the law of God, mostly to make themselves feel better. Misery loves company.

"The Law of Moses was to be a guide to live by, but also it was leading to Jesus. So now, if we live in Jesus, loving God with our whole heart, then the Law of Moses is no longer over us. Of course to love the Lord your God with all your heart will take much seeking, studying His Word, and praying."

By the look on Mac's face, Pastor John could see that he had understanding of what he was explaining. He paused a moment to give Mac a chance to comment.

"The real problem in Christianity, then, is that most Christians don't seek God the way that they should. So how can they love a God that they don't know? Or how will they love their neighbor if they don't love God? Some neighbors are just hard to love regardless, so without knowing God intimately and being able to draw from His love for people, how will we love those that are hard to love? Or how will we not sin, or transgress God's Law that he gave to Moses and the Israelites, if we do not first love God? He'll give us the ability to both love and not to sin, but we have to come to know Him personally and intimately as our beloved Father, or as a very dear friend." Mac's conclusion was right on the money.

Mac continued. "And if God remains to us as only a religious symbol, a theory, or just a good idea to live by, then we will always come up short where obeying the law comes in, because of the weakness of the flesh, for we cannot please God with our flesh. And then the guilt and condemnation move in when we sin, and so we have to make excuses for our sin, such as, I am only human; I am not under the Law but under grace; or the real good one—what sin? If we really know God, we will know when we sin, for if we are born again, His spirit is within us. He will let us know when we do wrong, and if we have a sincere heart toward God we will ask His forgiveness when we sin."

"And if God's people do not progress in their relationship with Him, then their life will always be a struggle with sin, and they will constantly be missing out on His blessings for their life here and now." Pastor John leaned back in his chair, gathering his thoughts, to bring the conversation to its end.

"And that brings us back to the original question: why are the blessings of God, as they are stated in Deuteronomy, not part of the fundamental Christian teaching? If it is taught that God will help us and bless us, and yet we are not helped or blessed as it is written in Deuteronomy, then it will be known to those around us that we are not receiving that blessing. If we are not being blessed, then we will be known as ones that are not pressing in to God as we should, and if we are insecure in our place with God, condemnation will result.

"That is not to say we won't go through any hardships or trials, for the enemy will always make sure that we do," Pastor John continued. "But rather, God is there to help us, lead us, and provide what we need to achieve victory, if we stay in faith and continue to do what we know to do. There are many variables in our attaining victory: knowing God intimately, spiritual warfare, staying in faith, keeping our mind stayed on Him, trusting Him, knowing that He wants us to have victory over all of our problems, and being obedient to His voice. Not just His written Word, but also obeying His voice when He talks to us. Sometimes He will give us the answer to our problem, and it usually includes something that we have to do, but a lot of the time obedience is put off until later or there isn't any faith behind it, and the victory eludes us."

Mac concluded the conversation with a rather direct statement. "But rather than bring the psychological dilemma of condemnation on the minds of those who are not where they should be with God, the mainstream doctrines have to ignore God's original plan of blessing, in the natural or physical sense, as seen in Deuteronomy. And in so doing they have removed any distinction that there should be between a Christian and a non-Christian. God said that all nations would see that we are blessed of Him, that He is our God, and they would then be afraid of us. It's a pretty good picture of the Moslem world toward the Christian world."

Mac knew that a lot of what they had talked about was directly tied to knowing the complete truth of God's word. There are so many false doctrines and teachings across the church world that it would take a move of God to eradicate all of them and to set the record straight. If people are not taught that God wants them to be blessed, how could there ever be any hope in them that God would extend His hand into time and help them in such a way? If they did not know God in that way, then how could they ever believe by faith that He would do it, or even that He wanted to? People can only believe God for what they know He wants to do.

The leper who came to Jesus and said, "Lord, if You are willing You can make me clean," believed in the power of Jesus to heal but did not know if Jesus wanted to heal him, a sinful man with leprosy. Of course, he probably knew himself and his sin well enough that he didn't think that Jesus would want to heal him. For, under the law, he was committing a sin just by being in public. But Jesus straightened out his thinking immediately by saying, "I will." And stretching forth His hand, He touched him and made him whole. The leper's doctrine on healing was set straight by the Son of Man Himself.

Mac desperately wanted people to learn that Jesus is not only able but also willing to help them. It took Mac several years to learn and accept that fact about Jesus. That was one of the reasons he found it hard to relinquish control of his life to God. He thought that once God was in control of his life, then he wouldn't have the things that he wanted. Little did he realize that many of the things that he wanted for himself and his family God also wanted. When he finally learned that God was a God of blessing, it became easier to give Him control.

Since the time that Mac had given control of his life over to God, he had become a better Christian, a better husband, a better father; he had gotten out of debt, made an invention, became a millionaire, had all he ever wanted, and had been able to help out numerous others financially.

God doesn't bless His people only so that they can spend everything on themselves, but rather so that they can help others in need. For there will always be among God's people those who need help. If they continue to trust in God and obey His voice, then He will bless them. They have His Word on it.

CHAPTER FOUR

Mac called Pastor John to tell him what God had sent him to do. Over a late lunch, Mac gave the story to Pastor John, who could only shake his head and smile that knowing smile. It seemed like there were more and more stories like this one that were happening across the church world. It was getting close to the reappearing of Jesus, and it seemed like the Kingdom was in a growing spurt to get as many people saved as possible. Believers all over were pressing in to God more and more, to know Him better, and in so doing were hearing directions from Him on how to be prosperous and to help others.

"There are so many stories that I've been hearing about," began Pastor John. "God is moving among His people like never before. Most of what I've heard is coming from pastors of churches similar to ours. As their people are receiving the Word and putting into practice what they are learning, they are drawing closer to God, and when He begins to tell them what to do, they are doing it. God's blessings are beginning to reach so many people that I'm astounded."

"When I start thinking about all of the possibilities as the ranks of God's faithful continue to increase, I'm almost over-whelmed," replied Mac.

"Yes, I know what you mean. I think God is a God of expanding possibilities. If His people will just continue to press in, seeking Him like there's no tomorrow, then He will bring those possibilities into reality. You know that Kathy has walked in the gifts of word of knowledge and word of wisdom for several years, but for the last several months now, she's been getting words of knowledge about people just about everywhere she goes. She sees someone, even strangers, and the Lord starts giving her details about them. She's been step-ping out in these gifts and speaking to them more frequently, just as you've been doing. You know how that is, Mac. As time progresses toward the blowing of the trumpet, the magnitude of these things will keep increasing until they have touched almost everyone. They might not all respond to it favorably, but they will have had a chance to be blessed. It's hard to believe that, by the time Jesus calls us up to meet Him, there will still be so many who will not believe."

"I know," Mac replied. "It's like some people have such a deep-seated hatred for Jesus that no matter how much evidence there is, whether supernatural or otherwise, they will still deny His existence. But next month we'll find out how many will refuse to believe even with the gifts in oper-ation. I'm really looking forward to this year's trip to Hollywood. As we walk in these gifts with a stronger anointing, it's going to be interesting to see the magnitude of what God can accomplish."

"I know exactly what you mean, Mac. I find myself antic-ipating the trip also. But there is a big difference between witnessing to those who are on the street living in poverty and to those who are affluent and who have all that they need. Quite often, the cultural elite sees no reason to need a savior; nor do they want one. Many times, the only thing that will break through their thinking is a healing miracle for themselves or someone that they love."

Pastor John and Mac were finalizing some details on an upcoming mission trip the following month to Hollywood. There were about twelve people going from the church to witness on the streets and evangelize the homeless and the hopeless. They were preparing themselves to assault the kingdom of darkness and to take back those that were being held captive by drugs, alcohol, depression, sickness, and dis-ease. They had both been to Hollywood before, but this year, by the Spirit of God, they felt that God was going to be doing something special. They were all getting excited over the prospect of God moving in their midst in a supernatural way to win the lost and to set the captives free.

Joe and Peggy were among those who were going, and they were very anxious over it, as it was going to be their first time on the mission field. Witnessing on the streets of America can sometimes be very trying. A lot of people don't have manners or morals, and if they don't want to hear about God, they let you know it in no uncertain terms. You will get snubbed, ignored, cussed out, flipped off, yelled at, and threatened with bodily harm. But sometimes you will make contact with someone who is searching for God, someone who has a tender heart, a person who will receive what you have to say and have a life-changing experience. These are the ones who make it all worth it.

But this year, things were going to be different, for the Spirit of God had spoken of the things that He was going to do among them as they went out to advance His Kingdom. They would be traveling and working under the power of the Holy Spirit; He would be moving and working with them in a greater way than ever before, even as in the last chapter of Mark, where it says, *"And they went out and preached everywhere, the Lord working with them and confirming the word through the accompanying signs."*

Is it any different today? Doesn't the Lord need to confirm the word through accompanying signs? Who do you think the signs were to be a confirmation for? The disciples, or the ones being preached to? Why did the listeners need signs for the confirmation of the word being preached? Possibly so that they would know that the word being preached was true and was from God. Even as the man who was born blind said to the Pharisees, "We know that if God were not with Him [Jesus], He could do nothing." In other words, the power of supernatural healings and miracles confirm that God is behind the message.

What the masses need is a good dose of hope that God is willing and able to help them, in any area of their life. This hope will only come from receiving knowledge of what the Word of God actually says. God says it is time for people to really know what He is like. He is looking for those who will follow Him and obey His every commandment, and He will show Himself strong on their behalf (2 Chronicles 16:9).

The group going to Hollywood was getting very excited about the trip. They were putting in much prayer time over it, asking the Lord for wisdom and guidance, quoting the Scriptures for His leading and His help, asking the Lord to prepare those who were going to be ministered to, and binding the enemy from interfering with the people that God was putting in their path.

They were all studying the Word of God diligently to memorize Scripture that they would need in witnessing to the lost. But most of all they were getting closer to the Lord. As they spent time seeking Him and drawing nearer to Him, He was also drawing near to them. That was the biggest advantage that they had when they were ready to go out: to be close enough to God to hear His immediate instructions and to follow them without question, because they knew the One speaking.

After lunch, Mac headed back home to do some chores and to start his bookshelf project. He had a feeling that the following day he was going to receive a call from Kevin, and it was going to be a lengthy conversation. He wasn't worried about it, because the Lord had already confirmed that they were going to be involved with one another, Mac and Linda teaching, Kevin and his wife, Sue, learning. Mac could tell by Kevin's personality and his spirit that it would be a good relationship. Kevin had been getting beat up by the enemy, but he loved God dearly. It was going to be a joy to teach them of the deeper things of God, and Mac was looking forward to it.

Late that afternoon, Linda was working on a sewing project when the Lord interrupted her thoughts and told her to go to the grocery store, right away. She went to Mac and told him that she had to get to the grocery store right now, that the Lord had just told her that there would be a young woman there who needed His help.

"Let's pray," said Linda.

Mac and Linda joined hands, and Linda began to pray.

"Lord, I ask that You give me wisdom and understanding concerning this woman. I ask for Your insight and clarity to hear what You want me to tell her. Lord, prepare her heart even now for Your Spirit to move upon her. I thank You for calling upon me to do your will. In Jesus' name, amen."

As Linda was heading to the store, Mac began to pray for the woman as well. He didn't always know in what manner to pray or what to ask for, so he began to pray in tongues. He began to pray in a language that he didn't know in his natural mind, but by the Spirit of God he was praying the perfect will of God for this young woman. As he was praying, he began to receive knowledge of the woman's need. She needed a miracle inside of her body immediately, for the doctor had already pronounced his diagnosis, and she was contemplating her decision for the next day. Once Mac knew what she needed in his natural mind, he began to pray earnestly for the miracle that would change her life and the life of her unborn baby that she now carried.

When Linda arrived at the store, she could feel God's power within her, rising up to meet this need. She also knew that Mac was praying for her and the young woman; she could feel it, but she also knew Mac. He cared deeply for people, and when he knew there was a desperate need, he was always ready to pray and to fight the enemy over it. He was very tenacious in prayer when it came to seeing the Lord win out over the enemy. Remember, Jesus came to destroy the works of the enemy, and the Bible gives many examples of how He did the destroying. It wasn't just His death on the cross and His resurrection that destroyed the works of the enemy, but also walking in the power and anointing of God, doing good, and healing all who were oppressed by the devil (Acts 10:38). And are Christians not called to walk as Jesus walked and to do the same works that He did? Jesus said, "*A disciple is not above his teacher, but everyone who is perfectly trained will be like his teacher"* (Luke 6:40). Christians are called to be Jesus for people, doing for them as Jesus Himself would.

Linda walked down the first aisle and turned across the back of the store, looking up each aisle. When she saw a young woman halfway up an aisle, she asked, "Is that her, Lord?"

"Yes. She is in her fifth month with child, and the doctors have discovered that the baby is deformed and does not have any legs. They have recommended that she abort the child, but this is not My will. Speak into her womb My will."

The young woman looked at Linda, almost staring, and then looked away. As Linda began to walk toward her, the woman looked again at her and then looked away, feeling a little embarrassed about staring.

Linda went to her and said hello. The young woman turned to her, looking like she was about to cry. Her eyes were red and moist, and when she looked into Linda's eyes her lip began to tremble. Linda took her hands in her own, and when the woman felt the Presence of God emanating from Linda, she wrapped her arms around her and began to weep.

"I know that you have received bad news today from your doctor," Linda began, "but the Lord Jesus sent me here to tell you that the doctors are wrong. Your baby boy within you will jump and run, and he will leap for joy when you tell him how God healed him while he was still in your womb."

In amazement and with the tears still flowing, the woman pulled back from Linda to look at her and ask, "How do you know about that? I just left the doctor's office a half hour ago, and I haven't even told my husband yet."

"A half hour ago the Lord told me about you and that you would be here. He also told me that you are His daughter and that you have asked Him for the miracle that I am now here to give you. I have come here to pray for you and your child, to lay my hands on you, and to speak life over you," said Linda.

Linda laid a hand on the woman's stomach and began to speak. "Little boy, the Lord has formed you and you are perfect; He has made all your parts and they are all perfect. You will be a joy to your mother and father, and they will marvel at your perfection. The day that you are born, you shall be kicking and screaming, and you will cause thankfulness to overflow in your house. In the name of Jesus, it shall be so."

The woman could feel Linda's hand on her stomach, and it wasn't moving; yet as Linda was speaking she could feel warmth and something moving within her. She felt as though something was getting larger within her womb, and when she realized what was happening she began to sob, but with joy. The tears were falling to the floor, and as Linda finished speaking, the woman hugged her tight, saying, "Thank you, thank you! Thank You, Jesus!"

Linda held her tight for a moment and then pulled back to arm's length to look her in the eye. "Honey, Jesus has healed your baby, so tomorrow I want you to go back to the doctor and tell them that you want another ultrasound done. They will be amazed, and when you tell them about today and this moment, they may begin to make excuses about what they thought they saw on your ultrasound today. But you need to keep all the ultrasound pictures that they gave you as evidence of your miracle. Okay?"

There were several people standing around by that time because of the woman's loud crying and sobbing, so most of them heard what was said. Some had smiles on their face, while others were more skeptical, and one woman even asked if she could go to the doctor with her. She wanted to verify the miracle, and yet she didn't even know her. But people are searching for the real deal, not something fake and phony. That is why psychic hot lines makes so much money, because people want a taste of the supernatural that cannot be explained. They want to believe that there is something beyond the physical, whether it is the truth and existence of Almighty God or some other supernatural power. They will believe in the thing that has the strongest evidence for its reality. If the children of God were to rise up in His power the same way that the early Christians did, they would not have to compete as much with all the other religions, New Age teachings, and the psychics.

Linda said, "If you like, Carrie, I will go to the doctor with you."

Carrie's eyes opened wide in surprise, and she said, "You even know my name?"

By this time the people were hanging on every word that was spoken. They knew that something very strange was going on, but it was hard for them to believe that Linda could know something by a supernatural means. And besides that, she wasn't claiming to be a psychic. It was easier for them to believe that Linda had psychic powers than that she had God talking to her.

"Yes," Linda replied. "Don't you think that if God can tell me what you needed, where you would be, and even point you out to me, that He can also tell me your name? If we seek God with our whole heart, we will find Him, and if we continue in our seeking, He will begin to speak to us and to use us, as He did here today."

Carrie said, still wiping the tears from her eyes, "Thank you for coming here, and yes, I would like for you to meet me there. I will be there with my husband, Jack, and I would really like for him to meet you."

"Okay. What time is your appointment, and where?"

"It's at ten o'clock at the Central Community Pediatrics Building. Can you get there about twenty minutes early?" asked Carrie.

"Yes," replied Linda. "I'll be there waiting."

Carrie stepped up to Linda and wrapped her arms around her. The tears began to fall again, and she said, "Thank you again. You don't know what this has done for me. God bless you!"

Linda held her tightly and said, "God loves you dearly, and now so do I. I'll see you tomorrow."

Linda let go of Carrie, and as she turned away, her eyes fell on a young man standing there in the crowd of listeners. She looked at him steadily, and then she said, "God would like for you to call your wife right now and apologize to her and ask for her forgiveness. And He would also like to see you in church more often."

The young man just stood there dumbfounded, and by the look on his face, no one doubted that what Linda had said to him was accurate and true. Linda turned and walked down the aisle and left the store.

She went directly home and found Mac in his study, where he had been praying, just as she thought.

"The young woman was pregnant, and her little boy didn't have any legs, right?" asked Mac.

She could only stare at Mac. She told him what had happened, every detail.

"It looks like I'm going to be busy tomorrow," finished Linda.

"Me too," Mac replied. "I'm going to receive a call from Kevin tomorrow, and we're going to go out for lunch and talk for a while."

After dinner, they both spent time in the Word of God, and before going to bed, they spent time praying together. They praised God for His wonderful mercy and His endless compassion; they thanked Him for counting them worthy to be used to help those that are hurting and needful of Him; and they asked for His wisdom and His guidance for the meetings that they were going to have with Kevin and Carrie. The Presence of God was a tangible thing when they prayed and was a major reason for their praying and seeking God. There is nothing to compare with God's Presence with you, and once you have tasted it, you will always seek it. They knew that as time progressed toward the appearing of Jesus at the sounding of the trumpet, these types of things were going to increase exponentially. Even now, there were thousands and millions of believers being trained up for service, being prepared to walk in the power and grace of God. They were going to be manifesting the Presence and the Glory of God to the world on an ever-increasing scale. In the history of the world, there have never been as many people alive at one time nor as many Christians as there are at this moment. God is now in the final preparation of the great harvest, and He will complete the good work that He has begun.

CHAPTER FIVE

Mac was up early the next morning; he wanted to spend more time in prayer than usual. He needed God's guidance today with Kevin, but he also wanted to pray for Carrie and her meeting with the doctor. Neither he nor Linda had prayed before for such a mighty miracle as with Carrie's baby, and he wanted God's victory to be complete. Before he got very far into prayer, Linda walked in.

"Do you mind if I join you this morning?" Linda asked.

"You're just in time. I was going to pray for Carrie, so I'm glad you're here," replied Mac. He started to pray, praising God for His great mercy and compassion. As he lifted praises and thanksgiving to God, Linda went to her knees and began to weep. The Presence of God was in the room, and it was so sweet. The love of God was washing over them and filling them. Mac also went to his knees before the Lord's Presence and bowed his head to the floor. Linda began to sing praises to God with her spirit, singing in another language. There was a great peace upon them, and they knew that at that moment they could ask God for anything and they would receive it. God was pleased with both of them, and they could feel His joy at their obedience to His instructions. To have God pleased with you brings a joy like no other, and once you enter into that there is no holding you back. It becomes the most important thing in your life, seeking Him, finding Him, and doing His will with all of your heart.

After an hour of prayer with Linda, Mac drove down to the church to pray with the pastor and several other men. Pastor John was at the church almost every morning for prayer, just like clockwork. He was the most devoted and faithful Christian that Mac had ever seen. He had energy and drive that were almost matchless, and it inspired those around him to also be committed to the Lord wholeheartedly. If you were not serious about your walk with the Lord Jesus, then Pastor John was one person you didn't want to be around. He was always praising God and encouraging others to do the same.

When Mac arrived at the church, prayer had already started. Pastor John was leading the praying, and when he subsided, someone else took over. They were praying for things in each of their separate lives and also for larger things that affected all of them—the president of the United States, government leaders, judges, court cases, laws that were coming up for voting (good ones and bad ones), other countries—but the one thing most prayed for was God maturing His people to take their rightful place in His creation.

Mac began by praying in another language, his mind being unfruitful, but his spirit was being edified. (In 1 Corinthians 14:4, it says, "*He who speaks in a tongue edifies himself, but he who prophesies edifies the church.*" And in Jude 1:20, it says, "*But you, beloved, building yourselves up on your most holy faith, praying in the Holy Spirit.*" As it says in 1 Corinthians 14:14, "*For if I pray in a tongue, my spirit prays, but my mind is unfruitful.*" So we let our spirit pray, because it is being led by God's Spirit. Our mind is unfruitful, but it is also outside of influencing our prayers. Because our mind doesn't know what our mouth is saying by the leading of our spirit, which is joined with God's Spirit, it cannot taint or influence our prayers by our own fleshly desires or our finite thinking. With practice and seeking God, we can develop our mind's understanding of what we are praying in another tongue or language. As in 1 Corinthians 14:13, "*Therefore let him who speaks in a tongue pray that he may interpret.*" And verse 15, "*What is the conclusion then? I will pray with the spirit, and I will also pray with the understanding. I will sing with the spirit, and I will also sing with the under-standing.*" So, it is possible to understand what you are praying in another language, even as you are speaking it.[1])

When Mac's turn came to pray, he began to pray for Kevin and his wife first and then moved on to Carrie's needs. They all listened to Mac's prayers, and when they caught the gist of it, they began praying fervently in the Holy Spirit, being led by God's Spirit to pray God's perfect will in the matter. After some moments, they could begin to feel the victory by the Spirit of God. They were overcoming the enemy by the power of prayer, and they ended with many thanksgivings and praises. "Our God reigns. Amen."

After prayer, Mac filled them all in on the details of what had already transpired, and all they could say was, "Glory to God." Mac stayed awhile longer to visit with Pastor John after the others had left to go to work.

In his office Pastor John said, "God's Spirit is beginning to move at a more rapid pace. He has a plan, and we are now moving into it. Kathy and I have been feeling the moving of His Spirit with stronger anointings in the church services and also in situations like you and Linda have been experiencing."

"I know," Mac replied. "For the last month we've both been feeling His Presence in our prayer time growing beyond anything that we've experienced before. Our spirits within us are rising up with expectancy and excitement at what He's about to do."

"Yes. God is raising up for Himself a faithful people who will believe His Word and who know His voice, and they'll go forth in the power of His might without questioning His directions. They will advance the Kingdom of God against the enemy relentlessly until the end comes. This is only the beginning of the glorious Bride that He has been waiting on to come forth for almost two thousand years," said Pastor John.

"I'm really glad that I gave my all to the Lord several years back so that He has matured me and prepared me for these days. There is nothing in my life that compares to His abiding Presence and His leading. I don't know how I ever got along without Him before," shared Mac.

"I know what you mean, Mac. It was hard for me to let go of the control too, and then one day I realized that He wanted me to succeed more than I did. Of course He had the means to make me successful in ways that I never dreamed of, but still it had to be a step of faith to say, 'Okay, Lord, it's all Yours. I give up control. I will do my best at doing everything You want me to do.' But once that moment finally came, then He called me to pray and to seek Him with my whole heart. I began to spend so much time praying and studying His word that I almost forgot to eat. But I found God, and He began to talk to me, just like His Word promises: 'If you seek Me with your whole heart, you will find Me.' We still have our trials, but the Lord gives us the victory over every one of them. The key is to seek Him on everything and then do what He tells you to do." Pastor John sat thinking for a moment.

"I've been hearing some stories from other churches lately. Some are similar to yours. People are pressing in to the Kingdom of God, seeking God like never before, and God is speaking to them and leading them to do things by the power of His Spirit. This move of God will be His final one that will continue at an ever-increasing pace until the trumpet blows and we meet Jesus in the air. There have even been a few stories coming out of churches ranging from the Baptist to the Catholic. God is raising up a people from all walks of life and from every denomination who are seeking Him like never before. They're beginning to find Him, and that is beginning to cause quite a stir in their home churches, especially the ones that don't have any understanding of the working of the gifts. I have even been getting some calls from some of the pastors of these churches, asking questions about the Holy Spirit and how it all works."

"It looks like God is going to bring us all into unity in this final outpouring of His Spirit. As He moves on the hearts and minds of His people, using them to perform miracles of healing, the ones who have been against the gifts will start coming in, and God will embrace them also and begin using them to do the same things," added Mac.

"Yes, Mac, you're right," replied Pastor John. "I can see that whole churches are going to receive the baptism of the Spirit when their pastors finally wake up to God's moving and

His power. When the pastors themselves get baptized with the Spirit, it will make such a huge difference in them that they'll want their whole congregation to get it. I've been seeking God about this, and He told me to get ready to accept speaking invitations to these types of churches. Once it starts, it will snowball in a hurry, and I want you to be there with me, Mac."

"I'll begin to pray about that too, then," said Mac. "That would be a real blessing to me, to stand at your side and minister with you, Pastor. I can feel my spirit within me already bearing witness to what you said. We are moving into exciting times, and I'm glad that God has placed Linda and me under Kathy's and your care."

"Thank you, Mac. I really appreciate that, and I don't think we would've wanted it any other way," replied Pastor John.

Mac stood up and said, "Well, I've got to go. Linda will be meeting with Carrie shortly, and I want to be home when she gets back. After that, I'll be meeting with Kevin, and I want to get a little studying done before then."

"Okay," said Pastor John, rising. "I'm glad you came in today. Let me know how everything goes today."

"I'll give you a call this afternoon," said Mac.

"Okay, brother. I love you, and I'll talk to you later."

"I love you too, Pastor."

They embraced, and then Mac walked out to his truck. "Thank You, Jesus, for Pastor John." Mac was always glad to spend a little extra time with the pastor.

Mac just got home when Linda was walking out the door to go to the doctor's office.

"We had a good time in prayer this morning," Mac began. "We prayed about your meeting this morning and mine this afternoon. We've got the victory on both counts."

"Good," replied Linda. "Pray with me now before I go."

They joined hands, and Mac began to pray. "Lord, we ask for your wisdom and guidance today. Give us the words to speak, and prepare the hearts to receive them. Give us boldness and courage to follow wherever You lead. In Jesus' name I ask, amen."

Mac hugged Linda and said, "Do what you know to do. He will show Himself strong on your behalf."

"I will. I love you Mac," replied Linda.

"I love you too, honey."

---

[1] For more information on the gift of speaking and praying in tongues for all believers, turn to addendum at the back of the book.

CHAPTER SIX

While Linda waited in the parking lot, she continued to pray in tongues. It was only a few minutes before she saw Carrie and her husband driving in. Linda got out of the car and walked over to Carrie, and when she got out, she hugged her.

"I'm so glad that you came," Carrie started. "The baby has been kicking me almost all night and didn't sleep until this morning. He just started kicking again the moment that I saw you. Isn't that strange?"

"Yes, that is a little strange. I wonder if he knows me already or if he senses the Spirit of God within me."

"I want you to meet my husband, Jack. Jack, this is Linda," said Carrie.

"Hello, Linda. I don't know how to thank you for what you've done, but we're both so grateful."

"Just thank Jesus then; He is the one who gets all the credit. I'm only His tool, but He is the reason for your blessing. He loves you both so much, and when Carrie turned to Him, asking for help, He sent me to bring what you needed," replied Linda.

"Linda, I was going to tell you that up until yesterday I never really felt my baby kicking. I felt movement and poking, but I didn't realize that it was all in one direction or that it wasn't kicking at all but just his arms and elbows. But now that I've been feeling what real kicking is, I know that the doctors were right." Tears started to run down her cheeks. "My baby didn't have any legs yesterday, but now I know that he does. Thank you so much for being there and doing what God told you to do."

"You're welcome, Carrie," said Linda, hugging her close. "God is full of mercy and compassion, and in these last days He is raising up His people to know Him and to do the same works that Jesus did. There is hope rising once again among God's people that He will answer all prayer that is spoken with faith, no matter how big the problem or how serious the situation. There are many of us, even now, who are listening to His heart's desire and are willing to carry forth His Word and speak it to the problems of life."

"Could you teach us about God, the way that you know Him?" asked Carrie.

"Of course," answered Linda. "It will take some time, but I'd be glad to. I can give you some specifics, but the best way to learn would be to attend my church and sit under some anointed teaching. That way you will experience God's Presence while being taught, and you will also see others in the same setting, just like yourselves, seeking to learn about the God who loves us and wants to help us in all that we do. We should go in now, don't you think?"

"Yes, it's time. I'm very anxious to see what the doctors have to say about this," answered Carrie.

Linda followed them into the building and then took a seat to wait for them to check in. When Carrie and Jack came over, they sat down facing Linda.

"I told them that I wanted another ultrasound done, but it sounded like they didn't think it necessary. Of course, that's because they don't know what we know. But I insisted that they set it up because of the importance of the situation, and so they finally agreed," said Carrie.

"Good," said Linda. "Little do they know that they will be witness to the goodness of God. I'm wondering if they will accept the truth or deny it?"

"There are a lot of doctors that would say something like this is a miracle. I read stories of things happening that the doctors have no explanation for, and many of them label it 'miracle,'" said Carrie.

"Carrie Johnson? We're ready for you," the nurse at the door called.

They all stood up and followed the nurse through the door and down the corridor. "Right in here," said the nurse, pointing into the room. Handing Carrie a gown, the nurse pointed to a curtained-off area to change. Once Carrie was on the table, the nurse pulled her gown up over her stomach and began to apply some gel to her skin for the ultrasound paddle.

"This will be a little cold to start. Are you ready?" asked the nurse.

"Yes," replied Carrie.

As the picture came up on the screen, they were all watching it, trying to make heads or tails of all the shapes. When the nurse obtained a good picture of the legs, they could all see the scrotum and the legs beneath it. There was no mistaking what was in the picture. The nurse printed out the picture, and when she took it off the machine, she said, "I'll be right back. I think the doctor would like to see this picture."

"Is there something wrong?" asked Carrie.

"No, it doesn't look like there is anything wrong. But I saw the ultrasound yesterday, and this is not the same one," answered the nurse as she hurried from the room.

Carrie was beginning to weep. Linda looked over at Jack and saw that he also had tears running down his cheeks. He leaned over Carrie and wrapped his arms around her, and they both began to cry in earnest. Linda put a hand on each one and began to pray.

"Lord Jesus, we thank You for Your wonderful mercy and compassion that You have shown here today. We thank You, Lord, for showing Yourself strong on our behalf and revealing Your goodness, and we give You all the praise and the honor, in Jesus' name."

After a moment, the nurse walked back in, and a few steps behind her was the doctor.

"Good morning, Carrie," greeted the doctor. "Karen tells me that there has been a change in the ultrasound picture, so I thought I would come over and take a look for myself."

He took hold of the paddle and began to apply pressure and to slide it around on Carrie's stomach until he had a good view of the two small legs. He sat there for several minutes, manipulating the paddle back and forth, staring hard at the screen, looking at the legs from every angle. When he was done, he began to take measurements of the baby's size and also the size of Carrie's stomach. He asked the nurse to hand him the file, and after examining it and comparing the new measurements, he turned to Carrie and looked at her for a moment before saying anything.

"Tell me what happened between yesterday and today," he said.

Carrie looked at Linda, and when she nodded her head, she began her story.

"When I left your office, I stopped by the grocery store to pick up a few things. I guess I was in a little bit of shock while I walked around in the store, wandering from aisle to aisle. I couldn't think straight. I just remember that from the time I left your office, I kept asking God to heal my baby. I remembered when the leper came up to Jesus and said 'Jesus, You can heal me if you are willing,' and Jesus answered him, saying, 'I will.' So, I knew that Jesus is not only able to heal my baby, but He is also willing to do it." Carrie looked straight at the doctor and asked, "Are you sure you want to hear the rest of it?"

"Yes, I do. Everything has changed over night. Right now, you are carrying a perfectly healthy baby, and I want to know why and how, so please continue," answered the doctor. The nurse was standing behind the doctor, listening to everything that was said.

"Well, as I was standing in the store thinking and praying, I saw a woman coming toward me. I noticed that there was something different about her as soon as I saw her. I...uh...don't know any other way to say this, but I sensed the Presence of God. I could feel His love surrounding me, and a great peace came over me. When the woman stopped in front of me, I began to weep, and when she took my hands, it felt like God was touching me. I'll never be able to explain it fully, but I felt a warmth and quietness sweep over me; it was like nothing I've ever felt before." Carrie's eyes were beginning to tear up again, and the doctor handed her a Kleenex. After wiping her eyes, she continued.

"She hugged me close and began to tell me what I had just experienced in your office. She told me all of the details before I said anything to her and then said that God had sent her to me, that God told her where I would be, and pointed me out to her, and even told her my name. I know it's hard to believe, but it happened exactly the way I'm telling you. She knew that my baby is a little boy even, and as she spoke these things to me, I realized that God had indeed sent her to me. She put her hand on my stomach and began to speak life to my baby, to proclaim perfect health and development. I began to cry, and a crowd of people began to gather around, listening to what the woman was saying. As she prayed for me, I began to feel something growing within me, getting larger and larger. When I realized what was actually happening, I broke down and began to sob. The woman told me to come back today and have another ultrasound done, and here we are." Carrie finished her story and waited for the doctor's reply.

The doctor sat motionless through the whole story, listening intently, catching every detail. Looking into Carrie's face, he began to speak.

"It's a hard story to believe all right, but I know what I saw on yesterday's ultrasound, and there was no mistake about my conclusion. Your baby has grown two complete legs since yesterday, and your story is the only thing that makes sense. This is the first miracle that I've ever seen, and it just blows my mind. That God healed your baby is the only thing that it could be. There was nothing there one day, and now there are two complete, healthy legs. I can't get over it, but here is the proof right in front of my face."

"I know. Isn't God wonderful? Jesus healed my baby, just like in the Bible," said Carrie, as tears started to run down her cheeks. Linda glanced over at the nurse and saw that she was wiping the tears out of her own eyes.

The doctor looked at Carrie and then glanced at Jack and Linda. As he looked away from Linda, he thought he could see a glow around her. He looked back at her, but he couldn't make it out. He slowly let his gaze slide away from her, and he could see it again. She didn't have any light behind her, so he couldn't figure out what was causing it. As he was looking for it again, Linda asked him if there was anything wrong.

"No, there's nothing wrong, but I thought that I could see a light behind you but there isn't one. Hmm." The doctor asked Linda to step over to the side of the room, and as she did so, he looked to the side of her. He could see that, as she moved, there was indeed a glow that surrounded her.

He looked at Linda and said, "You're the woman at the grocery store."

"Yes, I am," replied Linda. "I suppose you have some questions?"

"Yes, I do. First of all, was Carrie accurate in her story? Did she leave anything out?"

"She told it just like it happened," answered Linda. "The answer to your second question is no."

"No, what?" asked the doctor. "I haven't asked a second question."

"No, I have never met Carrie before yesterday."

The doctor had a surprised look on his face, and Carrie saw it. She found herself smiling even as she was wiping away her tears.

The doctor asked, "How did you know that was my next question?"

"Was it?" asked Linda.

"Yes, it was. Did you just guess that it was my next question, or did you arrive at that assumption through logic?"

"The way that I knew about Carrie's baby is the same way that I know about you. I know that your wife went to a women's retreat last year with a Christian friend and gave her heart to Jesus, that you attend church occasionally, and that you were taught about the Lord Jesus when you were a teenager but have only recently in the last year begun to seek God again. What is your next question?" asked Linda.

The doctor was dumbfounded. There is no way she could know that, he thought, unless she was psychic.

"No, I'm not a psychic either," said Linda. "God reveals things to me by His Spirit. It's a spiritual gift called word of knowledge, and it operates for the edifying and encouragement of His people. Do you now believe that God has sent me to help Carrie?"

The doctor nodded his head. He was also trying to keep his thoughts in a safe area, for he was afraid that she knew his very thoughts.

"To be honest with you, I've never seen or heard of anything like this ever happening. Where I've gone to church, they didn't teach anything like this," the doctor answered.

"I don't doubt that," replied Linda. "Most churches have decided to ignore that part of the Bible. Down through the ages, men who didn't know God were placed in leadership positions, and eventually the church lost all of its supernatural power of God. But now, at the end of the ages, God is restoring to His church all that she has lost. It will be the faithful sons and daughters of God who know God intimately that will manifest God's power to the world; this is only the beginning."

"Do you heal anybody, or are there limitations?" asked the doctor.

Linda looked at him and said, "I minister to those that God tells me to. I have faith to do what God tells me to do, but if I see someone who moves my heart, I'll ask God if He wants me to do anything for them. Sometimes it's my faith that opens the door for healing, and sometimes it's the person I'm ministering to who has asked God, in faith, for their healing. I do know that God is bringing His people to the point that we will walk in His compassion just as Jesus did, and many millions of miracles will take place."

"So if I ask you to heal my patients, you would say no?" asked the doctor.

"I would have to pray about it. If people don't know about God's goodness, it will be hard for them to receive anything from me. Healing is not something that you just turn on and off, and it would do more harm than good to lay hands on someone who is not prepared, through teaching of the Word of God, to receive a miracle. Many times, the one who is being prayed for needs to believe by faith for their healing."

As Linda paused, the doctor looked from Carrie to the ultrasound screen, then back to Linda. "How do I get to know God?" asked the doctor.

"You believe in Jesus?" asked Linda.

"Yes, I do," replied the doctor.

"Have you ever asked Jesus into your heart, to be your Lord and Savior?"

"No," answered the doctor.

"Have you ever been taught that you have to be born again to enter into the Kingdom of God?" Linda was trying to find his level of understanding and knowledge of the Word of God.

"I'm not sure what you mean," said the doctor.

"Jesus said that a man must be born again to be able to enter the kingdom of God. He meant that your spirit must have a new birth in Him, by the power of His Spirit. When you ask Him to be your Lord and Savior, confess with your mouth that He is the Son of God, and believe in your heart that God has raised Him from the dead, you shall be saved. It is at that moment that God's Spirit comes to you and gives new birth to your spirit. That is being born again. From then on, it's a matter of studying His Word and seeking Him in prayer, building a relationship with Him in much the same way as you develop any relationship. Would you like me to pray with you to be born again?" asked Linda.

The doctor hung his head down as Linda was speaking, thinking about all that she was saying. There was no denying the existence and power of God after today. Since God had proven Himself to be there, he could see no reason not to accept Him into his life. Looking up into Linda's face, he could feel God's Presence. He noticed that his own heart rate was beginning to climb, yet there was no reason for it.

"Yes, I want your God to be part of my life," responded the doctor. His voice was low and husky as he spoke.

Carrie began wiping the tears from her eyes, and as she looked up at Jack, she saw that he also was wiping his eyes. When Jack saw her looking at him, he took her hand in his and squeezed it tight.

Linda looked at the nurse.

"You are a Christian already, aren't you?" asked Linda.

"Yes, I am," answered the nurse. There was a surprised look on her face as it dawned on her that Linda didn't know her, yet she knew that she was a believer. "I love Jesus, but I didn't know that we could have this kind of relationship with Him. I've never had any teaching on these types of things, but there's no denying that God answers your prayers," answered the nurse.

"There will come a day in your future that you will see your prayers answered in the same way. If you begin to seek Him with all your heart and soul, you will find Him just like I have. God is no respecter of persons, so what is available to one He will make available to others," said Linda.

Linda took the doctor's hands in her own and said, "Repeat after me. Lord Jesus, I believe that you are the Son of God and that you died on the cross for my sins." Linda paused to let the doctor speak and then continued. "I ask you now to receive me as your own...to forgive my sins...and to be my Lord and Savior...I thank You Jesus for saving me and giving me new life in You. Amen."

As the doctor finished speaking, Linda looked at him, and she could see a new light on his face and a light in his eyes as he opened them and looked back at her. She smiled at him and said, "Welcome to the family of God." She leaned forward and hugged him.

"I guess it would be proper now to ask what your name is," asked Linda.

"Oh, yes," laughed the doctor. "My name is Alan Jones. You know what? I really feel different. That wasn't something that I was expecting."

"Of course! Your spirit has been born again within you, and you can feel it throughout your whole being," explained Linda. "People think that Christianity is just another religion of the world, but it's much more than that. It is the truth of the one and only God, who loves us and wants to help us, who wants us to be His children and to look to Him as a beloved Father. He has given us His Holy Spirit to live within us while we are here and as the guarantee of our future with Him."

Jack and Carrie were listening intently to everything that Linda had to say. Just listening to her explain about God was exciting; they had learned more about God in the last two days than they had in the last five years at the church they had been attending.

"Dr. Jones?" Carrie asked. "Jack and I are going to attend Linda's church. Why don't you think about going, too? We can all learn about God together."

"I just might do that, Carrie. My wife has been wanting to visit other churches lately, so I'm sure she would like to try it," answered Dr. Jones.

"My church is over on South Twelfth Street," said Linda. "The name is Victory Fellowship. Come on out on Sunday; services start at ten o'clock. I'm sure you'll all enjoy it. Don't worry about a dress code or anything like that, okay? We've got everyone from cowboys to executives of businesses, restaurant owners to teachers and nurses. Just come, expecting to meet God in the praise and worship service, and you'll grow to know Him and to love Him."

"Okay, I'll be there," answered the doctor. "I don't have anything else on my schedule this weekend, so you can count on my wife and me being there."

"Would it be okay if I come to your church, too?" asked the nurse.

Linda looked at the nurse and smiled. Taking her hands in hers, she said, "Certainly. I would be so glad to see you there, too."

"We'll be there too," added Jack. "We wouldn't miss it for the world."

"I guess we're all done here, then," said Dr. Jones. "I've got more patients to attend to. Carrie, I'm very glad that everything is fine with your baby now." He put his hand over hers and squeezed it. "I'll see you on Sunday, and be sure to come in if anything comes up, okay?"

"Okay, Dr. Jones, I will. And thank you so much for your help. Good-bye." The doctor walked out, and Jack helped Carrie to her feet. After she had changed into her clothes, Linda handed her a picture of her baby with his new legs.

"The doctor left this sitting on his chair. I think you should keep it as a testimony of your miracle," said Linda.

"I will," answered Carrie. They walked outside, and in the parking lot Carrie turned to Linda and hugged her close.

"Thank you so much for everything, Linda. If there's anything we can do for you, don't hesitate to ask, okay?"

"Okay, Carrie. I'll see you guys on Sunday. God bless you both."

When Linda arrived home, she went straight to Mac and told him everything that had happened. Mac listened to the details, smiling and nodding his head, and when Linda got to the part about Dr. Jones getting saved, he began to grin.

"That is so good and so like God," replied Mac. "Praise the Lord for His goodness and His grace."

"Yes, Jesus is wonderful," agreed Linda. "So you and Pastor John believe that we're going to be seeing more things like these ones?"

"Yes, we do. You've noticed a change in God's Presence during our prayer time?" asked Mac.

"I have. His Presence is so strong when I'm praying that it's hard to stand, I have to sit or kneel most of the time. Come to think of it, it's like that almost daily now. Before, I would feel His Presence like that only once in a great while," answered Linda.

"I think it's a combination of things that are causing that to happen. First, we are drawing closer to God, and in turn, He is drawing closer to us. Second, the end of the ages is drawing to a close, and God has His own agenda to carry out, and that includes His people walking in His Presence and His powerful anointing to accomplish His goal. Third, Jesus is coming back for a glorious bride, not one that has been whipped by the enemy in every area of life, and we must be very well acquainted with His Presence to walk in His power and to destroy the works of the enemy and to win the lost," said Mac.

"I'm so glad that we're together in these last days, honey," said Linda.

"Me too," replied Mac. "We make a good team, don't you think?"

Linda looked into Mac's eyes and smiled. As she wrapped her arms around him, there was a twinkle in her eyes as she replied.

"Yes, the three of us are a good team," replied Linda.

CHAPTER SEVEN

Kevin was waiting patiently all morning for the call from the general contractor. He stayed close to the phone, not wanting to miss it, just doodling around in his office, finding little things to take up his time. He and Sue had prayed together earlier in the morning, thanking God for His provision. They were beginning to notice the last two times that they had prayed together that God's Presence was stronger than they had ever felt before. It was as if they had broken through something with their victory in their finances and now they were able to sense the Presence of God in a whole new way.

"Don't be anxious, honey," said Sue as she walked into the room. "You know he's going to call, so just relax, and maybe you can do some Bible reading."

"The truth is I wasn't anxious about that call at all. What I'm anxious about is talking to Mac again, but that won't be until after the other call comes in," replied Kevin.

"Why don't you get your Bible and read some in the book of Acts and see how our situation might fit in with all of that?" said Sue.

"Okay, I'll do that. Thanks for the inspiration. I love you, Sue," responded Kevin.

Sue looked into Kevin's eyes and smiled. "I love you, too; now get busy." She turned and left the room, and Kevin got up, walked over to the lamp table next to the couch, and got his Bible.

He began to think about how a lot of the early disciples had sold their properties and brought the money to the apostles, so that it could be dispersed among those who needed it. That was a little different from his situation, but it was still a story of God providing for those who needed it. And then there was the time that the disciples took up a collection for the saints in Jerusalem because of an upcoming drought that would affect the financial status of the church located there. God was again providing for a need. Also, God provided Paul and his traveling companions employment as they went from city to city, to give them the finances they needed to live on. Sometimes there were even people that they ministered to who were well off financially, and they helped them on their way with money, food, and lodgings. So it would look like that God has people doing well financially just so they can help the church and the people connected with it, no matter what the need.

Even one of God's covenant names is *Jehovah Jireh*, meaning *the Lord Our Provider*. He wants to provide for us, but we have to look to Him for it or else we will boast about our own ability to get our own wealth. Since we are supposed to live by faith and not by sight, we need to depend on Him for our provision, seeking Him in faith and trusting in His ability to supernaturally meet our needs. What a situation for a testimony of God's care and provision!

Kevin was deep in thought and jumped when the phone began to ring. He went to his desk and looked at the caller ID. Yep! It was Dale Lancaster all right. He picked up the phone and said hello. It was hard to keep his voice normal; it was very exciting to know what was going to happen before it did.

"Hello, Kevin?" asked Dale.

"Yes, this is Kevin."

"This is Dale Lancaster. How are you?"

"I'm doing great. How are you doing on that big project? It must be about ready to start the excavation," asked Kevin.

"Yes, as a matter of fact it is. That's why I'm calling. I...uh...ran into some problems with the other excavator. He's not going to be able to do my project on time, and I was wondering if you had enough free time to start it early next week?" asked Dale.

"I can probably squeeze it into my schedule. What day were you thinking of starting?" asked Kevin.

"Well, the truth is I would like to get it started on Monday. I know it's on short notice, but if you can do that for me I'll give you a two-thousand-dollar bonus and give you a check for twenty-five percent of the bid up front. Could you swing that for me?" asked Dale.

"That sounds good to me," answered Kevin. "How about meeting me there in the morning and you can fill me in on all the details?"

"Okay, Kevin. I'll see you there at eight o'clock. And thanks. This really helps me out," said Dale.

"No problem, Dale. I'm glad to be able to help you out. I'll see you in the morning. Good-bye."

"Good-bye," replied Dale.

Hanging up, Kevin looked over at his wife, who had come into the room halfway through the conversation. He couldn't help but grin at her.

"You will never believe what just happened! God is so good, I can hardly believe it! Dale is going to give me a two-thousand-dollar bonus for squeezing his job into my busy schedule, and he's going to pay me twenty-five percent of my bid up front! How's that for our God?" laughed Kevin.

"Wow!" Sue whispered. "Do you realize what this means? Mac was right about everything that he told you. I can't wait to meet him for myself."

"I know how you feel, and I've already met him! I'm going to give him a call right away, but first I think we ought to pray and give thanks to God for this extra blessing." He walked around his desk, took hold of Sue's hands, and they both knelt to the floor.

"Lord God, we thank You for Your goodness and grace, for blessing us financially in such a great way and leading us into Your truth." God's Presence began to fill the room as they prayed; they could feel His love enveloping them both. "Lord, I love you." Kevin's heart was overwhelmed with God's Spirit. It was an experience that neither of them had ever experienced before; God touched them to the very depths of their being. They found themselves on their faces before Almighty God; they worshipped Him from their hearts for the first time in their life. They felt so free and so clean, their spirits refreshed in His Presence. He is so Holy, righteous, and compassionate. They began to comprehend how much God really loves them, not just a Bible teaching but a reality. They waited before the Lord, basking in His Presence. They could feel that God was pleased with them, and they wept freely before Him.

Jim Norman

"Lord Jesus," Kevin began, "we give our lives to You, to use as You see best. Help us to know You and to serve You, to trust You and to follow where You lead."

It was a while before they felt His Presence lessening, but even as they arose, they knew that He was still with them. They always knew that He was with them because of what they were taught from the Bible, but now they were aware of His abiding Presence like never before. They knew that their walk with Jesus was never going to be the same, something had broken through in their spirits, and they were never going to let it go.

Sue was still wiping away her tears when Kevin reached for her and hugged her close.

"Wow! God loves us," whispered Kevin. "I never knew how much until now. Mac knows this love; when I was with him, this is what I felt. Not quite as strong as this was, but it was the same love."

"I feel that God wants us to meet with Mac," said Sue. "He'll teach us what we need to know. I sense that God has a big plan going on, and He's now putting us into position in it "

"Yes," responded Kevin. "I think we've stepped up to a new level in God, and there's going to be a lot to learn in a short time. Let's give Mac a call and see what he has to say."

Kevin reached into his desk drawer, pulled out Mac's card, and dialed his number.

"Hello, Kevin," Mac said.

"Hello, Mac," answered Kevin. "How did you know it was me?"

"I wasn't being spiritual, if that's what you mean. Caller ID," laughed Mac.

"Oh yes. Caller ID. I forgot about that. I guess after yesterday I'm thinking that you know everything. But you don't, do you?" asked Kevin.

"No. As much as I've learned, I still don't know much, and as for the other kind of knowing, I only know what God wants me to know. But right now, I would guess that you want to tell me about your other blessing. Am I right?" asked Mac.

"Yes, you're right. I just got off the phone with the general contractor about a half hour ago. He wants me to meet with him tomorrow and go over the details at the site and to start work on Monday. This is the good part. Since he wants me to start right away on short notice, he's going to pay me a two-thousand-dollar bonus *and* pay me twenty-five percent of my bid up front. I'm learning how good God really is!" exclaimed Kevin.

"Praise the Lord! God can certainly surprise us sometimes, can't He?" laughed Mac.

"Yes. He has surprised me more in the last two days than I ever thought possible. Sue and I were just in prayer before I called you, and we got a surprise then, too. God's Presence came in, and we found ourselves on the floor. We've never experienced His Presence in such a way, and we didn't know what to do. All we could do was worship Him and cry," related Kevin.

"Sometimes Kevin, that's all we need to do. That has a way of opening our heart to Him like no other way. Once we reach that stage, we want Him more and more. You and Sue have a good beginning."

"Thanks to you, Mac," responded Kevin.

"Not thanks to me, Kevin. Thanks to your stand of faith. If you hadn't stood in faith for God's deliverance and provision, you would not have seen me yesterday, I can guarantee that. Do you recall this verse? 'For the eyes of the Lord run to and fro throughout the whole earth, to show Himself strong on behalf of those whose heart is loyal to Him.'"

Jim Norman

"Yes, I remember that verse," answered Kevin.

"In your stand of faith, your heart was loyal to Him, believing for His help, and when He saw that, He showed Himself strong on your behalf. He fulfilled His promise to your faith. Now do you understand?" asked Mac.

"Yes. He wants to help us, but His hands are tied if we don't believe by faith for His intervention," answered Kevin.

"You've got it. In the book of James it says, 'But let him ask in faith, with no doubting, for he who doubts is like a wave of the sea driven and tossed by the wind. For let not that man suppose that he will receive anything from the Lord; he is a double-minded man, unstable in all his ways.' James is talking about asking for wisdom from God, but it is still a principle for all of our asking," explained Mac. "We have to have it settled in our heart and mind that He is able and also willing to help us, and in studying the Bible we will learn all the ways in which He wants to help us."

"I'm beginning to see, Mac. I've heard a little bit of teaching on faith from my pastor, but it wasn't as clear-cut or authoritative as what you've been telling me," said Kevin.

"Tell you what, Kevin. Let's have lunch together, and we can talk about it some more, okay?" asked Mac.

"That sounds good to me. I'd like my wife to meet you too, if that's okay. Where would you like to meet?" asked Kevin.

"How about the Pizza House on 97?"

"That's fine. About twelve o'clock?" inquired Kevin.

"Yes. I'll bring my wife Linda along, too. She's got a testimony you might like to listen to. We'll see you there, Kevin," said Mac.

"Okay, Good-bye."

CHAPTER EIGHT

Kevin and Sue were already there when Mac and Linda walked in. Kevin raised his hand and waved them over.

"Hi, Kevin. And this must be Sue. Hello." Mac took her hand and shook it. Immediately, tears started to water her eyes. "This is my wife, Linda. Honey, this is Kevin and Sue Hendrix."

Linda hugged both of them, and after she pulled back, Sue cleared her throat and wiped her eyes. "Mac, I want to thank you so much for blessing us. I could hardly believe it, and I praise God for you," said Sue.

"You're certainly welcome, Sue. We all serve the same Lord, and Linda and I are so blessed to have been able to help you," explained Mac.

After their greetings, they walked over to the counter and ordered. When they were finally seated, Mac looked at Kevin and Sue to get their attention.

"Before anything else, I'd like you to hear Linda's story

about what happened yesterday and today with another couple that the Lord had her minister to," said Mac.

"Okay. Go ahead," replied Kevin.

"Well, to begin, I was home yesterday afternoon, Mac had already shared his story about your meeting, when the Spirit of God told me to go to the Safeway store. He said there was a young woman there who needed His help and that she was praying. Mac and I prayed right away before I left, and when I got to the store, the Lord led me to her. He told me that she was pregnant and that her baby boy didn't have any legs and that I was to lay my hand on her and pray for him. After speaking to her and letting her know what the Lord revealed to me about her situation, I placed my hand on her stomach and began to speak God's will into her womb. She began to weep, and then she started sobbing as she felt her little baby begin to grow legs within her womb. When I was finished..." Linda shared with them the whole story and finished it with the doctor's salvation prayer.

Kevin and Sue could only sit there and stare at Linda, listening with rapt attention. It was like nothing they had ever heard of before, and by the time that Linda was finished, Kevin had tears in his eyes and Sue was outright weeping.

"Carrie and her husband, Jack, are both going to be in church Sunday, and Dr. Jones and his wife are also planning on coming. Hopefully Carrie will give her testimony to the whole church, and with her doctor also being there, it will be something extraordinary to hear. You guys ought to plan on coming too. I think it's going to be a great day for God's Glory," said Mac.

While Mac was speaking, Kevin was wiping his eyes with a napkin and Sue was digging in her purse for a Kleenex.

"You know Mac, except for my mom and Sue, you've seen me cry more than anyone else has in my entire life. I feel like a real softie, but I guess God has a way of doing that to people," said Kevin.

"That story just touches my heart," added Sue. "I've always wanted to believe that God would do something like that, but I just didn't expect it to happen. That's just not something that you hear pastors teaching about."

"I know," replied Linda. "There aren't many churches out there that believe for God's supernatural power to be manifested. If the pastors don't teach it, then the congregation won't seek it. They may want it, but they don't have any sound biblical teaching on it so they don't have any idea of how to get it to operate."

"And without us having faith in God's ability and His willingness to intervene on our behalf, He won't move," added Mac. "His power is there for us, but it has to be activated by faith. Do you know that verse in Hebrews 11:6? 'But without faith it is impossible to please Him, for he who comes to God must believe that He is, and that He is a rewarder of those who diligently seek Him.'"

"Yes, I'm familiar with that one," answered Kevin.

"So many Bible teachers today have downplayed the fact that God wants to reward His people if they will seek Him diligently. If it's taught that He wants to reward us, then the question comes up: what kind of reward? Are the rewards financial, physical, or spiritual? Of course, the easy answer is spiritual rewards. Spiritual growth, spiritual knowledge, spiritual awareness—you get the picture. Those things are intangible; they are not necessarily seen, and they can also be falsified somewhat. But if the rewards are physical, such as healing in the body, then that is something that is very easy to see, whether the person actually got healed or not. There is no hiding it when you don't get healed of a visible sickness or disease. It's at that point when the question arises, 'Why didn't they get healed?' And the assumed answer is usually, 'I guess it wasn't God's will' or 'That Scripture verse must mean something else.' People actually talk themselves out of believing in God's goodness," explained Mac.

"I'm beginning to see what you mean," replied Kevin. "I think I was beginning to get an inkling of understanding about that just before I met you."

"Yes, you had to be, or you wouldn't have been believing by faith for a financial miracle. Do you know what is really sad about the way God's people are being taught today? They are being taught that good things are bad and bad things that happen are good, completely opposite to what Jesus actually taught."

Mac was interrupted by the loud speaker calling out their names.

"I'll finish that thought in a moment," Mac said as he stood up. Kevin also stood, and they walked over and picked up their order. After praying a blessing over the food, they began to eat, and Mac resumed his conversation.

"Do you remember the place where Jesus was in the temple on the Sabbath day, and there was a man sitting there listening to Jesus teach who had a shriveled hand?" inquired Mac.

"Is that the one where Jesus has the man stand up to be healed?" asked Kevin.

"Yes, that's the one. When the man stood up in front of all the people, Jesus asked the Pharisees if it was right to do good on the Sabbath or to do evil, to save life or destroy it. He was confronting their religious thinking about the

Sabbath day. But the point here is that Jesus likens the healing to doing good and not healing to doing evil, also healing to saving life and not healing to destroying life. Do you see that?"

"Yes, I do. I mean, I see it now that you explained it. It looks as plain as the nose on your face. I wonder why I never saw that before?" said Kevin.

"Mostly, it's because a religious mindset is like a pair of colored glasses. Every Bible teaching that is looked at through those glasses is tainted with that mindset. Down through the ages those colored glasses have tainted almost everything from the Bible with human reasoning and error. So, when people have their understanding darkened by false teaching and human wisdom, small things like this go unnoticed. It is only when the truth pierces that veil that light and understanding come.

"Think about this: when people ask God for healing and they don't get it, then their assumption is that God doesn't want to heal them. But according to this, then God is evil, because He doesn't heal. We know God is not evil and cannot commit any evil, so there must be something else that prevents God from acting. The religious thinking is that God is sovereign and can do anything that He wants here, so if you don't receive healing then God doesn't want you healed. Also, everything that happens here, whether good or bad, is God's will. If you get sick with a disease and God doesn't heal you, then that is God's will for you. But the thought that God wants you sick and diseased, even to the point of dying, is completely foreign to Jesus' teachings. Jesus clearly shows that healing is saving life and doing good. Do you know the verse in the tenth chapter of Acts, verse 38? 'How God anointed Jesus of Nazareth with the Holy Spirit and with power, who went about doing good and healing all who were oppressed by the devil, for God was with Him.' With everything within Him, Jesus combated sickness and disease throughout the entire time of His ministry. He clearly represented God's desire as wanting to save life and to do good to people. He has not changed just because the religious crowd teaches a different doctrine. The religious crowd will not or cannot accept this thought or teaching because it will expose their religious mindset as false," finished Mac.

"I see. That is definitely something to think about. But you are right about that mindset of everything that happens is God's will. There are people dying every day who go to hell, but we know that God doesn't want anyone to perish but come to the saving knowledge of Jesus. It's simple to see that God's will doesn't always come to pass," replied Kevin.

"You've got that right," agreed Mac. "Everyone has a free will to choose what he wants to do, good or bad. It isn't God's fault that people choose to ignore Him. It's just like if you tell your child to stay off the road or they might get run over by a car. You care so much about their well-being that you even build a fence for their protection. If they choose to ignore your command and do their own will, even to the point of climbing out of the fence, and a car hits them and kills them, whose fault is it—yours or theirs? It's their fault, not yours, and neither was it your will that they died. You tried to keep them safe, but because they were rebellious and wanted to do things their way, they brought on their own destruction."

"That's a good analogy, Mac. God tries to bring us to salvation, but when we ignore Him we end up bringing on our own destruction."

"If you two don't stop talking, your food is going to get cold," interjected Linda. "Enjoy your food first; then you can talk."

"Okay, honey. You're right; we've got plenty of time to talk later, and the food here is good," replied Mac. They finished their meal with a quiet satisfaction of enjoyment, but when it was over, they resumed their discussion.

"Let me ask you this," started Mac. "Do you know of anywhere in the Bible that when the people repented of their sin and turned to God with all their heart, God ignored them instead of lifting them up out of the mire that they were in?"

"No, I can't think of anything like that," replied Kevin.

"God wants people to turn to Him, so when we finally do turn, He will meet us right where we're at and begin to change us. If we are sincere about it, He will always help us. Think about the time of the judges, when the whole nation of Israel would turn away from God and His commandments. Their rebellion would open the door for their enemies to triumph over them in battle, but every time they would repent and turn back to God, He would raise up a strong leader for them to follow into battle, and they would be victorious over their enemies once again. He wants to help people because He loves them, but if they won't seek Him or listen to His instructions then they are on their own."

Mac paused for just a moment as a thought came to him, then started again.

"Here's an example. You remember Gideon?" he asked.

"Yes."

"Gideon's victory, was it brought about by something he read about in the Old Testament or was it accomplished by listening to and obeying the commandments and instructions of the Angel of the Lord?"

"By obeying the voice of the Lord," answered Kevin.

"Should it be any different today? We have our Bible to teach us how to live our life, but for specific instructions on how to walk victoriously in all the variables and complexities of life, we have to seek Him to get our answers. When we get those answers, we have to do what He tells us. If we get our instructions on what to do but then fail to obey them, we won't walk in the victory that He wanted for us. That's the way it works throughout the whole Bible, starting with Adam and ending with all the apostles. All of them had to follow personal instructions to walk in victory.

"Today, there are lots of Christians who don't walk in any kind of victory. Some have partial victory, and there are a few that have victory in many areas. And, of course, there are some that seem to have a certain amount of victory, not necessarily by the power of God but obtained through worldly wisdom or common sense. I want to make this clear: even if we don't have a victorious lifestyle, it doesn't mean that we don't belong to God; nor does it mean that He loves us less. But if we don't seek Him to lead us into victory, then we are just as susceptible to the curse of Adam and to all of the enemy's schemes as are the unsaved.

"The world is under the control of the evil one and is still under the curse of Adam. If we aren't God's people or if we aren't listening to and obeying Him, then we are susceptible to all the bad things that are out there. Sickness and disease, poverty, ruin, sin, death and decay, theft, destruction, and the list goes on. There is no promise of protection outside of God."

"That's good, Mac. You have a way about you that makes it easy to understand what the Bible is all about. There are so many questions I wanted to ask, and yet you have already answered most of them without me even asking them," replied Kevin.

"That's because God has anointed me to teach His Word. That is my main calling, to lead others to an understanding of the goodness and grace of our God. Because it's a gift from God, it is no longer me who teaches but the Spirit of God who dwells in me," explained Mac.

"Not to change the subject, but can you explain to me how it works that you can hear from God so clearly?" asked Sue. "We've never heard of anyone, outside of the Bible, hearing from God like you do."

"Yes, I can. But I think Linda would like to answer that one," replied Mac.

Linda looked at Mac and smiled.

"Thank you, honey. You're right on that one." Linda looked at Sue and started to speak, "The fastest answer would be that the more time you spend with God, the closer to Him you get, the better you know Him, and in time He begins to talk with you. He has always wanted to fellowship with us, beginning with Adam and Eve. He talked with them and walked with them. Do you think that His desire has ever changed?"

Sue answered, "No. But what makes it so different with some people that they do talk with God and He actually answers?"

"If God wants to talk with us and share fellowship with mankind, and yet there are so few that He actually does this with, then there must be some kind of barrier that prevents it from happening. From Adam down through the Old

Testament to Jesus, God has spoken in fellowship with a certain few. Mostly those were His spokesmen to mankind, His prophets and priests. But there were others who sought God with their whole heart, and they found Him. There's a few that are recorded, but many that are not.

"Then there was Jesus. Do you realize that He prayed to the Father all the time, that Jesus asked the Father questions about what to do, where to go, what was going to happen? I believe He got His daily instructions from His Father every morning. Many people today believe that Jesus knew everything, that because He was God in the flesh of man, He had all knowledge. But Jesus had to learn about God the Father the same way we do: by reading the Word of God. God revealed to Jesus who He was by revelation knowledge of the Old Testament Scriptures. Jesus' earthly father Joseph taught Him the Scriptures faithfully, but it was God Himself who opened Jesus' eyes to His true heritage, that He was indeed the Messiah. Even in Luke, the end of chapter 2, it says that Jesus increased in wisdom and stature and in favor with God and men. That means Jesus had to learn knowledge and wisdom; He didn't start out with all knowledge about everything.

"Think about this: if Jesus knew everything that God the Father knew; if He had known everything that He was going to do, how He was going to do it, and when; if He was in complete harmony and oneness with God all the time, then why did He pray at all? What purpose did it serve? Even at the last, in the garden, Jesus asked the Father if there was any way that the cup could pass from Him. This implies that Jesus didn't know for sure that His torture and crucifixion was the only way for man's redemption. I thank God that Jesus was fully submitted to His Father's will and didn't turn away from His mission."

"I think I'm beginning to see what you mean, Linda," answered Sue. "If Jesus shared complete thought and knowledge with God, then there would be nothing to pass between them in prayer, in either direction. Yet Jesus spent more time praying to God than anyone else recorded in the Bible."

"You've got it," replied Linda. "Jesus revealed to us, by His own relationship with God, the way to have a progressively closer relationship of our own with God. He passed this on to His disciples, and after His ascension, His disciples developed a relationship with God the Father; they had intimate fellowship with Him through the indwelling Spirit of God.

"And at the end of the Bible we see a close and intimate fellowship that the apostle John had with God the Father, Jesus, and the Holy Spirit. That is the kind of relationship that God has always wanted with His people, a one-to-one closeness. The ones who had that kind of relationship with God were committed to God before they developed that closeness. It was a developed relationship that progressed from an acknowledgment and acceptance of God to seeking Him with a whole heart in sincerity and truth. So, you see that through the whole Bible, God reveals that He wants and desires to fellowship with His people, to walk and talk with us even as He did with Adam and Eve. He has opened a way, through the atonement of Jesus, for us to have a closer relationship with Him than even Moses had, but it is up to us to make that decision to seek Him with our whole heart and to develop that closeness that He so desires," finished Linda.

"Wow! And you thought I was long-winded," exclaimed Mac, jokingly. "I didn't know you had that much in you."

Smiling, Linda looked at Mac and replied, "You know that I can't hold a candle to you in that regard. Sometimes,

I just expect to find you collapsed on the floor from lack of breathing."

They all began to laugh at Linda's remark. Mac took Linda's hand in his own as he was laughing, then looked at Kevin.

"I hope you got all your questions answered today, but if you have more, just say so," said Mac.

"I'm sure we'll have more questions. Maybe I'll start a list so I can remember all of them," replied Kevin.

"Kevin, I want to leave you and Sue with this instruction. You both want to come to our church, but you need to ask God if that is His will for you. It is very important that you have His release from the church that you are now attending. Never leave your church except under His instruction, and if you do leave, make sure your heart is right with your pastor. Give offense no place to take hold between you and the church you are leaving. Do you understand?" asked Mac.

"Yes. We'll both do as you said. And if we have His release for this Sunday, where is your church located?"

"Our church is Victory Fellowship, and it's located over on South Twelfth Street. If you end up coming Sunday, the service starts at ten o'clock," answered Mac.

"We both feel already that God wants us to attend your church, but we'll ask Him about it in prayer tonight to make sure that it's what He wants," said Kevin.

"Okay. Now, let's pray before we go." They all joined hands and Mac began.

"Lord, we thank You for Your goodness and Your grace in our lives. We ask, Father, for Your guidance and wisdom for Kevin and Sue; let them know Your will concerning their church and where You want them to be placed. Go before them, Lord, and prepare their path with peace and under-standing, and we give You all our praise and honor You. In Jesus' name, amen."

Kevin looked at Mac, then hugged him.

"Thanks, Mac, for everything. Your obedience to God has changed our lives forever. Thanks, Linda, for coming today and sharing your testimony; it stirred my heart as much if not more than the financial blessing we received." Linda stepped over to Kevin, gave him a big hug, and then hugged Sue. Sue had tears in her eyes again and when she turned to Mac, her lip began to quiver as she started to speak.

"Mac and Linda, I'm so grateful to have met both of you. I know that you were just following God's directions when you helped us, but there are a lot of Christians out there who have lots of money. But it was the two of you that God called on to help us in our time of need, and I think that is something very special. Thank you." As Sue finished, Linda hugged her again, and then Mac stepped up and gave her a fatherly embrace.

"Thank you, Sue. We are only too glad to be able to help. I've already been thanking God myself for bringing us together. Maybe we'll see you on Sunday. God bless you and take care of you. Good-bye, Kevin."

"So long, Mac." replied Kevin.

It was late at the hospital when Johnny and his sister, Alice, left their mother's room and walked over to the visi-tors' family room. At twelve years old, Johnny couldn't imagine his life without his mom. Johnny was starting to cry by the time they walked through the door. Alice, fifteen years old, put her arms around her little brother and hugged him close. She had to be strong for Johnny, but tears were also beginning to escape out from under her closed eyelids, although she was trying her best to stop them.

"Why doesn't God heal Mom?" asked Johnny, through his tears.

"Daddy says sometimes God loves someone so much that He wants them to be with Him in Heaven," answered Alice, her voice breaking.

"But I love her that much, too," replied Johnny.

"I know you do Johnny. I do too, but Daddy says God knows best," explained Alice.

"Well, I'm going to keep praying and asking God to change His mind. I don't want Mommy to leave me," cried Johnny.

"I'll keep praying too, Johnny. Maybe He *will* hear us."

The door opened, and they saw their dad standing there. Before he turned his face away, Alice could see the tears on his cheeks and realized that he was trying to keep them from seeing that he was crying. She let go of Johnny, stepped over to her dad, and put her arms around him. He looked down at her and then wrapped his arms around her.

"Don't cry, Daddy," whispered Alice through her own tears.

That was all it took. All of his strength was gone, and he broke, tears falling to the floor, his body wracked with deep sobbing. For several moments, the two of them stood there in each other's arms, comforting one another.

The nurse on duty behind the counter knew what was going on; she had been attending to Clare Shelton for the last few evenings. As she heard what passed between father and daughter, she had to turn away and step back into the interior office. Her throat began to constrict, and the heartache that began to grow brought tears to her eyes. She would never get used to this part of her job. Although she was out of sight of the Shelton family, she could still hear the continuing sobbing of Mr. Shelton and his son's declaration.

Johnny had stopped crying, and with a new strength, he stepped toward his dad and looked up at him. "Daddy, don't cry. I'm going to keep asking God to heal Mom, and I think He's going to change His mind." Johnny's dad stretched out his hand and pulled him up close in a tight embrace with his sister.

Joanna, the nurse, took a deep breath when she heard Johnny's declaration, trying to keep from breaking down into sobbing herself. After wiping the tears from her eyes, when she could finally speak, she uttered her own prayer for Johnny's sake. "Lord, please heal Johnny's mom. Don't let them be robbed of the one they love so dearly. Please, not this time. In Jesus' name, amen."

CHAPTER NINE

When Sunday arrived, Mac and Linda were at the church early for prayer. About forty regulars showed up at seven o'clock for pre-service prayer. They all wanted God's Presence to be at the services in a mighty way and were committed and faithful to do all they could to prepare the way in prayer. They prayed for God's direction in every service, to lead the pastor and the worship leader also in all that they did. There would always be people in the services who needed God's intervention in some way or another. Only God knew all of the details and how best to meet their needs, whether it was a particular teaching from the Word of God, a touch of God's Spirit during the praise and worship, a testimony, a timely word of encouragement, or just a hug. God needed to be the one in charge to accomplish His goals.

The prayer group was growing, and in the last few weeks, as God's Presence began to fill the room, more and more people began showing up. It was made known to all of them that the pre-service prayer time was devoted to intercession for the services, not for anyone to get prayed for personally. As the people prayed within the Presence of God, their hearts were bound tighter to the Spirit; they were led to pray God's perfect will and to battle the enemy with fervency; a new fire in their hearts lifted them to new heights in prayer. As they gave themselves over to God's Spirit, there arose within the people an expectancy of God's goodness, a new and living hope that began to spread throughout the congregation.

This morning, Mac and Linda arrived earlier than usual, for they wanted to spend some time alone with God before the rest of the prayer warriors showed up. When they entered the parking lot, they recognized the pastor's car, and the pastor and his wife were already in the prayer room when Mac and Linda walked in.

When they approached the door to the prayer room, there was a tangible Presence of Almighty God. With reverence and awe they walked through the door and knelt down in worship. As the four of them prayed, His Presence was almost overwhelming. They found themselves prostrate on the floor before Almighty God, His love enveloping them in a tangible way. They worshipped Him from their hearts, their spirits refreshed by His Presence. After some moments they were able to come to their knees and began to pray in other languages, sensing God's leading and His desire.

They all knew that God wanted to do something special today during the service, and as they continued to pray God revealed to them that He wanted Carrie and Dr. Jones to testify to their miracle. He wanted them to tell their story after the praise but before the end of the worship service, and then He would take over from there. He wanted to move into the service with His Glory, to touch His people like never before. Mac and Linda were overwhelmed with the magnitude of what God showed them that He wanted to do, but they began to pray what He wanted, following where His Spirit led them.

It wasn't often that His Presence was so strong, and they knew that God was going to do something very special today. God had told Pastor John and Kathy the previous morning how He wanted the service to go today and that they were to show up early before all of the others arrived. So, they arose earlier than usual this morning, anticipating the day, excited to watch what God was going to do.

They all began to intercede for the service, to block the enemy from interfering, calling in all the people who needed to be in the service today, binding doubt and unbelief. As they prayed, angels began to take their places around the building, positioning themselves to protect the service from any of the enemy's agents that tried to interfere in the work of God. Other angels went forth to awaken those who were called to be here this day, making sure that the enemy didn't prevent them from attending the service.

As the four of them continued in prayer, the door kept opening and closing as others filtered into the room. When people approached the door, some of them stepped back, beginning to weep, and turned the other way. The Presence of God convicted them of sin in their life, and they moved off to different areas of the church to be alone before God to confess and repent of their wrongdoing. They knew that they couldn't enter the prayer room this morning without a clean heart, for the fear of the Lord was standing guard. But as they were cleansed of their sin, the Spirit of God drew them back to the prayer room, to enter in and worship the Lord. The others who walked directly into the room did so with reverence and awe and stayed on their feet only long enough to find a spot to kneel down.

Soon the room was overflowing with people and prayers; many different languages were declaring the goodness of God, rising as a sweet aroma before the throne of God. The prayers were drifting throughout the halls of the church building, and as others arrived, they began to pray outside the prayer room, to kneel where they were, opening their hearts to God. As time went on, those who left the prayer room to do their assignments and their duties left open spaces, but they were quickly filled in with the latecomers who desired to enter into the Presence of God.

There was a growing anticipation in the house of God, spreading among the people, starting with those who had prayed and extending to those who didn't know or understand the Presence of God. The ones who had never experienced God's Presence were a little bit nervous, not understanding what was happening, but the Spirit of God kept them in the building.

Mac and Linda kept watch on the door, waiting for the arrival of Carrie, Jack, and Dr. Jones and his wife. When they saw Carrie and Jack approaching, they met them at the door.

"Good morning, Carrie," Linda began, hugging her tight. "Hello, Jack. I'd like you to meet my husband, Mac. Honey, this is Jack and Carrie."

"Praise the Lord! I'm so glad to meet you and that you were able to make it today." Mac gave both of them a big hug to welcome them.

"We'd like to introduce you to our pastor and his wife. I think he's over in his office. Come with me." Linda led the way and was soon standing before Pastor John and his wife, Kathy.

"This is Pastor John and his wife, Kathy. Pastor, I'd like you to meet Jack and Carrie Johnson." Linda stepped back as Pastor John stepped forward to shake hands with them.

"Praise the Lord, I'm so glad to meet you!" Pastor John exclaimed. "Mac told me your story. Praise God for His grace!" Kathy stepped up and gave them both a hug.

"I'm glad you came today," greeted Kathy warmly.

Carrie and Jack could both feel the Presence of God as soon as they entered the building, but standing here in front of the pastor and his wife, there was something else also. Here was a man and woman of God who walked in authority. They could sense it; it was so strong. There was a gentleness and meekness about them, but there was a strength and authority that just seemed to surround them. It wasn't arrogance, either, for there was sincere love shining in their eyes. They knew who they were in Christ, and they walked in that authority in the realm of the spirit. The love of God just surrounded them and went out to all those that were in contact with them.

Carrie's eyes were beginning to water as she began to speak. Pastor John held out a Kleenex for her.

"Thank you. I'm so overwhelmed with God's Presence in this place. It's not something that we're used to. I can honestly say that when I met Linda it was the first time that I really experienced the Presence of God. We didn't know that there was so much to know and to experience, so we decided that we needed to come here and learn about God the way that Linda knows Him," explained Carrie.

Pastor John took her hand and squeezed it. "We're glad to have you, Carrie. I'd like to ask you if you and Jack would come forward to give your testimony in front of everybody. It's something very special, and I know that it will be a blessing for all."

"We'd be glad to do it, Pastor. Just say when. The only thing I ask is that I'll need a box of Kleenex," replied Carrie.

"That's something we have plenty of around here," said Kathy. "We're notorious for crying in this place."

"I can see why. You guys know God in a way that we never dreamed of. I've always wondered why the Jesus we learn about today isn't like the Jesus we see in the Bible. But now that I've met Linda, I know that we haven't been taught right," said Carrie.

"We know now that there's a lot about God that we don't know," added Jack, "and we want to learn all we can so that we have a relationship with Him like all of you have."

"If you seek Him with your whole heart and learn the truth along with your seeking, you will come to know Him as your Beloved Father and develop the same kind of relationship that we have. It's all going to depend on how much you really want to put into that relationship. God will never slow you down or hold you back, because He desires you to know Him even more than you want to," explained Kathy.

"I think I'm about ready to sit down now. Pastor, feel free to call us up whenever you want us," said Carrie.

"Okay, Carrie. I'll see you two later."

Mac and Linda led them into the sanctuary and seated them next to their own seats.

""We've got to meet some more people before the service starts. Feel free to get up and mingle or look around, okay?" said Linda.

"Okay, we'll be all right. Go ahead and do what you need to," replied Jack. Mac explained where the rest rooms were before they walked away.

As they walked back to the foyer, Linda spotted Dr. Jones and his wife talking to another couple. They walked over, and Linda introduced Mac to them and met Dr. Jones' wife, Nancy.

"Dr. Jones, I'm glad to see that you could make it. Carrie and Jack are already here. You can come up and sit with us too," said Linda.

As she finished speaking, Karen, the nurse, walked up beside Dr. Jones.

"Good morning, everybody. This is my husband, Tim," greeted Karen.

After introductions, Linda led them into the sanctuary and seated them behind Jack and Carrie. Mac remained close to the door, waiting for Kevin and Sue to show up. He was pretty sure that they would be coming; it had sounded like they already had it settled in their hearts when they spoke last. It was only a couple of minutes before he saw them coming toward the entrance, their twelve-year-old son with them. Mac met them as they came in and hugged them.

"I had a feeling that you would be here today," said Mac.

"We did as you said and prayed about it, and we both felt strongly that the Lord wanted us here. We went to the pastor of our church yesterday and told him of our decision. He released us with his blessing, and we parted on very good terms. So here we are," explained Kevin.

"Mac, this is our son, David," introduced Sue.

"Hi, David. My name's Mac, and I'm glad to meet you." Mac reached out and shook hands with him.

"I'm glad to meet you, too. Mom and Dad said that God talks to you," replied David.

Mac began to laugh. "Yes, He does. But He also wants to start talking to you, too, and your mom and dad also," explained Mac.

"Did Carrie and her doctor come today?" asked Sue.

"Yes, they're all here. Even the nurse and her husband came in. God's got a special plan for today. He's already shown the pastor and his wife what He desires to be done, and Linda and I began to see part of it this morning in prayer. This is going to be a glorious day for Jesus," said Mac. They could sense the excitement in Mac's voice and were themselves anticipating the day's developments. They already knew what God was capable of because of their own blessing and also from hearing about Carrie's baby.

"Come on in. You can sit next to the doctor and his wife."

As they were walking up the aisle, they met the pastor. Mac introduced them and then seated them next to Dr. Jones. Linda had introduced Pastor John to Dr. Jones and his wife as he was passing by, and it was arranged for Dr. Jones to go up with Carrie and Jack when they gave their testimony. It was almost time for the service to start, and everyone could feel the excitement in the air. Most of them didn't know what it was, but they could feel God's Presence in the building.

The people kept filing in, the chairs filling up with purses, Bibles, and people. There were many people moving around, visiting with friends and with new people to make them feel comfortable. The pastor was still making the rounds, trying to make contact with as many people as he could before the service started. Just seconds before ten o'clock, the praise team began walking up onto the stage.

When the pastor saw the stage filling up, he walked up to the stage and took up a microphone.

"Praise the Lord. Did you come today expecting to meet God?" Cheers and praises came forth from the people, louder than Mac and Linda had ever heard before, drowning out the pastor's voice.

As the cheers started to slacken, the pastor said, "Did you come today to praise our God?" The cheers were renewed, rising to the throne of God.

Again, the pastor said, "Did you come today to worship our Lord?" And again the cheers and yells came forth. The pastor turned to the praise leader and nodded his head. The instruments began to play, and all their voices were raised to heaven, praising their Creator and their King. Song after song played out, leading the people into the Presence of the Lord.

When the first worship song started, many people began to weep; the Spirit of God was in the room, moving here and there, touching hearts and minds. Hands were raised and tears were falling; in the Presence of the Lord, hearts were being changed; some people were repenting of things that they had been holding on to for years. New people who were visiting were raising their hands to God for the first time in their lives.

Carrie and Jack were crying on their knees; Dr. Jones and his wife were sitting in their chairs, crying with their faces covered by their hands; and Karen and Tim had their hands raised to the Lord while their tears fell to the floor. Kevin and Sue were also on their knees, worshipping the Lord as they had so recently learned to do.

Pastor John walked back onto the stage, and at the end of the song, while the piano kept playing, he raised the microphone to his lips and began to speak.

"Isn't the Lord wonderful? He is visiting us today with His Presence, but for a few minutes I have some special people here today that have a testimony to share with us." He turned toward Carrie and Jack and waved his arm to bring them up.

"Carrie, Jack, and Dr. Jones, come on up." He stepped to the edge of the stage and took Carrie by the hand to help her up the steps. He continued to hold her hand as he began to introduce her. Everyone could see that she was pregnant, and Jack stood behind her with his hands on her shoulders.

"This is Carrie and her husband, Jack. And this is her obstetrician, Dr. Jones. A few days ago, she received some bad news from Dr. Jones about her baby. Am I right so far?" Carrie nodded her head a couple of times, and then the tears started to come. "Linda, would you bring that box of tissue, please?" Linda walked up beside Carrie, handed her some tissue, and then put her arm around her. Pastor John turned toward Dr. Jones.

"Dr. Jones, would you like to fill us in on the start of this story?" asked Pastor John. He handed the microphone over to the doctor.

"Well, as time went by, the growth measurements for the baby weren't lining up with the progress of the pregnancy. So, we scheduled an ultrasound to take a closer look at the baby. There hadn't been any problems thus far, so it was going to be the first ultrasound for Carrie."

As the doctor continued speaking, Linda leaned towards Carrie to whisper an encouraging word as she was wiping away her tears.

"Within minutes we could see what the problem was. Carrie's baby was without any legs. For some reason, the legs never developed. I encouraged Carrie to have an abortion rather than go through the heartache of raising a deformed child. She left my office heartbroken. She planned to return the following day with her husband and her decision. I think Carrie should take over at this point. Carrie?" he asked as he held out the microphone.

Except for the softly played piano in the background, it was so quiet in the sanctuary that you would think everyone was holding their breath. No one wanted to miss a single word of the story.

"I hardly know how to begin. I was in shock and didn't know what to say or do, and when I left the doctor's office, I went to the grocery store to pick up a couple of things. All I could think of is that God could heal my baby just like Jesus healed all of those people in the Bible. So I asked Him to heal my baby boy." Tears were running down her cheeks as she was speaking, and Linda handed her another tissue.

"I remember telling God that He never changes, the Bible says so, and that if He healed then, He should heal my baby now. Doesn't the Bible say that Jesus is the same yesterday, today, and forever? And Jesus healed everyone that asked Him. I remembered that part where the leper came to Jesus and said, 'If You are willing, You can make me whole,' and Jesus said back to him, 'I will.' So I asked Him to heal, knowing that He is willing. It was about then that I saw a woman coming toward me, and I could sense that there was something special about her. I couldn't keep from staring at her as she came toward me; there was a sense of godliness about her. When she stopped in front of me, I could feel the Presence of God, and it just flooded my soul. I broke down and started crying as she put her arms around me." She turned to Linda and put her arms around her as the tears were falling freely. Linda comforted her with a few quiet words, and when Carrie was able to continue, she held the microphone for her.

"When she started speaking, she told me everything about my baby, all of the details, and even that it was a little boy. She said that Jesus had sent her to heal my baby, and I believed her." Looking at Linda, she continued, "She put her hand on my stomach and began to speak to my baby, saying that the Lord had formed all his parts and that he was perfect, that he would be kicking and screaming when he was born. At that moment, I began to feel something growing and getting larger inside my womb. When I realized what was happening, I started sobbing; my baby boy was healed."

There was hardly a dry eye in the house as Carrie paused in her story to wipe away her own tears. Tissues were being raised to eyes and noses were sniffling, even Jack was reaching for a Kleenex.

"Linda called me by my name, after she finished praying, and I realized that God actually speaks to people and tells them what to do and say. She said she would go to the doctor's office with me the next day, and Jack and I met her there. I had another ultrasound done, and when the picture came up on the screen, we could all see both of my baby's legs. They looked perfect." Now there was a smile on her face as she spoke, and it spread to those listening. There were amens, hallelujahs, and Praise the Lords sounding off all over the sanctuary as the people were overwhelmed with the goodness and mercy of God.

"When the doctor came in to look for himself, I told him everything that I've told all of you," finished Carrie.

Pastor John asked, "Doctor, is there anything you want to add?"

"Yes, there is. I looked at all of our measurements in the file and double-checked everything. I took new measurements of her stomach to compare with the previous day, and they were even different. I looked at the ultrasound pictures that were in the file to make certain that I hadn't made a mistake, but everything was as I remembered it. Carrie's baby didn't have any legs one day, and the next day he did. It was just a flat-out miracle from God." Cheers and praises broke out all over again, and when it subsided, the doctor continued.

"I want to add that I believed in God and Jesus before that, but when I witnessed this miracle, Linda prayed with me to receive Jesus, and I haven't been the same since." More cheers broke out for the third time, and everyone stood to their feet, praising God.

As the praises lifted to heaven, God's Presence settled on the building. Some started weeping, and others began to laugh with the joy of the Lord.

Pastor John began to pray, giving thanks to God for His grace and His mighty power, for His intervention on Carrie's behalf.

"All of you who need healing, come forward. God's Spirit is present to heal the sick." Pastor John turned to Carrie and laid his hand on her head. She collapsed backwards into Jack's arms, and with Linda helping, they laid her on the floor of the stage. Dr. Jones could only stare at what just happened, wondering if he should check on Carrie to see why she collapsed, but a peace came over him and whispered, "*Do not worry.*"

CHAPTER TEN

As the doctor watched, a line of people assembled across the front of the sanctuary at the bottom of the stage, people of all ages; even a few children were mixed in, standing with their parents. He noticed Mac and Linda stepping up to stand behind the pastor and his wife. Several men, all wearing suits, spread out and took up positions behind the line of people. As the pastor and his wife Kathy laid hands on an individual and began to pray for them and to issue commands to the body and the sickness or disease, there were two men who stepped up behind the person to catch them in case they fell. More often than not, the one being prayed for would fall back in an apparent dead faint into the waiting hands of two capable looking men. They would lay them gently on the floor and move onto the next person.

When Pastor John came to about the eighth or ninth person in the line, there was an expectant hush that fell over the room, for it was a middle-aged man in a wheelchair. By the erratic movements of his hands and arms, the doctor could tell that the man was, for all intents and purposes, a quadriplegic. The nerve damage was total from the waist down, but he had retained minimal use of his arms and hands.

"Nick, the Lord Jesus has healed you. Rise up and walk." Taking him by the hand and with Kathy grasping his other one, they lifted him from his chair. As he began to rise, the doctor could see that his legs were like rubber, but the moment that they had lifted him to his full height, his legs stiffened and straightened, and when they released his hands, he stood there unsupported.

He raised his hands toward heaven and cried out, "Thank You, Jesus!" repeatedly, tears streaming down his face, and as he began to jump up and down, the congregation cheered and wept. He took off running back and forth on the stage, jumping and shouting, praising God for His grace. Pastor John continued down the line of people, praying and commanding, the people weeping and shouting praises as they received their healing.

As Dr. Jones watched from the stage, a man waiting to be prayed for all of a sudden fell to the floor and started convulsing. The Doctor's first thought was that it resembled an epileptic seizure. Not having any idea that the cause could be a spiritual issue, he started to walk toward him, but again, a whisper within him said, "*Wait.*"

As he watched, the pastor's wife, Kathy, stepped up beside the man. Looking down at him, she began to speak, "Unclean spirit, come out of him in the name of Jesus!" Instantly the man stopped moving and resembled a dead man. Bending over him, Kathy took his hand and said, ""Rise up and be whole!" Standing to his feet, the man began to cry as he embraced the pastor's wife.

Dr. Jones had never seen anything like this in his entire life and was having trouble processing all of it. If it wasn't for witnessing Carrie's miracle, he might not have believed what he was seeing here now, but there was no denying the over-powering Presence that he was feeling along with what he was seeing take place. As the ones who had passed out came to their senses, they were helped to their feet and then walked back to their seat to allow room for others who were waiting to be prayed for. Those who remained standing while they received healing were soon moved along also, for there were so many still lining up, especially after seeing Nick rise up out of his wheelchair.

While Dr. Jones stood there, he heard Pastor John praying for heart problems, blood disorders, arthritis, kidneys, livers, lungs, problems with shoulders, knees, and elbows, back problems, neck stiffness, and many other ailments. He even heard the word *cancer* a couple of times. People were shouting and jumping, dashing here and there, doing things with their bodies that was a struggle to do just a few minutes before. Dr. Jones began to think about his own problem with his back; it wasn't a big problem, just some degenerative tissue from wear and tear, hard work, and participating in sports from an early age. It wasn't a real problem as yet, just some discomfort now and then whenever he had to bend over to the floor. But as he watched people getting healed, he was thinking how ironic it would be for him, a doctor, to get in line to be healed in such a way.

Pastor John's voice lifted above all the noise, the praising, cheering, crying, and shouting. "It doesn't matter who you are or what you've done, Jesus wants to heal you today. So, come up to the front and receive this free gift."

Dr. Jones knew that God was saying something to him, so he made his way down to the floor and stepped into line. His heart rate was elevated, and he could feel it pounding in his chest; it seemed like his shirt was going to start bouncing with the rhythm of his heartbeat.

Pastor John stopped at the woman next to Dr. Jones, looked at her, and after a few seconds said, "Yes, Lord...all right." He took her by the hand and started to speak. "At this time next year, I will dedicate your little boy to the Lord."

"Thank You, Jesus," was all she got out before she began to tremble and then slowly fall back into the waiting arms of Pastor John's helpers.

When Pastor John stepped in front of him, he took his hand and put the other one on his shoulder.

"What would you like Jesus to do for you today?"

"My back has been giving me problems, and I'd like to have it repaired," answered Dr. Jones.

"Jesus, I thank you that You are the Great Physician and that You even heal our physicians when they come to You in faith. Bend down and touch your toes," Pastor John commanded.

Dr. Jones began to bend down, wondering when he would receive his healing. As he bent lower, he realized that there wasn't any pain. He touched his toes and then straightened up. He looked in the eyes of Pastor John, who had a big grin on his face. Quickly he bent to touch his toes again, and then repeated it twice more. The pain was completely gone, not even a single twinge. He began to laugh and hugged the pastor in a bear hug, and those around them joined in, their laughter spreading across the sanctuary until all the people were entering in to the joy of the Lord.

As soon as Dr. Jones pulled back, the pastor reached up and touched him on the forehead. When he felt the contact of Pastor John's hand, there was such a peace that flowed into him that he began to feel himself floating backwards away from the pastor. His eyes were still open, and he was conscious, but he had no control to keep himself from falling backwards. The only thing he could do was hope the two guys were behind him and ready to catch him; if they weren't, he was going to hit the floor. But for some reason, he wasn't even worried; the peace on him overruled every worry. He didn't even feel their hands on him, but as he settled gently to the floor, he found himself looking into their faces close above him as they were bent over his prostrate form.

Pastor John laid his hands on the few remaining people, giving them what they needed, each in turn raising their hands to God and thanking Him for His goodness and grace just prior to falling back into those capable hands of Pastor John's helpers.

As the doctor lay on the floor, he could feel God's Presence; his heart rate was racing, and he felt tingly all over his body. He had an overwhelming urge to praise the Lord, and when he began to speak, the language that he heard coming out of his own mouth wasn't English. It had an almost Middle Eastern sound to it, but he had no idea for sure what language it was or how he was speaking it. He was trying to evaluate what was happening, but he could find no answers. One second he was standing, with full control of his faculties, and the next second he was falling, completely awake and aware but unable to do anything to prevent it. And then to start speaking in a different language—wow!

A few moments later he found he could begin to move, and someone else helped him to his feet. Dr. Jones moved back to his wife, where she gave him a tight embrace, tears rolling down her cheeks. He looked around at those who were close to him, the only ones in the room that he knew, and saw hands raised to heaven, tears falling, and heard voices flowing with praises and thanksgiving. And the strangest thing happened again. He could hear a different language, but it wasn't coming from him or from someone far away but rather from his own wife. He looked at her. Her eyes were closed, hands raised to heaven, and a very clearly pronounced foreign language was pouring from her lips. Amazed with the wonder of God, he went to his knees in worship.

The band started up, and Pastor John led the congregation in worship. He went to his knees, singing to the Lord with one hand uplifted. Everyone who was already in the aisles or next to them dropped to their knees also, worshipping the Lord their Healer.

Linda looked up from her seat, where she had returned when the pastor was finished ministering to the people, and she let out a small gasp. Mac had his eyes closed but opened them to see why Linda had cried out. His eyes turned to where she was looking. On the stage, standing between Pastor John and Kathy, who were on their knees, was Jesus. He had a hand resting on each of them as they were worshipping the Lord. Mac and Linda could only stare; no words would come forth. Jesus was wearing a shining white robe, and there was a smile on His face. As they watched, His face turned toward them, His eyes piercing into their own, to the very depths of their heart. They saw Him for only a few seconds, and then He was gone. Mac and Linda went to their knees, praises on their lips, hands raised to God.

They sang the worship song several times through, and when it was finished, Pastor John began to sing a song of worship from his spirit.

"We worship You; we worship You; we worship You Lord, Lamb of God. God of heaven and earth, Creator of the universe, we worship You, our King. We worship You; we worship You; we worship You, O Lamb of God. We worship You; we worship You, King of heaven and earth. O Lamb of God, O Lamb of God, Thou art the One who was slain; O Lamb of God, O Lamb of God, worthy is the Name. He is worthy; He is worthy; He is worthy; He is worthy; He is worthy; He is worthy; He is worthy of the Name. O open up your hearts today and sing a new song before Him; O open up your hearts today, worshipping His Holy Name."

Pastor John began to pray and to thank the Lord for His manifested Presence and His Glory.

After the praise team took their seats, Pastor John began to speak.

"Isn't God good to His people? His Presence is so wonderful, it's hard to comprehend, but He has visited us here today like we've never seen before. I'd like to take the next few moments and teach about what just happened. I see a lot of new faces here today, and a lot of you haven't had any teaching about this sort of thing." He looked around at all the faces. There were many smiles, but there were still a lot of people wiping their eyes and noses with tissue, evidence of so many hearts being touched so deeply. Pastor John was moved with wonder and compassion. To have so many touched and healed by the Spirit of God at one time almost overwhelmed him to tears again.

"Jesus walked in the Presence of God every day, and what we have experienced here is the same thing that He experienced. When God's Presence is on the scene, things happen. I know that God is always with us, everywhere we go, but His manifested Presence is on a much higher level than the normal, everyday Christian living. The body of Christ, in these last days, is being raised up out of its complacency and religious traditions. For so many years the church has been void of the power and Glory of God, so that it has been reduced to just another religion of the world. Because there have been so many leaders without a proper relationship with the Lord, in control of the teaching and the thinking of the church as a whole, the church has lost the Glory of God that it had started with. If the leadership is not listening to God's instructions, then how will the church function according to the design that God set forth?

"But in these last days God has begun to place people in leadership roles who have a heart for Him and are willing to seek Him and obey the voice of His Spirit. And in so doing, God is opening the door for His Glory to enter back into the Church, which is exactly what we have experienced here today.

"I'd like to give you an example of why it is so important that we have God's manifested Presence at work in the church, so please open your Bibles to Exodus, chapter 33, verses 12 through 23. In the context here, God has told Moses that He will not go up into the promised land with them, lest He consume them on the way because they were a stiff-necked people. This happened right after the people made a golden calf to worship, because they thought that Moses had died on the mountain, for he had been gone for about forty days and nights. So, God told Moses that He would send His angel before them into the promised land, but He Himself would not go. So, starting with verse 12:

"Then Moses said to the Lord, 'See, You say to me, "Bring up this people." But You have not let me know whom You will send with me. Yet You have said, "I know you by name, and you have also found grace in My sight." Now therefore, I pray, if I have found grace in Your sight, show me now Your way, that I may know You and that I may find grace in Your sight. And consider that this nation is Your people.' And He said, 'My Presence will go with you, and I will give you rest.' Then he said to Him, 'If Your Presence does not go with us, do not bring us up from here. For how then will it be known that Your people and I have found grace in Your sight, except You go with us? So we shall be separate, Your people and I, from all the people who are upon the face of the earth.' So the Lord said to Moses, 'I will also do this thing that you have spoken; for you have found grace in My sight, and I know you by name.' And he said, 'Please, show me Your Glory.' Then He said, 'I will make all My goodness pass before you, and I will proclaim the name of the Lord before you. I will be gracious to whom I will be gracious, and I will have compassion on whom I will have compassion.' But He said, 'You cannot see My face; for no man shall see Me, and live.' And the Lord said, 'Here is a place by Me, and you shall stand on the rock. So it shall be, while My glory passes by, that I will put you in the cleft of the rock, and will cover you with My hand while I pass by. Then I will take away My hand, and you shall see My back; but My face shall not be seen.'"

"I want you to see this: there will be no difference between God's people and the people of the world unless God's Presence is with us. It is His Presence that makes us different. It is His Presence that sets us apart from everyone else. It is His Presence that exhibits to the world that we *have* found grace in His sight. Look at what Moses said. 'Show me now Your way, that I may know You and that I may find grace in Your sight.' If we come to know Him, we can find grace in His sight. What is the grace that this text is talking about? The word 'grace' means 'favor, kindness, or graciousness.' It is a bestowed kindness from God to an inferior. The grace that we do find will be seen in a tangible way by those around us, for it will be enough to make others say, 'God is really among you and is helping you.' It will be as His Presence is with us that we will be separate from all other peoples on the earth. Without His Presence, we will not be separate.

"Are you seeing this?" asked Pastor John.

"Yes."

"Amen."

"That's right."

"Preach it, Pastor."

"Now look at this. When the Presence of God was with Moses on the mountain, God was going to show Moses His Glory. But God said, 'I will make all My goodness pass before you.' It looks like God's Glory is His goodness, and His goodness is His Glory. They are inseparable. Also, you will never have God's Glory without His Presence. They are inseparable. When God's Presence is with His people, His Glory and His goodness are also there. In verse 22, God says, 'while My Glory passes by,' so God Himself links His Glory with His goodness. Now, think about Jesus. Did He walk in God's Glory and His Presence? Of course. What was manifested in Jesus' ministry but the goodness of God? The people witnessed God's grace, power, forgiveness, mercy, compassion, favor, and healing. Jesus said 'I do nothing on My own. I do what I see My Father doing and say what I hear Him say.' He also said, 'If you've seen Me, you've seen the Father.' The Jews had the writings of Moses, the psalms, and the prophets, but it took Jesus' coming to remind them what it meant to have God's Presence among them and to find grace in His sight. He was showing mankind exactly what God was like, every facet of His character.

"Let's continue in Exodus for a few more verses. chapter 34, verses 5 through 7. This is the account where God actually passes in front of Moses with His Glory. 'Now the Lord descended in the cloud and stood with him there, and proclaimed the name of the Lord. And the Lord passed before him and proclaimed, "The Lord, the Lord God, merciful and gracious, longsuffering, and abounding in goodness and truth, keeping mercy for thousands, forgiving iniquity and transgression and sin."'

"What was God showing to Moses? What did Moses ask to see? God's Glory. Why would God reveal all of this to Moses unless it was His Glory? This was a very solemn occasion. Moses did not ask for a common favor, nor did God treat his request lightly. This is a very special thing going on. Let me read what God said with an expanded sentence: 'Jehovah, Jehovah Almighty, compassionate and bending to bestow kindness and favor, longsuffering, and abounding in kindness and goodness and stability, certainty, truth, trustworthiness, keeping mercy for thousands, forgiving iniquity and transgression and sin.'

"When we picture God's Glory, we see a bright light shining forth from God, a sort of glow emanating from Him. Well, I'm here to tell you today that God is shining with His Glory. He is shining with compassion, shining with grace, shining with longsuffering, shining with abundant goodness and kindness, shining with truth and stability, shining with mercy and forgiveness. This is God's Glory. It is His renown. This is the weight and substance of our God. This is who He is 'I AM WHO I AM.' There is no separating these attributes from God. He is the same yesterday, today, and forever. In Him, there is no shadow of turning.

"This is whom we met today. Hallelujah! Stand to your feet and praise Him with me!"

Everyone jumped to their feet, shouting and praising God, lifting hands high. The praise team made their way to the stage and began to play. Two hundred voices joined in, people jumping and clapping, singing with abandon, praising Jesus like never before. The man who had been in the wheelchair ran up to the front of the sanctuary, bear hugged the pastor, then ran back and forth at the bottom of the stage several times. Then he went to his knees with his hands raised to God, tears starting to run down his face.

Dr. Jones looked past the kneeling man at the wheelchair that had been pushed over to the end of the stage. Wow! Was he going to wake up any moment to find out he was only dreaming? No! This is for real. Why had this not been getting more attention? He was a practical man, and he was always trying to analyze everything, but this was beyond analyzing. God is more real than he ever imagined; he was just so overwhelmed with everything that had happened. He could hardly wait to start asking Mac and Linda questions about everything. But in the meantime...he started singing with the others, praising his God and loving Him.

Song after song they sang, no one wanting to depart, all of them enjoying the Presence of God and worshipping Him. For over an hour the people praised and worshipped the Lord, some on their knees while others remained standing. People's hearts were being knit together with one another and with the heart of God.

The pastor started to speak, quieting the band.

"Isn't our God precious? He has revealed Himself to us today in a magnificent way. When you go out these doors, remember that the Lord is with you, no matter where you are or what situation you might find yourself in. Look to Him for direction and help, for He cares about you and all your needs. Start spending more time with Him, and get to know Him. Even as Moses knew Him and found grace in His sight, so also all of you start seeking God and begin to build a strong and faithful relationship with Him, beginning with your experience here today if need be. I know that not all of you are Wednesday night churchgoers, but come to the service and learn more about God, expecting to meet Him again.

"Thank You, Father, for Your graciousness today and for being who You are, the great I AM. I ask that You lead Your people this coming week, give them wisdom and understanding and a new boldness to witness about Your goodness. In Jesus' name, amen.

"Love one another before you go, and be sure to give your testimony to your family and friends, telling them what great things the Lord has done for you today."

CHAPTER ELEVEN

Monday morning, the telephone started ringing off the hook. By the time Pastor John arrived at six o'clock, the message recorder was already full. Apparently, the calls had started the night before. He listened to the calls and took notes on whom, what, and where. That way the recorder wouldn't miss any more calls and he could spend some time in prayer. Before he made it to the prayer room, Mac walked in.

"Good morning, Mac. It's good to see you," greeted Pastor John.

"Good morning, Pastor. Ready to get your directions for the day?" asked Mac.

"Heading that way right now."

They walked into the prayer room and began to praise God, thanking Him for the previous day. Before they progressed very far, two more men walked in. They all continued to pray, and before thirty minutes had passed, there were about thirty men present. They were praying for all kinds of things, lifting to God all sorts of petitions that needed answers. Many of them were praying in other languages, raising their hands to the Lord. Some were kneeling, some standing, and a couple were prostrate on the floor, pouring their heart out to God.

The Spirit of God was present in the room, touching hearts and minds, which is what He wants to do. If His people will earnestly seek Him, He will reveal Himself to them. He has the answers that they need and wants to give them to His people, but they have to seek Him diligently to receive them. Christians must spend time with Him, dwelling in the secret place, and then they shall abide in the shadow of the Almighty, as it says in chapter 91 of Psalms. Then they shall have deliverance and protection; no evil shall befall them nor any plague come near their dwelling. They shall receive authority and power to tread upon the lion and the cobra; the young lion and the serpent they shall trample underfoot. Because they have set their love upon God, He will deliver them and He will set them on high because they have known His name. He will be with them in trouble; He will deliver and honor them. With long life He will satisfy them and show them His salvation,[1] which is "deliverance, aid, victory, and prosperity."[2]

As the men in the prayer room learned of God's goodness, they began to spend more time seeking Him and laying down the things in their life that were an obstacle to their growing relationship with Him. More of them were showing up at church in the mornings to pray in a corporate setting as well as their personal prayer time at home. It is the goodness of God that leads to repentance and draws people to Him, entwining their heart with His, ready to lay their desires aside to take up His.

But the immediate increase of men in the prayer room this morning was in direct relation with God's manifested Presence the day before. Again, the goodness of God leads to repentance. As people see and come to know God's goodness, it touches their heart and mind like nothing else ever will. They will want to know God to the depths of their being, with each passing day, progressively spending more time with Him, anticipating the day that will come when they will begin to hear Him speaking to them in return.

As time progressed, the men who had to work began to filter out of the room, until only Pastor John and Mac were left. Joe was one of the last ones to leave; since he worked at the church and was able to work on his own schedule, he could stay a little longer in the prayer room than most of the others.

When prayer was finished, they walked over to Pastor John's office to visit for a while. After the service on Sunday the two of them didn't get a chance to talk about what happened.

"What did you think of yesterday's service when God showed up?" asked Pastor John.

"Absolutely glorious and amazing. It was what I've been dreaming about and hoping for. To see God working among His people on such a large scale and watching so many people receiving His goodness was almost overwhelming," answered Mac.

"I know. When I think about everything that happened yesterday, I feel like going to my knees and worshipping Him again."

"That reminds me of something that you ought to know, John. When you were finished ministering to the people and began to lead us in worship, you and Kathy knelt down on the stage together. Remember?" asked Mac.

"Yes. I remember that. Kathy and I even talked about it later. While we were kneeling, we had our eyes closed, and we both felt a hand resting on our heads. The Presence of the Lord was stronger at that moment than either of us had ever felt before. Why did you bring that up, Mac?" asked John hesitantly.

"I had my eyes closed at the time when I heard Linda gasp. I opened my eyes and looked at her, and she was staring up at you and Kathy. When I looked at the two of you, I saw Jesus standing between you with one hand on each of you. We both saw Him for several seconds, and then He vanished," explained Mac.

"Wow! I bet that was something to see. Kathy and I thought that's what it was, but now that you've told me, I feel goose bumps all over. Have you talked with anyone else? Has anyone said anything about seeing Him, too?" asked John.

"No, we haven't heard anything."

"He must have had a reason for allowing you to see Him. I think He might have done that just to show you and Linda that He's pleased with you."

"He couldn't have blessed us more. But I think of equal importance is the fact that He is very pleased with the two of you. He knew that you felt His Presence between you, and this way, you now know that He was standing right there between you, blessing you personally with His touch," explained Mac.

"Maybe you're right, Mac. Either way, His Presence and the working of His Spirit blessed us all. I wanted to let you know that when I arrived this morning, the answering machine was full of messages. I went through them right away, taking notes, so the machine wouldn't miss any more calls. Three different pastors left a message, all of them wanting to know what happened yesterday. They asked if it was for real or just a rumor. It's sure something how fast word can get around to different churches, isn't it?" asked John.

"It sure is. It would be interesting to see a list of the chain of people that a bit of news travels through. So, what do you think they will do when they find out it was all true?"

"I think they will want to meet with me and ask a lot of questions. It might even lead to something bigger. It all depends on where their heart is with God. This could be the beginning of what we talked about the other day—pastors seeking and receiving the baptism of the Holy Spirit."

"I believe you're right on track, Pastor. So, how many people do you think will be in the service next Sunday? I think yesterday is going to have quite an impact on everyone that was here, and all of them will be here in full force," suggested Mac.

"I think that's an accurate assumption, Mac. But there's no telling how many new people will show up because of all of the witnessing that will be done this week. Everyone knows someone who is sick or diseased with something or who has some kind of injury or debilitating situation. Doctors can only do so much, and then the patient is faced with living with the problem or dying. Once God starts moving within the church with miracles of healing that are easily documented, then there will be mass migrations into the church. People at their wits' end on what to do or how to survive will jump at the chance to get healed, although it doesn't matter to them how it happens. It could just as easily have been some New Age way to get healed; the only thing that will matter to them is that they get the real deal," explained Pastor John.

"I think many of them are going to meet God for the first time in their life, and when they receive God's mercy and healing, they're going to fall down and worship Him," added Mac.

"Yes, I think that about sums it up. God's working in the midst of the church with signs, wonders, and miracles has always been an evangelistic tool, and in these last days it's going to be very important in the ministry of God's Word. There are a lot of lying and deceitful voices out in the world, trying to lead people down the wrong path, and when God begins to move all over the world with miracles of healing, there will be hundreds of millions of new believers."

"Healings and blessings really touch people where they live, don't they? You can tell some people about God day in and day out without making any headway, but when they get healed by God's Divine touch, their heart is changed in an instant," said Mac. "You know, we may even be standing room only. If this thing grows too quick, are you ready to start having two services a day to accommodate all the new people?"

They were interrupted by a knock on the door. Mac stood up and opened the door to disclose Julie, the church secretary, standing just outside.

"Yes, Julie?" asked Pastor John.

"There's a call for you, Pastor. It's Pastor Bob from the Community Church."

"Please tell him I'll be right with him," answered Pastor John.

"I'll get out of here and let you catch up on all your phone calls. If you need anything, Pastor, just let me know."

"Okay, Mac. There are still a few things I wanted to talk to you about. You want to do lunch?" asked Pastor John.

"Sounds good. Give me a call and let me know where. Have a blessed morning, Pastor."

"You too, Mac."

---

[1] *Strong's Exhaustive Concordance of the Bible*, Psalms 91:16, *salvation*, # 3444, Hebrew.

[2] For more information on Satan's schemes to prevent our victory, turn to the addendum at the back of the book.

Chapter Twelve

David Hendrix, Kevin and Sue's son, was in school Monday morning and noticed that his friend Johnny was very sad about something. David knew that Johnny's mom was very sick; she had been in and out of the hospital several times recently for some kind of treatment. The week before, Johnny told him that his mother might die. The doctor didn't think that the medicine was doing any good. This morning was the saddest that David had ever seen him.

He began to think about what happened in church yesterday, remembering how the man in the wheelchair got healed completely and about the woman who said her baby's legs were made in just a few seconds. His mom and dad had told him about the woman and her baby the day before they went to the new church. If God could do that, then maybe He would heal Johnny's mom, too. He decided to tell Johnny about Pastor John when they went to recess.

When recess came, David led Johnny away from everyone else and asked him about his mom.

"She's in the hospital right now, but my Dad said she won't be coming home again." Tears started to run down Johnny's cheeks. "I've been praying and asking God to heal her, but she isn't getting any better."

"*Tell him about yesterday*," came a whisper, but with firmness.

David jumped a little and turned to look around him. There wasn't anyone close by. It was then he remembered what Mac said, that God wanted to start talking to him too.

"*Yes*," came the whisper again.

"I know how she can get better," said David. His heart was beginning to beat faster; he could feel something was taking place beyond what he could see. He was full of enthusiasm to tell Johnny about God helping those people.

Johnny looked at him, wiping the tears off of his face. He could see that there was something different about David, but what was it?

"How?"

"We went to a new church yesterday, because someone that goes there talks to God and he helped my mom and dad. His wife talks to God too, and she prayed for a woman's baby that didn't have any legs, and God made them grow out. At the church, Pastor John prayed for a whole lot of people, and they all got better; he even prayed for a man that couldn't walk who was in a wheelchair. The man stood up and started running around, and he was crying. I think if Pastor John prayed for your mom, she would get better," finished David with an excited exuberance that was contagious.

Johnny looked off in the distance and whispered, "I

could write him a letter and ask him to come to the hospital and pray for Mom." He looked back at David with a renewed hope shining in his eyes and said, "Your dad could give it to him tonight. I'll go write the letter right now so you can take it home with you. Okay?"

Johnny took off running without waiting for a response from David and disappeared into the building. About ten minutes later he burst out of the door, running back over to David, and handed him a folded piece of paper.

"Here it is. Do you think your dad can take it to him tonight?" asked Johnny.

"Yes. I think when I tell him how important it is, he'll find a way to do it," replied David.

There was new hope in Johnny's voice, but when he spoke next there was also a note of desperation. "He has to do it tonight. I don't know how much longer Mom will last. She can't even get up and walk around." Johnny's voice began to break as the picture of his mom came into focus; there was anguish and pain on his face as he recalled his last moments with his mom the previous night. "Last night when I hugged her good-bye, she couldn't even put her arms around me. I don't want to lose her. David, you have to go with your dad and talk to Pastor John for me. He has to come right away. Promise me you'll do it."

Johnny's desperate plea brought tears to David's eyes. With his newfound faith in God's power, he responded to Johnny's plea with confident assurance. "Don't worry, Johnny, I'll make sure that he gets your letter and that he comes to help. After seeing those people in church yesterday, I know your mom's going to be okay."

David's faith washed over Johnny's heart and mind, and there was a release of the worry that had been weighing so heavily upon him. He looked at David, gratitude shining in his eyes as he spoke. "I'll be your friend forever."

David's heart began to swell with love, and all he could do to answer that heartfelt confession was to put his arms around Johnny and hug him tight.

Pastor John arranged for Mac and Linda to meet with him and Kathy for lunch. There were a few things that he wanted to talk over with the two of them, some new arrangements for the services because of all the new people that were going to be coming in.

After their meal was brought out, Pastor John began to fill them in on the new arrangements.

"With all of these new people, we have to start taking steps right now to prepare ourselves for having two services a day. It's the only way to adequately minister to all of the new people that will be coming who are seeking God for their miracles of healing. I know that once word gets around about the way God showed up so powerfully yesterday, there will be many people who are in desperate situations coming to us to find answers." Pastor John spoke with an assurance of what he was relating to them.

"It looks like we'll need a leaders' meeting very soon to address this issue," agreed Mac.

Kathy looked at Linda and began to explain. "Until we can get more teachers and helpers to come forward to share the workload, everyone may have to do double duty. At the very least, one set of workers will have to work every early service and attend the second service for their own strengthening and edification while another set of workers can attend the early service for themselves and work during the second one."

"But the one disadvantage will be for the praise and

worship team. They'll have to play through both services until we can bring more musicians and singers on board and get them trained," added Pastor John.

Mac was thinking, and when he had his thoughts in order he began to speak. "Looks like we'll need to start seeking God on leading us to people that will fill the growing needs of this ministry. There are a lot of faithful people who have been attending here long enough to step up and take their place in the ministry. Not to mention that after yesterday there are going to be a lot more people here who will become a lot more serious about their relationship to the Lord and to this ministry."

"I believe you're right, Mac. But we still have to be careful about who we bring in on the ministry team. The enemy will try to infiltrate with as many people that he can, with immature Christians who put on a good front but underneath are envious, self-seeking, and ambitious. They might seem to be what we need at first, but when things don't go their way, then we will see them for what they are. And by then it might be too late to halt the trouble and strife that they might have already started." Pastor John and Kathy had more wisdom on leadership than what Mac and Linda could comprehend. All they could do was listen and learn, be obedient to them, and pray for the needs of the ministry.

When Pastor John had finished, Kathy began to tell of the directions that the Lord had already given her. She listed about twelve people that the Lord told her would step forward as teachers and another ten that would be stable helpers. Mac and Linda agreed with all of the names—they were all faithful and committed to the House of God, and as far as they could remember, they had all been present the day before to witness the Presence of God and the working of His Spirit.

"We have to keep in mind that the enemy will try to bring this ministry into disrepute and, failing that, will try to bring it down from within. But we're not going to give him a foothold or even a toehold. Everything we do must be birthed in prayer, bathed in prayer, and consummated in prayer." Pastor John was very firm on his stand against the enemy, and everyone agreed with all he had to say.

"I also wanted to let you know, Mac, that I received six calls today from other pastors. All of them had heard about yesterday, and they wanted, first of all, to verify that it was the truth. And then they wanted firsthand details of the story, what exactly happened and how. Of course, after that they wanted to know why it didn't happen at their church. That part got a little sticky, but I think that the evidence alone was enough to get their attention and to cause them to reconsider their position on certain doctrines."

Mac and Linda were listening intently, deeply interested in these new scenarios. When Pastor John paused, Mac asked his own question, revealing some of his own insight on the matter. "How many of them wanted to set up a meeting with you?"

"Four of the six are meeting with me tomorrow, at the same time. After talking with all of them separately, I called them all back and arranged a joint meeting that all of them readily agreed to. The other two acted like they wanted to attend but just couldn't come to the point of acknowledging that they needed to learn new doctrines that were going to displace other ones that they had taught and lived by for many years. But I think as this final move of God continues to grow they will be more than happy to join in, especially when they see the benefits of God being manifested in those around them."

"This thing is going to grow and spread faster than we can imagine, and I think the multitudes of Christians that begin to embrace it will cause more of the church leaders to join than the move itself."

Mac was thinking of how pride in the lives of church leaders who have taught against the spiritual gifts in the church, particularly the gifts of healings and working of miracles, would keep them from embracing God's move until they were in danger of losing their entire congregations. Some of them would hold out to the bitter end, and if they were not loved into accepting this new move of God, they would continue to reject it until they found themselves standing in a world devoid of Christians, left behind because of their pride and their rejection of God's Spirit that was constantly trying to lead them in the way they should go. Mac expressed his thoughts to the pastor.

"Mac, you're right on the mark," answered Pastor John. "It's hard to believe that with everything that God is going to do through His people, revealing His Glory to the world, that there will be some leaders in the church who will refuse to accept God on His terms. Their pride will cause them to miss the blowing of the trumpet and to go through the tribulation with unbelievers, and even then they may be so angry with God that they will eventually end up in hell."

Linda finally stepped into the conversation with an observation that was thought-provoking. "I wonder if those people who say they are God's people and yet reject His moving in these last days will hear the trumpet when it does blow and will immediately realize with horror what they have done?"

"That's an interesting thought, Linda. All I know for sure is that I would not want to be in their shoes at that moment," replied Kathy.

"It's hard to tell exactly what will happen at the time that the trumpet blows," began Pastor John. "I've wondered if, just previous to the trumpet, all true believers will sense the time is at hand, if when Jesus stands up to come gather us to Himself, we will feel in our spirits that within minutes or even seconds we will hear the trumpet blow. Will we all, just seconds before the blast of the trumpet, raise our heads and eyes to heaven in anticipation of seeing Him? Or will we just be going about our business, knowing that the time is near but not knowing it is upon us until we actually hear its welcoming declaration of His return? But one thing is for sure: to hear the trumpet, knowing what it is, and to realize that you are still here while all your Christian friends are gone would be the most horrible thing I can think of."

"Perish the thought!" exclaimed Mac.

After a few moments of silence, Pastor John remembered where he was heading with his meeting with the other pastors. He looked at Mac and asked, "Are you busy tomorrow, Mac?"

"Nothing that I can't do later. Do you want me to join your meeting with those pastors?"

"Yes, I would appreciate your being there. They're all coming over to the church at nine o'clock tomorrow morning. I'm praying and hoping that they will be receptive to the leading of the Spirit. It'll take a lot of prayer beforehand and some teaching when they get here, but I really believe they are going to receive what I have to say. This is in God's timing, and His Spirit is already at work on their hearts and minds. With the witness of God's miracles that happened yesterday and the Presence of His Spirit at the meeting tomorrow, I think they'll be only too glad to receive everything that God has to offer," explained Pastor John with his voice full of enthusiasm, hope, and excitement.

"We'll pray about it tonight, and I'll meet you in the morning for prayer."

They all stood up to go. It had been a long lunch but one full of information and good conversation.

"We love you guys. And I'll see you tomorrow, Mac."

"We love you, too."

When David walked through the door at home, he went straight to his mom, who was in the kitchen. "When's Dad going to be home?" he asked excitedly.

"I don't know for sure. He started that new job today, so I don't know how late he'll work. Why? What's the rush?" She could tell that he was excited about something.

"Do you remember my friend Johnny?"

"Yes. Isn't he the one whose mother has been sick?" Her thoughts began to rush. Yesterday at the church, the healings and miracles—David saw all of them.

"Yes, that's him. He was really sad today when I got to school. I didn't tell you, but last week he told me that the medicine his mom was taking wasn't doing any good and that he heard that she might die."

She drew in a quick breath of air and then let it out slowly. "Is she okay? She didn't die, did she?" It was a question that she didn't want to have to ask, and she wasn't ready for the wrong answer. Johnny was David's age, and she couldn't imagine what that must be like, a twelve year old watching his mother die from a disease.

"No, but she's not doing well. Johnny said his dad told him that she wouldn't be coming home any more. Last night when he hugged his mom good-bye, she couldn't even put her arms around him."

Sue had to turn away from David; she didn't want him

to see her tears. This was too sad for her, so how could a twelve year old handle it? She reached up and wiped away her tears before David realized why she turned her back to him. She cleared her throat before she spoke to make sure that her voice wouldn't break.

"We have to pray for her, for God to heal her, like He did to those people at church yesterday." Her voice was cracking, and David heard it.

"Mom, don't cry. She's going to be all right. When I was talking to Johnny, God told me to tell him about yesterday at church. You remember when Mac told me yesterday that God wanted to start talking to me, too? Well, He did. It seemed weird at first, but I know it was God. I told Johnny that if Pastor John would pray for his mom that she would get well, so he wrote a letter to him and gave it to me and asked if Dad could take it to him tonight."

When David started explaining, she turned back toward him so she could look at him while he was talking. "You have the letter?"

"Yes." He reached into his backpack and pulled it out. He handed it to her, and since it wasn't in an envelope, she felt compelled to unfold it and read it. David watched his mother's face as she read the letter. He saw her eyes squint a little with pain, and then tears started flowing down her cheeks. When she was finished, she closed the letter and set it on the counter, then wiped away her tears with the back of her hand.

She knelt down in front of David, wrapped her arms around him, and before she dropped her face to his shoulder, the tears started coursing down her cheeks. She hugged him tightly and whispered into his ear, "I'm very proud of you, David. The way that you handled today was very good. I love you."

David's eyes were beginning to run also as he hugged his mom in return. "I love you, too, Mom." After a minute of holding him, she let go and pulled away from him enough to look into his face.

"I promised him that I would make sure Pastor John got his letter tonight and that I would talk to him myself. He wanted Pastor John to come to the hospital tonight, because he didn't know if his mom would make it till tomorrow."

"Let's pray right now that Pastor John will get there in time to heal Johnny's mom, okay?" They both knelt on the floor, holding hands, and she began to pray for Johnny's mom. God's Presence moved into the room and received their prayer, and angels were sent off to do their work.

When Sue had finished praying, they stood up, and she hugged David to her again. "I'll make a call to your dad and also to the church to see how we get hold of the pastor."

She called Kevin's cell phone, and after several rings he answered.

"Hello."

"Kevin? This is Sue. Honey, what time are you expecting to be home tonight?"

Kevin could hear a note of urgency in her voice. "About five o'clock. Do you need me home earlier?"

"David came home from school today with news that the mom of his friend Johnny is very sick. She's in the hospital right now, and they don't know how much longer she can hold out. God spoke to David and told him to tell Johnny about church yesterday and that Pastor John would pray for her and heal her. So, Johnny wrote a letter to Pastor John and gave it to David so that you could take it to him tonight. It sounds like Johnny is very distraught, and David's words have given him new hope, and it's very important to him that Pastor John goes to the hospital." Sue quickly and concisely gave all of the pertinent details to Kevin so that he could make his own judgment.

"Is David sure that God spoke to him?"

"Yes. When he heard it, he even looked around to see where it came from, and then he remembered what Mac said to him just yesterday at church. And right then, he heard God say, 'Yes.' I think David knows what he heard was from God, and that only means one thing."

"If God told him, then it's a done deal," Kevin finished for her. "I can be home in about forty minutes. Why don't you call the church and see how to get hold of the pastor?"

"That was next on my list. I'll see you when you get home. Kevin, I love you."

"I love you, too, honey. Good-bye."

When Kevin arrived home, it was a few minutes after four. Sue met him at the door, and when David heard his voice, he came running from the kitchen. When David ran up to his dad, Kevin put his arms around him and lifted him from the floor for a moment before setting him back down.

"Mom told me what you did today for your friend. I'm very proud of you, David."

"Johnny was so sad, I had to do something, and when God spoke to me, I just did what He told me." David made it sound pretty simple, but still Sue could tell that he enjoyed the praise from his father.

"I talked to the church secretary, and she said that Pastor John would be there until almost five o'clock. There wouldn't be any trouble trying to see him," explained Sue.

"Let me change out of these dirty clothes, and we'll head down there."

Chapter Thirteen

"Hello, Pastor John," greeted Kevin as he shook his hand.

"Hello, Kevin. Hi, David. How are you doing today?"

"I'm doing pretty good, Pastor."

"So, Kevin, is there something I can do for you?" asked Pastor John. He could sense that they were here for something important and that it involved David in some manner.

"Well, Pastor, I guess I'll just jump right in. David has a friend at school whose mom is in the hospital. She's been fighting cancer, and they're not expecting her to last out the week, maybe not even a couple more days. David wanted to talk to you about it." Kevin wanted to open the conversation enough that it would make it easier for David to fill in the details. Pastor John turned to David and, after seeing the nervous look on his face, gave him a reassuring smile.

"Tell me all about it, David."

"My friend's name is Johnny, and his mom isn't doing

very well. This morning in school he looked really sad, and when he told me why, I told him about you and what happened yesterday and that if you went and prayed for her that she would be all right. He wrote you a letter, and I promised to give it to you." David reached into his shirt pocket, pulled out a folded piece of paper, and handed it to the pastor.

He unfolded it and read it quickly, not failing to notice the tear drops that had fallen on it and smeared the ink. When he was finished, he slowly folded it back up, then looked at David.

"Why did you tell him about me?" Pastor John thought he already knew the answer, but he wanted to make sure.

"God told me to. And I know that you can help her." It was a straightforward and honest answer. "You'll go, won't you? I promised Johnny that I would talk to you and that you would go." There was a tone of desperation beginning to edge into his voice and the pastor was quick to catch it.

"Don't worry, David. I'll go and pray for her. First of all, I need to pray about it and see what the Lord tells me about it. You did good, David, to tell him what you did. I can tell you that God is pleased with you."

David's face lit up with a big grin, which brought a smile to Pastor John's face. He turned to Kevin and shook his hand. "Thanks for coming down and bringing this to my attention. As soon as I know anything, I'll give you a call."

Kevin reached for his wallet, pulled out a business card, and handed it to the pastor. "Here's my number. And thank you, Pastor, for being a faithful servant of God."

As soon as they were gone, Pastor John went into the prayer room and knelt down on the floor. He took the letter, opened it up, and read it again. He closed his eyes and began to pray. "Lord, I bring this petition before you. I know that

You want her to be healed, and I ask for Your direction on what to do."

"Right now, Johnny is praying for Me to send you to heal his mom. I have told him that you will be there tonight. You know what to do."

"Thank You, Father, for Your goodness and mercy. I thank You for Your Presence and the anointing of Your Spirit. Go before me and prepare the hearts to be ministered to, and give me wisdom and guidance to do all that You want me to do." Pastor John worshipped the Lord.

At 5:30, Pastor John called Mac to ask him to accompany him to the hospital and then called Kathy to tell her he wouldn't be home for dinner and fill her in on the details. Both Linda and Kathy spent the next forty-five minutes praying for Johnny's mom and her healing, taking authority over the cancer and doubt and praying in tongues for God's perfect will to come to pass.

Mac drove to the church and picked up Pastor John. It was only twenty minutes to the hospital, and they spent most of that time praying in tongues, edifying and charging up their spirits within them for the coming encounter.

Johnny and his sister Alice were standing at the foot of their mother's bed, their father standing at the side holding onto his wife's hand, which was limp and lifeless. Alice's cheeks were wet with tears, and the tissue in her hand was drenched. Her mother hadn't opened her eyes or spoken a word since her aunt had brought her and Johnny into the room. Her aunt and uncle were standing behind them with their hands on her and Johnny's shoulders, and occasionally she could feel the drop of a tear. Her grandpa and grandma were also standing beside the bed across from her dad, holding on to her mom's other hand. Her mom's breathing was stopping and starting, and occasionally she would gasp and struggle to get air into her failing lungs.

Alice looked up at her dad, and she could see the pain written on his face, the tears that he could not stop dripping steadily and rhythmically onto the sheet of the bed.

The priest had just left the room, performing the last rites over the patient before he left. Alice's aunt bent down to her ear and whispered, "Alice, maybe you should take Johnny out into the hallway."

Alice turned to Johnny and looked at his face. There weren't even any tears, and she became worried about him. Hiding his grief wasn't good for him and could cause some emotional damage that would have an adverse effect on him later.

She whispered, "Johnny, let's go out to the hallway. I want to talk to you about something." She led the way, holding onto his hand, and when the door had closed behind them, she turned to him so she could look into his face.

"Mom is dying, Johnny. It's time for you to let go of the idea that God is going to heal her." She spoke with firmness but didn't want to upset him. Her attention was drawn past Johnny, and she noticed that there were two men coming down the hallway toward them. There seemed to be something different about them, but she couldn't figure out what it was and didn't really care. She had a more pressing matter that demanded her attention.

She looked back to Johnny's face. He could be so stubborn sometimes. "Didn't you hear me, Johnny? God isn't going to heal her; it's too late." She was trying to talk softly, but his stubbornness exasperated her and caused her to speak louder than she meant to. She looked back at the two men and realized that they had probably heard her.

"God told me that Pastor John was going to come and pray for her, and I believe God over you or Dad or even the doctor. He's going to come, Alice. I know he is." Johnny was carrying this thing a little too far, and she was about to give him a piece of her mind when she realized the two men had stopped right beside them. She looked up at the one that she sensed to be the leader, and as she looked into his eyes, there was something there that drove out all of her worry.

Pastor John and Mac got off of the elevator on the designated floor and looked at the main sign with the room numbers posted on it, with an arrow to point the visitors in the right direction. When they saw the room number they wanted, they started walking, and as they turned the corner and started down the long hallway, they noticed a teenage girl and a younger boy standing together just outside one of the rooms.

It looked like the girl was pleading with the boy about something, and then she noticed them walking in their direction. As they got closer, her voice became louder and they could hear every word.

"Didn't you hear me, Johnny? God isn't going to heal her; it's too late."

And then the boy's reply came, with faith, firmness, and no room for doubt, which excited both their hearts. "God told me that Pastor John was going to come and pray for her, and I believe God over you or Dad or even the doctor. He's going to come, Alice. I know he is." As Johnny was talking he could hear approaching footsteps, and when he finished, the footsteps stopped at his side. He could feel his heart beating within his chest, not necessarily faster but with a deep thumping that was very noticeable. He knew before he turned to look up at the man that it was Pastor John. He could actually feel God's Presence. He didn't know how he knew; he just did. It was similar to what he felt when he was talking to David at school.

"Pastor John? I've been waiting for you." Johnny looked quickly over to his sister, the surprise on her face revealing her thoughts.

"I know you have, Johnny. But I had to wait until God told me to come." He reached out to take Johnny's hand into his own. "This is my good friend Mac."

"Hello, Johnny. I'm glad to meet you," said Mac as he held out his hand to Johnny.

Johnny took Mac's hand into his own, and as he did he said, "You must be the man that helped David's dad."

"Yes, I am. And this is your sister?"

"Yes. This is Alice."

"Hello, Alice," greeted Mac.

"Hello." Her voice was low, and she was unsure of what she should say, if anything. There was something about these men, and slowly she began to believe that what Johnny said about them was true.

Pastor John held out his hand to her, and reluctantly she extended her own. "Hello, Alice. We're here to help your mom." As her hand made contact with Pastor John's, there was a shock, almost like an electric current, but without any pain. Peace flooded her mind and heart, and she began to weep and smile at the same time.

"Johnny, can you take us into her room?"

Johnny led the way, pushing open the door, and Pastor John and Mac followed him, with Alice bringing up the rear.

When the taller shadows began to register through his blurred vision, Johnny's dad looked up, wiping away his tears. Johnny took the initiative and started to speak before his dad had a chance to even clear his throat.

"Dad, this is Pastor John; he came just like I told you he would."

When Johnny's dad could see clearly, he looked at Pastor John and Mac. He hadn't thought that anyone was going to show up on Johnny's behalf, but now that they were here, he didn't know what to say. He didn't think that there was any hope for his wife now; she was down to her last breaths, thirty or forty seconds between each one. How could there be time for a turnaround? And yet, there was something different about these men, the way they carried themselves; there was a calm confidence about them. It was nothing like what he felt with the priest just moments before. But what if there was something that they could do? Anything was worth a try; he couldn't lose his beloved. He couldn't. He looked at Pastor John again. There was something in his eyes, something that he had never seen before; something was shining forth from both of them that he had never experienced before.

"Mr. Shelton, I'm Pastor John Logan. Johnny wrote me a letter asking me to come. I'd like to pray for your wife."

"Is there any hope? I mean, look at her. Is there anything that you can do now?"

Johnny's grandparents were wiping their eyes while they listened to their son-in-law speak to Pastor John. As soon as they could see, their eyes were drawn to look at the pastor; there was something about him that demanded attention.

"There is always hope. Look at your son. He has enough faith himself right now to do what I have come to do.

Johnny, stand beside your dad." The grandparents moved back beside their son and daughter-in-law to give the pastor access to their daughter. They were beginning to feel the Presence of God themselves and were going to give this stranger all the room he needed to do God's work. Faith was building within the family; one by one they were beginning to believe that there was still hope for their loved one.

Dan Shelton was trying to remember what it was that Johnny had said about these men earlier today. Something about healing. There was a man in a wheelchair in church. He was healed and started running around. His heart was keeping pace with his mind, beating fast and hard, drumming against his ribs. Could this really be? His son was now standing beside him. He put his arm across his shoulders, and when he touched him, he could feel a Presence within him. Surprised, he looked down at his son, into his eyes, seeing a faith and hope shining from deep within. He looked at Pastor John and nodded his head.

"I believe that God has sent you. Do what you came to do."

There was an audible intake of breath from the rest of the family at the assent given by Dan, all except little Johnny.

Pastor John stepped up beside the bed while Mac stepped over behind Dan and put his hands on his shoulders. The flood of total peace flowing out of Mac almost caused Dan's knees to buckle. Pastor John took Clare's hand in his own and reached across the bed and took Johnny's small hand in his other. Johnny had already taken hold of his mother's other hand. Pastor John looked up toward heaven, closed his eyes, and began to pray.

"Lord God, I thank You for Your great and wonderful mercy, for Your limitless compassion, and for the faith that

You have placed in this young boy. I thank You, Jesus, for Your Presence here tonight and for Your manifested Glory in bringing this total healing to Your servant."

The Glory of God was so thick in the room that all of them could see a cloud-like substance in the air. The feeling was beyond human description; it touched their hearts to its deepest regions, washing over them and yet refreshing their minds and their spirits.

Pastor John opened his eyes and looked at Clare. There was no sign of breathing, no movement of any kind, nothing to indicate that life remained. They all had their eyes open, watching, holding their breath, anticipating the moment of truth.

"Clare!"

"Clare!"

Clare's eyes opened wide.

"Arise, in Jesus' name!"

There was a sharp intake of breath as she filled her lungs with air.

Pastor John let go of Johnny's hand to take hold of Clare's arm and to pull her forward, lifting her head and shoulders from the bed while Johnny and his dad were doing the same on their side. Just seconds had passed, and she was sitting up on the bed. As she swung her legs to the edge and placed her feet on the floor, her parents stepped forward, tears cascading to the floor as they took her into their embrace. Pastor John stepped back as Johnny and his dad came around the end of the bed to squeeze into the huddle around Clare. Already, Alice had her arms wrapped around her mother, having squeezed her way between her grandparents, her muffled sobs making their way to Pastor John's ears. Clare's brother and his wife had their arms around each other, both crying like babies.

Clare's parents stepped back a little to give Dan and Johnny unhindered access to their beloved.

Mac had tears in his eyes as he watched the proceedings, and he slowly went to his knees, raising his hands to the Lord, giving forth praises and thanksgiving to the eternal Father. Pastor John also went to his knees, worshipping the Lord, loving his God and King.

There were loud voices in the hallway, footsteps of several people coming close to the door. Pastor John and Mac were the only ones who heard the commotion going on, and they stood to their feet and moved to the door. Before they reached it, it began to swing inward. There in the doorway stood an old man dressed in a hospital gown, and behind him there was another patient, a young man likewise attired. There was a nurse behind them, trying to pull one of them back from the door.

"You can't go in there. There's a family grieving for their loved one."

As Pastor John and Mac watched, another nurse came up from behind and took hold of the older man who was standing in the doorway.

"There's no mourning going on in here." The old man started to speak. A third nurse stepped up behind him and hurriedly stepped around him and into the room.

"I'm sorry about this," she began to say, looking at Pastor John. And then her gaze slid past him to see Clare standing, with her loved ones around her, her eyes bright and shining. It didn't even look like the Clare that she had come to know. She held her breath as she stepped farther into the room. When she could see the bed, her eyes turned to it to see if the Clare that she knew was lying on it, passed to a better life. But the bed was empty. Her gaze was pulled back, drawn like a magnet to the beautiful woman standing there. How? How could this be? It was impossible!

"Clare?"

The shining woman looked at her and smiled, a beautiful and radiant smile. Faces turned toward the nurse, all of them decorated with smiles and tears.

The nurse stepped up to her and took her hand, feeling her to make sure she wasn't dreaming. "I don't understand."

The old man had worked his way into the room, and the other two nurses, sensing something strange was going on, came through the door to see what was happening. Pastor John could see other people out in the hallway, craning their necks this way and that, trying to get a glimpse of what was happening inside Clare's room. There were many voices causing a cacophony of noise, hard to distinguish any one in particular. One nurse had stepped up to Clare and had her stethoscope against her chest, listening to her heartbeat, while another was examining her eyes, and the third was holding on to her wrist, checking her pulse rate.

While Pastor John watched, his eyes fell to Johnny, standing beside his mother with tears still on his cheeks and a smile on his face. Johnny turned his head to look at Pastor John, and when he saw his eyes on him, he released his mom and walked up to him.

Through his tears, Johnny looked up and into Pastor John's eyes. "Thank you, Pastor John. I—" As Johnny's voice faltered and broke, he wrapped his arms around Pastor John's waist and buried his tearstained face against his shirt. Pastor John's arms instinctively went around the boy's shoulders and held him tight. He looked across at Mac and smiled. Mac smiled in return.

"Thank You, Jesus, for this wonderful miracle." Before Johnny could pull away, the old man was standing before Pastor John, with the younger one moving up to stand beside him.

"Please. Pray for me!" the older one let out his plea.

Immediately the younger one added, "Me, too."

When their words began to register, two of the nurses turned to look at the two men. They hadn't figured out yet just why or how the two men had gotten out of their beds. They had both been almost as close to death as Clare had been, and now they were both up and walking around. Something strange was going on, and they had no clue what it was.

Several more people were pushing into the room, apparently the relatives of the two patients, trying to retrieve them and escort them back to their deathbeds. Mac stepped over to stand behind the two men just as Pastor John began to speak.

"What do you want me to do for you?" asked Pastor John. His straightforward question, asked with calm assurance, immediately quieted the growing crowd. Johnny stepped back over to his mom but continued to watch Pastor John and the two men.

"I have lung cancer."

"You haven't noticed that you aren't coughing and wheezing any more?"

There was a look of consternation on the man's face as that bit of news began to register, but before he could reply, Pastor John reached up and touched him on the forehead. "Thank You, Jesus, for complete healing in this man's lungs." Before he uttered the last word, the man began to topple backwards, falling into waiting arms, and as Mac laid him gently on the floor the two nurses were stepping up to him to check his vitals, thinking the worst.

Pastor John turned to the young man, looked him in the eyes, and asked, "What would you like from Jesus tonight?"

"I want to be healed of leukemia."

"In the Name of Jesus, your blood is purified and your bones are strengthened." Again, as soon as Pastor John's hand made contact with the man's forehead, he toppled backwards in the same manner, and Mac laid him gently on the floor beside the first one. The two nurses, not understanding what was happening, turned to the second patient and began to check his vital signs. Strong heartbeats, pupils fine, both conscious—this wasn't reasonable! They were both thinking: Why did they faint? Faint? They were completely conscious. Why did they just fall over? This didn't make any sense.

Family members began to kneel down beside their loved ones, asking them questions, trying to understand what was going on.

"Listen, everyone. All of you want to know what happened, and I'm going to tell you. Jesus sent me here as an answer to Johnny's faith that God was going to heal his mother. There she stands, the evidence that Almighty God has visited you this night with His grace. God's Glory was here in such magnitude that it extended beyond the walls of this room, and these other two men tapped into it from their own rooms. And now they are healed, so don't expect them to go back to their deathbeds. I am here as a witness that Jesus loves you and that God wants to help you if you will seek Him."

The two men who had received their healing were now sitting up, with their family members still on their knees by their sides.

"How do I get saved?" The older man was looking up at Pastor John, tears in his eyes.

Clare's brother also had tears in his eyes when he spoke up. "I need to be saved too, Pastor."

"Me too."

"Me too."

"Jesus is the Son of God, and He came to earth to reveal God to mankind and to take all of our sin upon Himself and to die on the cross. He laid down His life, suffered in hell for three days, and then was raised to life by the power of God's Spirit. He paid the penalty for our sin that was our due and was raised for our justification. He has purchased, by His blood, our redemption unto God. If you believe this and ask Jesus to be your Lord and Savior you will be saved." Not knowing how much any of them in the room knew about Jesus, Pastor John was quite thorough in his explanation of salvation. "Do you believe this to be true?"

"Yes."

"Yes."

There were several answers, more than there were people who had expressed a desire and need to get saved.

"If you believe this, then repeat after me…" Pastor John led them all in the sinner's prayer of salvation. He knew that several of the people present were already Christians, but everyone in the room was repeating his words, even the three nurses. The Spirit of God was hovering in the room, touching their hearts and minds, and by the time Pastor John was finished, there was a multitude of tears falling to the floor. Only this time the tears that were being shed were tears of life and rejoicing rather than tears of death and mourning. As the Holy Spirit fell on them, they began to speak in other tongues and to magnify God, praising Him for His mercy and grace.

"Welcome to the family of God, dear brothers and sisters." There was such sincerity in the pastor's voice that they all stepped up to him to hug him and to extend their gratitude for bringing them to Jesus. When things began to quiet down, Pastor John began to explain to them about the working of the indwelling Spirit of God, especially about speaking in other languages, which all of them had just shared, the new converts as well as the ones who had been believers already. Even Johnny and Alice had been speaking in tongues.

When Dan stepped up to Pastor John, there was a light of gratitude shining on his face. When Dan began to thank him, his voice broke, and as he began to sob, Pastor John enfolded him in loving arms. When the shaking and sobbing began to subside, Pastor John pulled back so he could look Dan in the eyes. "God loves you, Dan. Today you have experienced that love in a magnificent way. Seek the Lord with your whole heart from now on, and He will lead you in the things that you need to do."

"Thank you, Pastor."

Clare stepped up to Pastor John. They looked at one another for a long moment. Everyone was quiet and listening.

Pastor John was the first to speak. "You saw Jesus."

"Yes. I was standing with Him when you called my name. He told me that He wanted me to come back, there were some things that I needed to do for Him. At that moment, I didn't want to come back; being with Him is indescribable. But now that I'm here, I know my life will not be the same one that I had. Now, my walk with Jesus is more precious to me than my family is." There were tears in her eyes as she turned to look at her husband and her kids, love shining from her face. She then turned back to Pastor John and took his hands in her own. "Thank you, John, for being a faithful servant of the Lord. Jesus told me that from now on you are my pastor."

John hugged her and then turned to the others. "Jesus is with you now. He will guide you and lead you concerning everything in your life, if you seek Him with all your heart as you've done here tonight. He will begin to speak to you like He does to me as you come to know Him better. All of you, listen to Him when He speaks and be obedient to what He tells you, and you'll be blessed in what you do. For the victory shall be yours."

After a few more words of encouragement, Pastor John and Mac left the room. All three of the patients were going to begin gathering up their things to leave the hospital. The nurses preferred that they remain overnight so their doctors could check them out the following day, but since they knew in their hearts that they were all completely restored to health, they didn't push that decision very hard. There was going to be some creative explaining to do in their reports as to why they lost three patients in such a remarkable and unexplainable way.

On the drive back to the church, Pastor John called Kevin and David to let them know the good news and to relieve any worry that they might have had. When that conversation was over, he also called Kathy to let her know how things went and that he and Mac were going to stop and eat out somewhere. As Pastor John was relating the story, Mac's heart was blessed again and again. It was an astounding story, and although he had participated in it and watched it with his own eyes, it still moved him to tears. Again Mac thought about how God's goodness leads to repentance, and looking back on the evening, he could see how true that was. After being witness to God's goodness and mercy, there were seven people that night who received Jesus as their Lord and Savior and another four who rededicated their lives to Him, and the rest of them who were already believers now had an even closer relationship with Jesus. God was amazing.

CHAPTER FOURTEEN

The following morning, Mac and Pastor John were both at the Church at six o'clock. Full of praises and thanksgiving, they entered the prayer room to prepare for their day. They laid everything before the Lord, seeking His direction and wisdom about all of their plans, those dealing with the church, their meetings with those from outside the church, and their own personal plans. The Lord is interested in every aspect of the lives of His people, and when they seek His advice, He will give it to them and lead them into success. Sometimes it takes some work; every time it will take prayer and intercession; and every now and then, the answer is a real easy fix. Those who trust in the Lord are blessed, but those who trust in the flesh will not even recognize when good comes. The victory for God's people is in trusting in Him, knowing the truth of His word, and acting upon that truth. Paying lip service to it will not get the victory, but doing His word pays big dividends, both here and in life everlasting.

Again, there were about thirty men or so that attended the early-morning prayer. Their hearts were thirsting for God, and they knew that the only way to quench that thirst was to seek God diligently. God would satisfy their hearts' desire, meeting them and speaking to their hearts and minds. As they draw nearer to God, He also draws nearer to them. That is where God's people are going to find their victory, in the prayer room and in that secret place with God, the place where God meets with you and begins to change you from within.

After prayer, Pastor John and Mac went out for a quick breakfast before their meeting with the other pastors. They invited Joe, who had also been in the prayer room since six-thirty. After they ordered, Mac shared the story of Clare's healing with Joe.

"Glory to God! That is so powerful. God never ceases to amaze me with His love and compassion," exclaimed Joe. "How many of them will we see this Sunday?"

"I'm not sure, Joe. Some of them may want to attend their home churches to let them see their healing and to testify of God's mercy. I told them where our church was located, and I do know some of them haven't been attending church at all, so some of those ones will probably be here," explained Pastor John.

"I think we'll be full to overflowing. I've been telling some of my old cronies about what happened, and there are a couple of them that are real interested in coming. Just think what will happen if everyone that was here last Sunday tells two new people about what they saw with all of those healings."

Pastor John and Mac could both see that Joe was very excited about the coming service.

"I know what you mean, Joe. It may be standing room only, but we'll just have to trust that God will be able to meet our needs. We've already begun planning for two services a day to handle the extra flow of people that will be coming to seek God's help." Pastor John paused for a moment.

"If we have to, all of our leaders, teachers, and helpers can stand, and we can also set up some chairs in the hallway as we need them. I'm sure we'll be able to accommodate them until we can go to two services a day."

"When I told my mom about God's moving during the service, she really wanted to be able to come, but since she lives in Idaho, she'll have to wait until she comes over for a visit," said Joe.

"Joe, did you hear that the pastor is going to have a meeting with a few of the other pastors in the area?" asked Mac.

"Yes. I overheard something about it. That's today, isn't it?"

"Yes, it is," replied Pastor John. "In about an hour from now."

The waitress came over with their order, and after she was gone, Pastor John prayed over the meal. For a few moments, they ate in silence enjoying the food. Pastor John was the first to speak.

"Yesterday afternoon, Kathy talked to a few people about Sunday and found out that there are a couple of other churches in the area that also had the Presence of God show up at their service. Faith Community and Living Word Christian Center. They're both similar to our church, holding to all of the same doctrines, believing for God's best in the lives of His people. It would seem that God has put His stamp of approval on the ones that have developed that special relationship with Him and who are subsequently rightly dividing the Word of Truth and teaching it."

"That's a pretty strong statement, Pastor. It won't go over well with all of the other churches," replied Mac. He wasn't in disagreement in the slightest bit, just stating a fact.

"I know, Mac, but the Word says in 1 Corinthians 11:19, 'For there must also be factions among you, that those who are approved may be recognized among you.' If God had showed up at any one of a number of churches that don't teach about His goodness, healing, or any of the spiritual gifts, it would be like giving His approval to their teachings and doctrines. I don't think that is going to happen. I'm not saying, either, that God doesn't work in those churches, that He is never there; it's just that He won't be welcome or invited to do great and mighty works. It's a house of unbelief, as far as His moving in a mighty way is concerned, and would be similar to what Jesus faced in Nazareth when He could do no mighty miracles."

"I totally believe you're right, Pastor. The Word says that when the apostles went out and preached His Word, the Lord worked with them, confirming the Word through the accompanying signs. If there are churches that aren't preaching the full word of His Good News, then the Lord can't confirm the part that's being left out. He will confirm the salvation message that they preach by touching people's hearts and minds and bringing them to an acceptance of Him, but when it comes to the Word of healing, wholeness, prosperity, or the manifestation of the spiritual gifts, then there won't be anything to confirm, because they aren't teaching it or believing it." Mac's logic and its conclusion were infallible. That was something Pastor John really admired about Mac. His thinking and teaching were precise and accurate, not leaving any room for wavering.

"I like the way you worded that, Mac. It lays it out like it is, take it or leave it," replied Pastor John.

"So, it looks like the only way for God to move in those churches, in the same manner that He did in ours, is for God to somehow change their teachings and doctrines to come in line with the same Word that the early church taught." Even Joe was catching on to what was happening.

"That's right, Joe. And it looks like God is planning on using us to do that."

"How so?" asked Joe.

"As the miracles and God's moving increases in the churches that are like ours, the pastors of these other churches will eventually come to the conclusion that we have something that they don't. And don't mistake this: it *is* something that they want; they just don't know how to get it. When they come to that conclusion, after much soul searching and seeking God, the Lord will lead them to us, to find out what they need to change. They will finally realize that if God were not with us, then we could do none of the things that have now begun to happen. Just like the blind man that Jesus healed, he said to the Pharisees and chief priests when they questioned him about his healing that if God was not with Jesus, then He would not be able to heal anyone."

"What happens if their pride keeps them from changing?" Joe was asking all the tough questions, but Pastor John had the wisdom of God in his answers.

"The Lord showed me that if they refuse to follow His direction and leading, that they will start losing the members of their congregations Slowly at first, but as surely as the sun rises, they will lose all of the ones that have a true heart for

God. When miracles start to happen, stories begin to circulate. People who are in those congregations will hear those stories and will be moved by them. Some of those people, who are in desperate situations themselves, won't even wait for the move of God to come to their church, but will go to the church that they've heard about that has the moving of God's Spirit, hoping against hope that what they heard was true and that they will receive divine healing.

"I am talking about those who have a disease or sickness that the doctors can't heal; they will be among the first ones to leave. And then, when they experience God's Presence and receive their healing miracle, they'll call all of their friends that are still going to their home church and tell them about it. When the stories of miracles start to come from people that they know and trust, then more of them will change churches, until the only ones left for the pastor to preach to will be the ones who won't let go of their pride and traditions. If they continue, even then, to hold onto their traditions, that church will dry up and die.

"I want to make this clear also: at any stage of this development, when any of them turn to God with sincerity, He will accept them, change them, restore them, and begin to use them in the same way as He does us. God will hold nothing back from them, nor hold anything against them, just like the Father with the prodigal son. He restored him to his position without anger, resentment, or unforgiveness. And we also must do the same." Pastor John's voice was filled with tenderness and love as he spoke about the restoration of God's people. There wasn't any question about where his heart was.

"That definitely answers my question. That will be something else to add to my prayer list," stated Joe.

"We'd better get going, Pastor, in case some of them decide to show up early," suggested Mac. He had already grabbed the ticket earlier, so he arose and went to pay it.

When the pastors had all arrived and the greetings and introductions were over, they all went into the prayer room to spend some time seeking God together before any teaching or instruction was given. All four of the pastors were Spirit-filled full gospel believers. They believed in the working of the spiritual gifts in the church assembly, the laying on of hands, and the moving of God's Spirit to accomplish what man could not. So in the prayer room, none of them felt ill at ease with praying in tongues before one another, although none of them were well acquainted with any of the others.

It wasn't long before the Spirit of God was moving, touching the hearts of His leaders, refreshing them in a way they had never experienced before. As Pastor John went to his knees, worshipping the Lord, the other pastors were overwhelmed with the Presence of God and fell to their knees, bowing their heads to the floor.

The other pastors all loved Jesus with all their heart, but because of a few hang-ups on some doctrines and disillusionment from some past failures, they had fallen into the trap of the enemy that was designed to stifle their faith and zeal for the Lord. One and all they had tried to pray and believe for God's best for their congregations, but when the enemy succeeded in stealing health, lives, and prosperity from too many of their people, disillusionment had set in, and they had never fully recovered. Because of that, they had little faith to really stand up against the enemy in prayer.

But now, kneeling in God's Presence, they began to see their shortcomings and where they had failed. God brought them to the realization that, although they had lost many battles to the enemy, there was restoration available to them. The war was not over; there would be many battles yet to fight; and if they would respond to His ability in them, they would begin to walk in victory from this day forth. God would meet them right where they were and begin to lead them in triumph over the enemy, but it would be contingent on their seeking Him in all that they do and being obedient to His voice.

Pastor John stepped up to Mark, placed his hands on Mark's shoulders, and began to speak by the unction of the Holy Spirit.

"*'My son, you have not done poorly. If you had known the schemes and the devices that the enemy has brought against you, then you would know that you have not failed. His plan was to destroy you and drive you out of My service, but you still stand; My right hand has upheld you. The enemy has had some victories over you, but not as many as you think, and as you seek Me and listen to My voice, his work in your life and ministry will begin to fade away. The battle is Mine, and as you follow My orders, the victory will be yours.'* Thus says your God." As Pastor John began to pray in another language, the power of God surged into Mark and he began to fall backwards. As the other pastors watched, Mac laid him gently on the floor.

Pastor John stepped over to the next pastor and began to speak the Word of the Lord over him in the same fashion as he had to Pastor Mark. It seemed odd that, as Pastor John spoke over each pastor, there was a lot of similarities between them. The attacks of the enemy against all of them were similar in their working, and all had the same outcome—to stifle their ministry from revealing the true power and nature of God.

Through the prayers, declarations, and intercessions of Pastor John and Mac, the power of the enemy was broken in their lives and in their ministries. Their spirits within them were refreshed with God's goodness and love, the Presence of the Lord becoming more real and tangible to them in that prayer room than He ever had in their past. They ended their morning with worshipping the Lord and praising Him for His Divine intervention in the lives of men.

After their prayer meeting, they stood around in the hallway while Pastor John and Mac told stories of God's miraculous healings and provision for His people. More than one of their stories brought tears to their eyes.

Mac explained to them, "For so many years, God's goodness has not been revealed in the teaching of His Word, only men's traditions and opinions. Just as Jesus told the Pharisees, 'making the word of God of no effect through your tradition which you have handed down.' But in these last days, men's traditions are going to be made of no effect by the power of God's Word spoken through His faithful servants. So now, you can see the responsibility that we all have to speak God's Word as it was meant to be. As we seek God for His direction and obey Him in all things, we will bring change to the body of Christ and to the world and will usher in His return."

When the pastors left, they were fired up and energized with a new hope and fervency, determined to fight the good fight of faith to the very end.

Chapter Fifteen

The day after Clare was healed, Johnny slept in late and missed school. Getting home late from the hospital and then staying up even later with his family, he didn't get to bed until three in the morning. Between crying, praying, and reminiscing about the evening's events, there had been too much excitement for anyone to even think about sleeping.

That same day, when David got to school, his teacher was wondering how Johnny and his mom were doing, fearing the worst. An opportunity to speak to David didn't come until the class was dismissed for lunch. She wasn't sure if David knew anything about it, but since he was good friends with Johnny, she thought he might know how they were doing. But watching David all morning and seeing how happy he was, she didn't think that he was aware of how bad off Johnny's mom actually was.

As the kids were heading out the door, she called out to David to wait a moment.

"David, could you come here for a moment?"

Walking over to her desk, he stopped and looked at her with a smile on his face.

"Yes, what do you want?" he asked.

"Johnny isn't in school today. I was wondering if you know anything about how his mom is doing?" she asked hesitantly.

David began to think that this was going to be a good opportunity to have some fun with some witnessing. "I haven't talked to him since yesterday, but someone I know was at the hospital with them last night. He called my dad afterwards to let us know that Johnny's mom had died."

"Oh, no. How sad! Did he say how Johnny was doing?"

David could see the pain and concern on her face and started to feel a little guilty about the way he was starting the story. "Actually, he's taking it pretty good. My family's going over to see them later today when my dad gets off work," replied David.

She began to wonder why David was still smiling, like there was something funny about Johnny's situation. Maybe he was having a hard time understanding exactly what had happened. "David, do you understand what it means when someone dies?"

"Yes, I do. But I also know that as long as they come back to life everything is okay." Now he was really smiling, and she began to wonder if he was lying to her about what happened.

"So you mean that she didn't actually die?" she asked.

"No, that's not what I mean. She actually did die. But the man that went to visit them at the hospital went there to pray for her to be healed. But she died just before he got there."

"But you're saying that she's still alive?" She began to wonder if David even knew what he was talking about.

"Oh yes. Even more than just alive, she's completely well and is back at home."

"She died, but now she's alive and well? How can that be? And are you saying that she doesn't have cancer any more?" This was starting to be confusing, but David seemed to be very confident in what he was telling her.

"The man that went to pray for her was the pastor of my new church. After she died, he called her back from death, and Jesus completely healed her at the same time. Jesus also healed two other men in the rooms next to her, and then they all got to leave the hospital and go home. Do you believe in Jesus, Mrs. Caldwell?" asked David.

"Yes, I do. But are you sure that what you told me is true?"

"It's true. On Sunday when I went to church, I saw Pastor John pray for a man who was in a wheelchair, and Jesus healed him, too. And there were a whole lot of other people who got healed."

Mrs. Caldwell was beginning to believe that there was something to David's story. He certainly believed what he was saying. "Maybe Johnny will be here tomorrow, and I can hear the story from him."

Tuesday night, before the youth group meeting, Daren and Leah Newman, the youth pastors at Victory Fellowship, met with their helpers to pray for the meeting. Like all of the leaders in Pastor John's church, they had learned that their victory was only going to be found in the prayer room. Praying for their kids, fighting spiritual battles for their hearts and minds, and finding wisdom and understanding from the Spirit of God was their top priority. But now, with the anointing of God so strong in their midst, they needed to know His voice without question. They wanted to have maximum impact on all of the kids that attended their meetings, some of whom were in serious situations in their school or home life.

As some of the early kids began to show up, they could sense the Presence of the Holy Spirit and were soon entering into prayer along side of the adults. With praises and thanksgiving, they were building a deeper intimacy with the Spirit of God, which would help them face the challenges of life. Before long there were about fifty kids in the building, excited about the moving of God in the previous Sunday service. Several of the youth group kids had received a healing miracle of some sort in the Sunday service and were quick to witness to their friends at school about what had happened. So now there were about ten new faces in the group, visitors who had heard about the miracles of healing from their friends and were now here to seek God in hope of finding help for themselves.

As they poured out their hearts before the Lord, the Spirit of God began to move among them, touching them and refreshing their spirits.

"*Pray for Lisa.*"

Leah knew that no one in the youth group was named Lisa, so she began to look over the new people, four guys and six girls. As she glanced at each girl, looking to the Holy Spirit to point her out, she could sense the different needs that they all had. She walked around and through the kids, praying in tongues as she moved. When she came to the last new face, she could feel the witness of the Holy Spirit.

"Lisa?" she asked softly.

The girl was young, about fifteen, and as she looked up at her with surprise on her face, Leah could see the pain in her eyes from some problem that she was facing. As Leah continued to look at her, tears began to form and then begin their slow slide down her cheeks. Leah reached out to her and took her in her arms, holding her tight as she began to sob, her body wracked with uncontrollable shaking. Lisa's two friends that were part of the youth group had stepped up beside her.

"It's okay, Lisa. Jesus is here to help you. Peace to your soul."

Lisa could feel the Presence of God; peace flooded into her mind and heart as the shaking and trembling began to subside. Stepping back, Leah looked into her eyes. By this time, Daren had moved up and was standing beside Leah.

"Lisa, Jesus loves you and wants you to know Him. Have you accepted Jesus as your Savior?" asked Leah.

"No, but Tracy and Tina have told me about Him. Do you think that He will accept me after what I've done?" Her voice was trembling, and there was a tone of condemnation in it. All she could think about was that God was punishing her for the sexual relations that she had with her former boyfriend. After giving in to his pressure to sleep with him, she found out that he had also been sleeping with other girls. When confronted about it, he soon dumped her to go after other girls. It was shortly after that when she found out that she had herpes. Tears began to water her eyes again as she looked at Leah, desperation beginning to edge into her countenance.

"Lisa, nothing you've done will change the way He loves you. He loved all of us when we were still lost sinners, and yet He accepted us all when we turned to Him. He even knows about your visit to the doctor, and He's not worried about what the doctor told you."

Lisa's head came up in a hurry at those words. Her lip began to tremble, and she lowered her eyes to the floor in shame, not wanting to see a look of revulsion on Leah's face for what she had done. Her tears began to fall to the floor as she raised her hands to cover her face. She was wondering how she knew about the doctor, for she hadn't even told her closest friend.

"Jesus came to earth to not only die for our sins but also to show us what God is really like. He's not a mean ogre in the sky with a big club waiting for us to mess up, but rather a God of mercy and forgiveness." Leah paused, reaching up to take Lisa's hands away from her face. Cupping her chin with a hand, Leah gently lifted her face up until she could again look into her eyes. "And Jesus also revealed that God's mercy is expressed in the healing of our bodies. Jesus wants you to know Him right now, but He also wants to heal you of your disease. Do you want to accept Jesus as your Lord and Savior?"

Nodding her head, she replied, "Yes, I do."

"I'll lead you in prayer, so just repeat after me and you'll be saved."

Again, Lisa nodded her head in acceptance.

"Jesus, I believe in You and that You died for my sins…and I ask for your forgiveness and mercy…I invite You into my heart to be my Lord and Savior…help me to live my life for You…and I thank You for healing my body…in Jesus' name. Amen."

When Lisa finished speaking, she felt warmth coming over her, beginning at the top of her head and flowing down her sides all the way to her feet. She felt so clean and free, and she knew beyond a shadow of a doubt that she was healed of the sexual disease that she had recently been diagnosed with. Her heart was leaping in her chest with love and joy at this new life that she now had with the Savior of her soul.

Going to her knees, she began to cry out, "Thank You, Jesus! Thank You for loving me!" The tears were again falling, but hers were not the only ones. Over half of those watching were now crying, expressing their joy in the goodness of God.

The following day, Johnny arrived at school a few minutes early to be able to talk to his teacher about his mom; David had told him the previous night of his conversation with Mrs. Caldwell. She listened to his story, and as it unfolded, she couldn't keep from crying. The Holy Spirit was touching her heart in a way that she had never experienced before. She had always wondered why people don't get healed today like they did in the Bible, and now she was listening to a story of just such a healing. She was soon asking about the church where Pastor John worked, so that she could go check it out for herself.

Just before class began, David walked in and gave Johnny a hug. Some of Johnny's other friends came in and asked him about his mom. As he started to tell the story, Mrs. Caldwell again listened to it, but she kept her eyes on the other kids to watch their reactions to such a remarkable story. As the story continued, more and more of the students were tuning in, a look of wonder on most of the faces. One of the bigger boys interrupted him with a remark of disbelief.

"I've heard some whoppers, Johnny, but yours takes the cake."

"Lonnie, would you just shut up. If you don't want to hear the story, then go out in the hallway," said Penelope. Dismissing him with a look, she turned back to Johnny and said, "Go ahead, Johnny; we want to hear the rest of it."

"I'm telling the truth. It happened just like I said. My

mom died and went to heaven and even talked to Jesus. All of you can come to my house today and see my mom. Jesus healed her in front of my whole family." Looking at Penelope, Johnny could see that her eyes were watering. "Penelope, do you want to know Jesus?"

"Yes! Tell me how." Her voice wavered, almost breathless. She could feel something in her heart, something pulling her toward knowing Jesus.

"It's easy. Just repeat after me. God, I want to know Jesus…I believe that He died on the cross for my sin…and that He rose from the dead…Jesus, please come into my heart. Amen."

Mrs. Caldwell could feel the Presence of the Lord as Johnny led Penelope in the sinner's prayer. Her own eyes began to water as she watched Penelope receive Jesus, her countenance changing before everyone's eyes. Johnny and David both placed a hand on her shoulder and then began speaking in another language, to everyone's surprise. After only a moment, Penelope herself began to speak in a foreign language, and as Mrs. Caldwell listened, she began to recognize the language as French. She didn't understand what was happening. She began to wonder if she should stop what was happening or let it continue. If this got back to some of the parents who were against Christianity, she might face some serious repercussions from the fallout. Yet, still there was something holding her back from stepping in. She felt that she should let it continue to its conclusion.

When the other students watched and listened to the three speaking in other languages, their interest in what was happening began to grow, questions ready to burst forth. As Penelope began to laugh with joy, the questions started, the first one from her friend Lisa.

"Penelope, what's going on? I didn't know you could speak in another language."

"I can't. I mean, I don't know any other language. I don't know how I'm doing this."

David felt the need to slip into the conversation at this point, although he didn't know much about it. "By yourself you can't do what you just did, but the Spirit of God that just made your spirit to be born again also filled you. It's called the baptism of the Spirit. I got it last Sunday at church, and Johnny received it when his mom was healed in the hospital."

"Penelope, don't you feel good? Isn't it a great feeling?" asked Johnny.

"It's wonderful!" said Penelope, and then she began to speak in another language again.

Lisa looked at Johnny and then David. "I want to know Jesus, too."

Lonnie, Timmy, and Julie also stepped up close to say that they also wanted to know Jesus. Mrs. Caldwell was dumbfounded. She had never seen this kind of evangelism before, but there was no denying that the Spirit of God was in the room. When Johnny had led them all in the salvation prayer, they all began to speak in other languages. This time Mrs. Caldwell didn't recognize any of the different languages, but they definitely sounded like legitimate tongues of different nationalities. She could still understand Penelope as she was speaking French, giving praises and thanksgiving to God.

On Sunday morning, there were so many people showing up for pre-service prayer that again there wasn't enough space for all of them in the prayer room. The Spirit of God was stirring the hearts of so many of the regulars in

Pastor John's congregation that almost all of them arrived early at the church for intercessory prayer. The ones who couldn't get into the prayer room moved into the sanctuary to pray; kneeling, sitting, standing, and pacing, they prayed fervently for God to again move in the service, visiting His people with His goodness and grace.

As the leaders and workers went about their duties, they could sense the Presence of God already in the building. Everyone who walked through the door could sense His Spirit, softly and gently hovering over everything. As the newcomers arrived, whether they came early with family or friends or showed up later in the morning, all of them began to weep as they entered the building.

Johnny and his entire family—even his grandparents and aunt and uncle—were all present. They were all sitting next to Kevin's family, and Johnny and David were side by side. Looking at Clare, no one would have known that six days earlier she had died of cancer. She had a beautiful smile on her face, and there were tears on her cheek when Pastor John greeted them and introduced his wife. Dr. Jones, his wife, his nurse and her husband, and Jack and Carrie were all in attendance. There were a few strangers mixed in with them also. It seemed like everyone who was in the service the previous Sunday had brought someone new. The ushers had every seat in use and had even set up a few extra chairs out in the main hall.

The praise team started up, leading the congregation in praising God, excitement and joyous singing resounding throughout the building. After about twenty minutes of singing praises, they were led into worship, people going to their knees and raising their hands to God. The Spirit of the Lord, sweeping through the congregation, was touching hearts and minds once again. Tears were falling, and there were many quiet pleas rising before the Lord.

Pastor John moved onto the stage and began to pray. When he had finished, he turned to Johnny and asked that his family come up on the stage. After introducing them, he had them testify about Clare's miracle healing at the hospital. Johnny even told about the other two men who were healed and how they had come into his mother's room. When they were done, there was weeping and shouting and praises to the King, people standing to their feet, praising their God for His great mercy.

Once again Pastor John asked for those who needed healing to come forward to the front of the sanctuary to receive prayer. Immediately people rose from their seats and began to work their way to the front. There were not as many as the previous Sunday, but there were still plenty of new people who had come just for that reason. They wanted to be rid of a physical problem that the doctors couldn't fix. As people were moving forward for prayer, there were ushers moving forward to stand behind them as they were receiving God's touch. Kathy, Mac, and Linda walked up on to the stage to minister with the pastor.

Pastor John worked his way down the line, laying his hands on the people with Kathy by his side. They were healed, delivered, and set free by the power of God's Spirit, most of them falling into the hands of the ushers as the pastor finished with them.

The rest of the congregation watched and worshipped the Lord as He touched His people with His goodness and healing power. The Kleenex boxes were again emptied of their tissues as the people were touched by God's care for His people. After everyone that needed prayer had been ministered to and was again at their seats, Pastor John led the congregation in more praise and worship. Afterwards, when he had dismissed the children to their classes, he began to teach the people on healing.

"Why is there sickness and disease in the world? In the beginning, when Adam and Eve were in the Garden of Eden, there wasn't any death, sickness, or disease. It was only after they sinned, by disobeying God and eating the fruit of the tree of the knowledge of good and evil, that death and decay entered into the world. Before sin entered, life and not death was the natural order of creation. After sin, the natural order was perverted, and death came. Corruption of the creation had taken place, and with it came disease and sickness, which were the agents of death. Now there was a new natural order, and it included death in nature as well as in man. Everything that had life in it was now subject to decay and death. And we know that death and disease is random in many ways. Disease will attack one person but skip over twenty others; it cares not for race, class, or culture. It is no respecter of persons.

"But also, the Bible clearly shows that Satan had influence over disease in the account of Job when his body was infected by the boils and the account of the woman who was bound by Satan for eighteen years, whom Jesus healed. Also, the numerous accounts in the Gospels of a demon being cast out of a sick or diseased person and the person instantly healed. So, not always does sickness and disease remain random, but it is guided or controlled by Satan's kingdom. These things are the natural order of nature and have been for thousands of years.

"But I want you to know this. When Jesus came, He introduced a new natural order. As the Man that never sinned, He revealed to mankind the authority and power that God desired for men to walk in. Everything that Jesus did supernaturally He was training the disciples to also do, regardless of the magnitude of it or the seeming impossibility of those things. Jesus said that a student who is perfectly trained would be just like his master. Training His disciples to walk as He did and to do the same supernatural works was one of Jesus' top priorities while He was here on the earth. And I believe that the Book of Acts clearly shows the success that Jesus had in training His disciples."

"Amen."

"That's right."

"Preach it, Pastor."

"Jesus clearly reveals the authority that He had in the earth to not only forgive men's sins but also the authority over all of creation. He commanded the elements of the weather, the forces of nature, and the life of the plants or trees that were not operating according to God's design. And He commanded sickness and disease, the flesh of man to be restored to wholeness after the ravages of disease or injury, the creative making of body parts that were missing or inoperative, and even commanding the demons and spirits that were under the control of Satan. He said that all authority had been given to Him, and He proved it. He set back into motion the God-given authority to mankind and sealed its legitimacy with His own Blood. This new natural order is specifically designed for the Christian to walk in. We are to exercise this authority in Jesus' name to destroy the work of the devil everywhere that we encounter it.

"This authority is operated by faith by those who believe in it, so those who do not have a close, intimate

187

relationship with the Lord will not be successful in its use. But what has been happening here and in other churches across the world that are similar to ours is that the full gospel of Jesus has been taught first and foremost, and people's faith has been increased to the point of believing for God's supernatural intervention in the lives of mankind. People must know the truth of God's Word and the things that He has freely given us by His Spirit before they can truly believe for His grace and goodness to be manifested. And that is exactly what has taken place in all of the churches where God is now moving, revealing His magnificent goodness and Glory. Praise be to Jesus."

CHAPTER SIXTEEN

During the following week, Pastor John began to get phone calls from around the nation from friends who were in ministry. All of them had stories to tell about the moving of God's Spirit in their services and the manifestation of His Glory. Many people had been healed in a miraculous way of all types of diseases and sicknesses, even of debilitating injuries that could not be fixed by the medical profession.

Apparently, God was moving all over, even overseas in many countries, but it did seem as if there was a limit as to where His Spirit was being manifested in miraculous occurrences. All of the stories were coming out of the full gospel churches, the ones that were teaching and promoting God's goodness and grace, believing for divine intervention in the lives of men and women who were turning to Him whole-heartedly.

Again, it was impressed upon Pastor John that God was moving and confirming His Word where His Word was being taught in its fullness. God was moving upon the hearts of men to draw them closer to Himself, to instill in them a profound trust in their Almighty God. Although the church had moved into the last days and God's agenda for the completion of the ages had begun, Pastor John knew of a certainty that it had really begun many years back in the past.

As Pastor John sat in his office, he thought about how this move of God had actually begun. To get the Church to the point at which it was now at, God had to get the truth of His Word and the revelation of His character and love back into its teachings and doctrines. As men and women began to seek Him with their whole heart and to search for His power and goodness that was such a big part of the early church, they found Him. They found that God had not changed through the years, but man and his understanding of God's Word was lacking and deficient. As they prayed and sought God diligently, they received revelation knowledge of His ways and His Word and began to act on it. They opened the door for God's Spirit to move among them with supernatural signs and the gifts of the Spirit. Some of them began to move in the Holy Spirit and to exercise the spiritual gifts listed in the twelfth chapter of 1 Corinthians. Revivals began to spring up, first one and then, as the participants spread out to different areas, more revivals. Christians were hungry for the moving of God's Spirit, to see that God was real enough to actually participate in the lives of men.

Through the early twentieth century, many people joined in on the move of God, and there were many hundreds and even thousands of people that were healed of all kinds of sicknesses and diseases. In Spokane, Washington, under John G. Lake's ministry, there were over one hundred thousand physician-documented cases of miraculous healings of terminal diseases. There was no denying that God was at work once again in His church, moving with signs and miracles that had been absent for centuries.

Although He was moving among new denominations that had sprung up that were teaching the original truths of His goodness and healing, none of the old-line traditional churches were seeing His miraculous intervention, because they refused to accept and teach what had been freshly revealed by His Spirit. Not that He did not want to move in their midst, but rather that they would not let go of the traditions that caused His Word to be of no effect. Their own pride kept them from entering in to God's fullness and receiving of His goodness.

Through the years of the twentieth century, the moving of God's Spirit spread across the United States and to other countries. Pentecostal churches sprung up all over the country, and as they received more revelation of the truth of God's Word, the charismatic movement began. The Greek word for the spiritual gifts that God gave to the church in the New Testament was pronounced *charisma*, meaning *a divine gratuity, deliverance, a spiritual endowment,* or *a miraculous faculty.*[1]

In the traditional churches, the most evidently supernatural spiritual gifts were thought to be done away with, but as the new denominations accepted, taught, and walked in the gifts of the Spirit, or the charisma of the Spirit, they took on the name *charismatic.* As the number of people who believed in the gifts increased into multiplied millions, their churches spread all across the world. The latest estimates for the number of followers of the charismatic teachings are over 500 million. The charismatic movement is the fastest growing of any denomination in the Christian faith and also outranks the growth of any religion in the world. The teachings of God's love and goodness without the bondage of religion and ritual is making inroads into every other religion and nation on the planet.

But even among the charismatic churches, there have been differences of teachings and doctrines. The overlying agreement among all of them is that God wants to help His people and move among them with the spiritual gifts. Because of the growth of the charismatic movement and the reinstatement of so many of God's truths of His Word into the lives of men, God has been able to raise up multitudes of individual believers who know Him intimately and obey His voice. And as individual pastors raise up congregations that know Him, they create an atmosphere of faith and expectancy within the church that allows the moving of God's Spirit without any hindrance of doubt.

When Jesus walked the earth, He taught the people about God so as to open their eyes to the truth, and when they accepted that truth, they were candidates for His divine intervention. Thus, thousands of people received miracles and healings from God. As His ministry progressed and the word about His ability to heal diseases spread to more people, the greater the expectancy and faith that grew among the people, and so the door was opened wider for the miraculous to happen. Jesus taught that all things are possible to those who believe. What Jesus did by His teaching was to increase the listener's faith that God could and would help them, no matter what the situation. Faith comes by hearing, and hearing by the Word of God. As Jesus taught the Word of God, faith within the listeners was increased to the point that they would believe that He would accomplish what they needed.

In the same way, Pastor John and other pastors like him had created an expectant faith within their congregations by teaching the Word of God in its fullness, themselves believing the Word and acting on it, and by praying for those who needed God's intervention in some area in their life. By encouraging his congregation to seek God with all of their heart, mind, soul, and strength and giving them a living example of how to do it, he promoted their faith to a level to receive. Of course, not everyone will put into their relationship with the Lord what they need to achieve faith and victory, but over the years Pastor John and Kathy had seen numerous answers to prayer for the members of their congregation: many miraculous healings, breakthroughs, turnarounds in situations, financial blessings, job opportunities, and many other blessings from the Lord.

They had seen their number of failures, also, but had refused to compromise the truth of the Word of God. Just because some situations don't turn out the way that they should according to the Word of God, even with their prayers and believing, doesn't nullify the integrity of God's Word. Pastor John had decided a long time ago that he believed what he had learned about the Word of God and would continue to teach it the way the Lord wanted him to. There are a lot of factors and variables involved with a Christian's walk with God, and that will affect the outcome of their walk of faith, and also there are some things that happen that are hard to understand or explain. But Pastor John also knew that you cannot interpret the Word of God according to experience. If Christians try to do that, the enemy will have them running in circles, not having any firm faith in any teaching of God. They would be like a wave of the sea, tossed about by every wind of trial or persecution.

If, when a Christian loses a particular battle of faith, they lay aside that particular teaching that they were believing in to produce the desired results, then they will be succumbing to the schemes of the enemy. As in the account of the sower and the word, the second stage of the enemy's attack is to bring trials or persecutions to test God's people on the teachings that they have received. If he can make them think that a particular teaching is falsely represented or is not accurate, then they will discard that teaching. And once it has been discarded, it will be harder for them to pick it up again in the future.

Pastor John and Kathy had experienced many setbacks in their walk of faith as they were learning and growing but had refused to let go of those teachings. And now, they had reached a point in their personal life, through their knowing the voice of the Spirit of God and being obedient to what He tells them, that they were walking in victory in everything that they applied their faith to. And in so doing, they were setting an example for their people as well as building the faith of their congregational members to receive from God in their own lives, through and by their own faith and prayers.

In the last couple of days, Pastor John even received calls from the four pastors that he and Mac had prayed for. They hadn't had God's manifestation in their service yet, but both their prayer time and their teaching from the pulpit had such a stronger anointing upon it that many members of their congregation had commented on it. Pastor John continued to encourage them to seek God with their whole heart and to be ready to do what He asks them, and when the time was right, God would begin to move in their service in the same way and manner that He had in his own.

All four of them were so excited over their new relationship with God that Pastor John overflowed with praises and thanksgiving to the Lord. Their wives had even been quick to grab hold of their husbands' newfound strength and faith in God and to begin to build on their own relationships with the Lord. Pastor John could see that this move of God was going to spread like a wildfire in the August heat and would not be put out or even dampened before the blowing of the trumpet and Jesus' return.

Pastor John's musings were interrupted with a knock on the door. "Come in." The door opened and Leah Newman stepped into his office. She was, with her husband Daren, the head of the youth group and a gifted evangelist.

"Hello, Pastor. Do you have a few minutes?"

"Sure. What is it you need?" returned the pastor.

"I was praying this morning, and the Lord asked me if I was ready to take our group out on the streets, here in town, to start witnessing about His Presence. That way we could get some early preparation for our trip to Hollywood. It's going to be different now, witnessing for Jesus with this stronger anointing, and it might be nice to break in the new people here at home."

"Well, Leah, I think that's a great idea. Do you have a day in mind to do this?" asked Pastor John.

"This Friday. There'll be a lot of people out and about, and we can split up into four groups and cover several areas. I'd want for us to meet here at the church at 5:30 and pray for about an hour before we go out."

"That sounds good to me, but let me pray about it first and I'll get back to you later tonight. Okay?"

"Okay, Pastor. I'll pray about it some more and see if there's anything else that I need to know. Thanks, and I'll talk to you later," answered Leah.

When she was gone and the door was closed, Pastor

John began to pray about it right away. He knew that Leah was champing at the bit to go out and do something, so he needed to get her an answer as soon as possible.

"Lord, You heard that conversation. What do you think about Leah taking the group out on Friday?"

"*It's a good plan. I helped make it.*"

"Okay. I just wanted to check first. Thank You for such a quick answer."

"*You're welcome.*"

---

[1] *Strong's Exhaustive Concordance of the Bible*, 1 Corinthians 12:1,4,9,28,30,31, *gifts*, # 5486.

CHAPTER SEVENTEEN

When Friday night arrived, everyone was at the church early, excited about going out and witnessing. As soon as Leah had settled which night that they were going out, she had contacted all of them to let them know what was in the works so they could put it on their schedule and so they could start praying about it, preparing themselves spiritually and mentally for street witnessing. At the church, after praying for about a half hour, seeking the Lord but also doing spiritual warfare for the lost, they were ready to go out. Leah was leading one group with Joe and Peggy; Mac was leading another with Jay and Sandy; Pastor John was with Kyle and Katie; and Daren was with Alan and Justin.

Two groups went down to the movie theater, while two others walked the streets, from one tavern to another and over to the local strip joint. At the theater, one group went across the street to a popular eating joint, which catered to the movie patrons but was mostly a hangout for the younger crowd. The second team began to witness to the crowds in front of the theater building, handing out gospel tracks and trying to start up conversations with various people. They were getting quite a few snubs and snide remarks when Pastor John stepped up to a young woman in a wheelchair.

She had several friends standing around her, but when he looked down at her, the Spirit of the Lord touched her heart. As she stared at Pastor John, tears began to water her eyes and to slowly trace a line down her cheeks. When one of her friends noticed that she was crying, he stepped up to Pastor John and put his hand out against his chest.

"We don't need your kind around here, so why don't you take your little group of do-gooders and get out of here before I go tell the management that you're out here causing a disturbance?" There was a snarl on his face as he was talking, but when he had finished, he had an overwhelming feeling that he better take his hand off the man. He didn't know why, but there was something about him that made him feel very uneasy.

"Miss, what would you like for Jesus to do for you tonight?" Pastor John asked. He looked straight into her eyes as he was talking, and he could see that the Holy Spirit was all over her, touching her heart and her mind. He knew that she was a Christian but didn't know what her church affiliation was or the depth of her knowledge of the Word of God. What he did know was that Jesus wanted him to minister His healing power to her tonight in front of all these people.

She looked back at Pastor John, and she saw something in his eyes, something that made her believe that he was serious about his question and that he could and would do whatever she asked for. And then there was that feeling in her heart, a Presence that she had felt before, long ago, just after she had the accident that had crippled her. But it was so much stronger now. She didn't understand what was happening, but she knew that God was here and that this man walked with Him and had a personal relationship with Him that she herself wanted. She looked up at her boyfriend and reached out her hand to him.

"Alan, don't." Alan looked at her, and her face was shining, even through the tears. He didn't know what was going on, but he wasn't going to say anything else to that guy. He had a gut feeling that if he said anything, it better be something good. When she saw that Alan understood her, she turned her attention back to the man of God. By this time, their little byplay had the attention of all the people within thirty feet.

"I want to walk again and to be able to dance before Jesus." Once the words were out, the tears again began to wash their way down her cheeks and fall onto her lap.

There was an expectant hush among those that were close by as they listened to her request and waited with bated breath for Pastor John's reply. They were all wondering what was going on; it wasn't like anything that any of them had ever experienced before. Both Kyle and Katie knew what was going to happen as soon as the pastor stepped up to the paralyzed woman and had immediately stepped up to take their place beside him, all the while quietly praying in tongues.

Pastor John bent down and reaching out his hands to her cheeks lovingly wiped away her tears. Looking into her eyes, seeing her hope and also her expectant faith rising to reach out and to grasp hold of what he was offering, he took hold of her hands. In a firm voice, he began to speak.

"Be whole in the name of Jesus!" And with Pastor John lifting her hands into the air, she began to rise, slowly at first, but as she began to feel muscles and movement in places that she hadn't felt in over eight years, she began to pick up speed, and it seemed to the onlookers that she leapt to her feet. With wild joy at being able to stand, she threw her arms around Pastor John, burying her tear-stained face against his shoulder, muffled cries drifting to the crowd as she was simultaneously crying and laughing.

Letting go of Pastor John, she began to jump up and down, and looking up to the sky, she cried out repeatedly, "Thank You, Jesus!" She turned to her boyfriend and hugged him tight for a moment, and when she let go of him, she began to dance before the Lord. The Holy Spirit was upon her as she danced around, moving in and out of the people, and as they began to step back to make room for her, she began to twirl around with a beautiful smile on her face. As the people watched her heartfelt dance for the Lord, they began to cry and to cheer. As the Presence of the Lord began to move among them, revealing their need for Him, almost all of the people that were witnesses of His miraculous healing began to cry out to God to be saved.

One man who was in his early fifties stepped up to Pastor John, tears rolling down his cheeks as he asked his question. "Would you pray for my kidneys?" The man's voice was breaking with emotional stress, but his hope could be clearly seen on his face by the people that were close by. Wanting to be respectful to the man of God, he kneeled down before Pastor John, clasping both of his hands in his own. Immediately Pastor John pulled him back to his feet.

"I am only a man like you. Jesus is the one you are to honor and worship." Pastor John spoke to him tenderly, not wanting to bruise his heart or cause him to doubt his compassion. As he was talking, he placed one hand on the man's shoulder and held onto one of his hands. Looking him in the eyes, Pastor John asked, "Do you believe in Jesus?"

"Yes, ever since I was a young boy. I asked Jesus into my heart when I was twelve years old."

"Are you aware that you entered into a covenant or contract with God when you asked Jesus to be your Lord and Savior?"

The man looked a little bewildered when he replied, "Kind of. But what do you mean exactly?"

"When you believed in Jesus and asked Him to be your Lord, you gave yourself to Him. You belong to Him, and in return, He is your God. He has made Himself and all that He is available to His people. But it is by faith that we are to draw from Him the things that we need in this life, and it is by faith that you now stand before me, asking for your healing. Jesus said, 'If you've seen Me, you've seen the Father,' and healing was included in that. God is your Healer." Pastor John paused for just a moment to look at Kyle. Instantly, Kyle knew that he needed to stand behind the man to catch him when he fell, and he quickly moved to take position.

"In the mighty name of Jesus, kidneys be healed and return to your designed function!" Placing one hand on the man's forehead, the power of God flowed into him and effected an immediate change and reversal in his kidneys. Only a few seconds went by before the man began to topple backwards into Kyle's waiting arms and was laid gently on the sidewalk.

Excited whispers began in the crowd, asking what happened and wondering if the man was okay. His wife and his daughter were both kneeling beside him with concern on their faces. His wife looked up at Pastor John and asked,

"What happened to him? I've never seen him faint before. Is he okay?" As she was talking the man's eyes fluttered open and his hand tightened on hers, which brought her attention back to his face.

Pastor John looked down at the two women, and with love and compassion in his voice he answered, "Your husband is just fine. When the Holy Spirit touched him with healing power, it knocked him out, so to speak. It's almost like a temporary paralysis that only lasts a few seconds. But your husband is now whole, and he'll begin to feel his healing almost immediately."

After the young woman had been raised from her wheelchair, several other couples had walked up, intending to buy their tickets for a movie, and all of them had been witnesses of the older man asking to be prayed for. One man, in his late twenties, after witnessing the older gentleman falling down, stepped up to Pastor John. The man looked a little uncertain, but when he came to a decision, he looked Pastor John straight in the eye and began to speak.

"Last month I went to the doctor to check out why I've been having really bad headaches, and after running some tests and doing a CAT scan, he informed me that I have an inoperable brain tumor. He said that it's fairly well advanced and that I may only have two or three months to live. Is there anything that you can do for me?" His voice wavered, and it sounded like there was a lot of pent-up emotion behind it. The woman that was standing close behind him, the one who had approached while holding his arm, had a surprised look on her face.

Pastor John felt a check in his spirit; something just wasn't right. He looked into the man's eyes, and the Lord revealed to him that the man was lying. He was a reporter for the newspaper, and he thought that he would run a scam on Pastor John to make him out to be a fake. As Pastor John continued to stare into the man's eyes, he began to fidget, shifting his weight from one foot to the other.

"Why do you want to test the Holy Spirit? Do you think that because you can lie to people you can also lie to God? Do you want to have an inoperable brain tumor? If you continue in your ways and do not repent, beware that something bad may come upon you." As Pastor John was speaking, the man's face became red with shame and embarrassment, and before long the crowd could see that Pastor John was right. At Pastor John's last word, the man turned around, and with his head hanging low, he pushed his way through the crowd and hurried to find his car, leaving his girlfriend behind.

"I've only been dating him for three weeks, and he's never mentioned to me anything about having a tumor or that he was dying. He's never even complained about a headache since I've known him. But I do know that he's a reporter for the newspaper." She was speaking loud enough that the whole crowd could hear her words.

The older man who was healed of kidney failure had stood up and had been listening to the whole encounter. Since everyone had quieted down to be able to hear the girlfriend's explanation, they also heard the man say to his wife that he needed to use the rest room. As he began to walk away with his wife, the daughter turned to Pastor John and with tears in her eyes, she began to explain about her dad.

"He's had total kidney failure for over six years and has been having kidney dialysis performed four times a week during that time. He hasn't passed any urine in that time, because his kidneys don't pass any to his bladder." She paused to wipe away her tears with her hand and to rub her nose, which was beginning to run. Pastor John reached for his handkerchief and handed it to her, and when she wiped her nose dry, she continued, "If he needs to use the rest room, then his kidneys are working again. Thank you for coming here tonight and healing my dad." She stepped close to Pastor John, hugged him, and then turned to follow after her parents.

A car screeched to a halt in front of them, and the reporter yelled out the window to his date, "Are you coming or not?"

"No! I'll get a ride with someone else."

As the car lurched forward, they could hear his voice drifting back from the window, and it didn't sound very happy. As they watched him drive down the lane through the parking lot, their attention was brought back to Pastor John when he began to pray.

"Lord Jesus, protect the people."

CHAPTER EIGHTEEN

The sound of screeching tires and a dull thud cut through the night air, followed by a woman's scream. The crowd turned toward the sounds, and they could see the reporter's car stopped in the street one block away. All eyes turned toward Pastor John to see what he was going to do, and when he took off in a trot toward the accident, all of them followed close behind.

As Pastor John neared the scene, he could see that Mac, Jay, and Sandy were already there, for they had been standing only a half block away when it happened. The reporter was pacing in front of his car, talking to himself, frantic over what happened. Pastor John could hear him saying it wasn't his fault, that the boy had darted out in front of him without any warning. He had a cell phone in his hand and was dialing a number even as he was ranting about whose fault it was.

Mac was kneeling next to a small form lying on the pavement, and across from him were the mom and dad, also kneeling. The mother was crying, but the father was able to keep his tears back as he tried to determine how bad the injury was. Pastor John could hear Jay and Sandy praying in tongues, and when he stopped behind Mac, he was also praying. Someone had stopped their car with the headlights shining on the scene, and he could see a small pool of blood on the pavement. Kneeling down next to the boy, who looked to be about seven years old, he could see blood dripping out of the boy's ears. He wasn't conscious, but Pastor John could see the rise and fall of his small chest as his broken body struggled to get air.

Pastor John looked across at the mother and reached out his hand to place it over hers as it rested on her son's stomach. When his hand made contact with hers, she felt the power of God, almost like an electric tingle, surge through her hand and up her arm. Quickly she looked up to see whose hand it was, and when her eyes made contact with Pastor John's, she felt a peace envelop her, a peace such as she had never felt before.

"Do not fear, but only believe, and your son will be made well."

She nodded her head, and her tears began to subside. There was something about these two men that surprised her, and their confidence overwhelmed her, causing her to trust them with her whole being.

"I don't think any of his limbs are broken, but he might have some busted ribs, and he's bleeding out his ears. His head injury worries me the most." The father's voice was shaky as he spoke, not wanting to believe what he was seeing, but as he was talking, there was fear beginning to edge into his voice. "Has anyone called an ambulance?" The worry and fear in his voice as he shouted confirmed the fears of the crowd. Pastor John reached out his hand and put it on the father's shoulder. He jerked slightly at his touch and then turned his eyes to look at Pastor John. When his eyes made contact with the pastor's, he could see God's love and care shining forth, and he could sense the power that resided there, flowing from the Spirit of God. Jay and Kyle took up positions behind the father and put their hands on his shoulders while Sandy and Katie kneeled behind the mother and did the same. They were all praying in tongues; everyone could hear them, and even though the peace that was flowing from them into the parents could not be seen, it began to spread to the onlookers until they could all sense the Presence of God.

Many of them who were themselves Christians were also praying for God's intervention, for divine healing and restoration. Pastor John even heard the reporter asking God to help the boy to recover. Although the situation was serious, Pastor John found himself smiling, thinking about how people can be so hypocritical.

Looking up toward heaven, Pastor John began to pray. "Lord God, we come before You to ask for the life of this boy, for You to touch him now with Your mighty power, to raise him up without injury or pain. For Your Glory we ask this, in the name of Jesus." Turning his attention back to the boy, everyone leaned forward to see what would happen. There were over two hundred people surrounding them, all of them sensing something of a great magnitude was about to happen.

Pastor John took the boy's hand in his and said in a firm voice, "Little boy, get up." Immediately, his eyes opened, and he sat up. Looking from Pastor John to his mom and dad, there was a look of wonder on his face.

"Mom, what's going on?"

She let out a cry and hugged him to her, squeezing him tightly as her tears ran down her face. The father was also crying, his arms reaching out to hold them both. The people that were close by could see his body shaking, wracked by sobs. Pastor John's team was all praising Jesus for His mercy and grace, some of the people joining in also. There wasn't any misunderstanding among the crowd as to what happened or who was the one that brought the miracle, for the name of Jesus was on the lips of the majority of the onlookers.

There was excitement in the air as word of the boy's healing spread to the people in the rear of the crowd of onlookers. The boy stood up with his parents, who still had tears running down their cheeks. Sirens began to make themselves heard just as the crowd began to cheer when they saw the boy standing, apparently without any serious injury, but the people that were up close knew better. When they had watched the boy laying there in a pool of blood that had been dripping out of his ears, they knew that his injury was life threatening or at the very least there would probably be some kind of brain damage.

Within sixty seconds, sirens could be heard approaching from the street as two police cars made their way to the accident. As they turned into the lane to pull to a stop just behind the car with its headlights shining on the scene, the ambulance siren could be heard as it was drawing near. About ninety seconds later, an ambulance was driving up the lane, its lights flashing, to stop beside the car whose headlights were covering the accident. The policemen were backing up the crowd to make room for the paramedics to move in and set up and then began to ask their questions to find out all the details of the accident. Once they saw the victim standing up and talking, apparently with little injury, the tenseness of the situation disappeared, and it turned into just another minor traffic accident. Of course, they didn't understand why the report said that the victim was near death, because there he was, standing and talking. Again, they glanced at the dent in the hood of the car, the broken pieces of the grille on the ground, and the small pool of blood on the pavement where the boy had fallen.

As the paramedics moved the boy to the ambulance, they were listening to the mother tell the story of how he got hit. They noticed the blood on the boy's head and neck and the line of drying blood that had run from his ears, realizing that his head must have had a very severe impact on the pavement to cause it, and they became concerned about a fractured skull or at the very least a serious concussion.

Pastor John looked around at the crowd, bringing his thoughts into focus to begin witnessing. There was much talking and excited speculation among the crowd, and he realized that he needed to capitalize on the moment.

"Listen, everyone. Some of you have witnessed three miracles here tonight. You saw the woman in the wheelchair receive total healing and rise up to dance before the Lord, the man whose kidneys had failed and are now once again functioning properly, and now this last miracle. This boy was close to death, as his parents can testify, but now he is up and walking without a single scratch on his body." As he spoke these words, the crowd could see the paramedics removing the boy's shirt to check for any bruises and breaks, especially for broken ribs. Pastor John turned to the paramedics and asked, "Does the boy have any bruises, cuts, abrasions, or broken bones?"

With a look of incredulity, one of the paramedics looked at Pastor John and then swung his attention to the crowd. "This boy doesn't have a single mark on him. We can't even find where the blood on his clothes and his head came from!"

At the words of the paramedic, excited whispers began among the crowd, and Pastor John began to explain. "These healings were all brought about by faith in Jesus, who is the Son of God and who died for our sins that we may be reconciled to God and to live for Him. Some of you are already Christians, but there are many of you who have never made a decision for Jesus before. Jesus loves you, cares for you, and wants you to know Him, but you have to come to Him by faith and ask Him to be your Lord and Savior. All of the sins of your past will be washed away, and you will receive times of refreshing, your spirit within you being born anew by the Spirit of God."

Pastor John began to notice that there were a few people at the back of the crowd beginning to walk away. He knew that not everyone will believe; there had even been people who ignored the notable miracles in Jesus' ministry and refused to believe that He was the one that He said He was. Pastor John knew that it wasn't any different today. Many people had a sour outlook on religion and didn't want anything to do with it, including Christianity. They lumped all religions together, assuming that it was all something made up by the human intellect to assuage their guilt and their shortcomings, not realizing that Jesus and His sacrifice were all true and were for their own benefit.

But Pastor John knew that there were some who felt the Spirit of God tugging on their heart, asking to be let in, and those were the ones that Pastor John was interested in right now.

"How many of you are already Christians?" About forty or so hands went up in the air. "Look around you and see how many of you are believers. Jesus wants the rest of you to also believe in Him. He is here right now, touching your hearts. He has enabled me tonight to heal these people by the power of His Holy Spirit so that you would believe in Him and ask Him to be your Lord and Savior." Looking around at the crowd, he could see the Holy Spirit moving among the people; some were beginning to weep as they felt His Presence for the first time in their lives. His gaze drifted past the paramedics and swept across to the four policemen that were scattered around the scene. Two of them were just bringing their hands down, and one of the other ones was wiping his eyes with a handkerchief.

"Those of you who want to invite Jesus into your life, right now, please raise your hands." Pausing for a moment to let them respond, Pastor John watched as several hands were raised, and then after another minute, there were at least a hundred hands raised into the air. "Praise the Lord. This is the greatest decision of your life, and you will never regret it. I'm going to lead you in asking Jesus to be your Savior, so please repeat after me. Lord Jesus, I believe that You are the Son of God…and that You came to earth and died on the cross for my sins…I ask You now to forgive me and to receive me as Your own…to be my Lord and Savior and to help me to live my life for You…and I thank You, Jesus, for Your sacrifice that gives me new life in You. Amen. Praise the Lord!"

Shouts and cheers erupted as the people felt renewed in their spirits, the Spirit of the living God touching them and giving them new birth in Him. Raising his hands in the air, Pastor John began to sing in another language, praising and worshipping God, and as Mac and the others began to join in, the Holy Spirit fell on all those present, and they all began to speak in tongues as the Spirit gave utterance.

Pastor John turned to where the reporter had been standing by his car to see him sitting inside with his head down. He wasn't praying but rather still angry over the whole scene. He did not want to accept the idea that there was a God and that Jesus was real. Even after experiencing and seeing what had happened, his pride wouldn't let him accept the fact that Jesus was for real. Pastor John realized that some people didn't want to believe because it would upset the structure of their whole life; it would put their whole way of thinking in the trash bin, and they just didn't want to have to face that reality.

"*Go to him.*"

Pastor John walked over to the reporter and stood beside the open door. Looking down at the man, love began to well up in him, God's unconditional love. Knowing this was a turning point in his life, Pastor John was very careful with his words, not wanting to cause any condemnation but rather love and acceptance.

"God loves you, Alan. Nothing you've done changes that fact. The enemy tried to use you to do harm to my ministry, and when that failed, he discarded you to this accident to destroy you, but Jesus has turned this around for your salvation." Reaching out and placing his hand on the reporter's shoulder, Pastor John continued. "Do you feel His Presence and power?"

As the reporter lifted his face to look at Pastor John, tears were rolling down his cheeks. He had felt the Presence of God, and when Pastor John placed his hand on him, he could feel power or something flowing into his shoulder, almost like an electrical current. He began to nod his head in answer to the question, and then words of remorse began to tumble out.

"I'm so sorry. I don't know why I did that to you, but I do believe in Jesus now. I realize now that I've been wrong about God, and I want His forgiveness and His help. Can you pray for me to be saved, too?" Part of the crowd had moved closer to hear the words between Pastor John and the reporter, and even the father of the boy had walked over to listen.

Taking his hand, Pastor John pulled him to his feet. Mac and Jay stepped around behind the reporter, just in case he needed catching. Wiping the back of his hand across his eyes, the reporter glanced at the two men and then looked at Pastor John with a question on his face.

"Don't worry; they're my helpers." Keeping hold of one hand and placing his other hand on his shoulder, Pastor John began. "Alan, repeat after me. Lord Jesus, I believe that You are the Son of God and that You died on the cross for my sins…and I ask Lord that You receive me now and give me new birth in You and help me live for You, amen." Embracing him, Pastor John said, "Welcome to the family of God. Now I'd like to pray for you." Keeping one hand on his shoulder, Pastor John began to pray for Alan. "Lord Jesus, I thank You for bringing Alan to this decision, for changing his heart and his mind, and I ask that You help him in his work place and to give him boldness to live his life for You. Open the eyes of his heart that he may come to know You as his heavenly Father and to trust and obey You in all things. In Jesus' name, amen." Raising his hand and placing it on Alan's head, Pastor John could feel a surge of power flow out of him as Alan toppled backwards into waiting arms.

Meanwhile, Leah with Joe and Peggy had taken a stand at the local strip club, witnessing to the patrons as they came and went. Early in the evening, a young lady drove up and parked, and as she got out of her car, she noticed the three people standing at the edge of the street.

"Miss, could I talk to you for a moment?" asked Leah.

"Sure." Walking up to her, she began to sense something different but not anything dangerous. "What do you need?"

"My friends and I are here to tell you about Jesus. He cares about you and wants to help you," answered Leah.

Crystal's heart began to beat harder and faster as soon as she heard the name of Jesus. She didn't know why it was happening; she had faced this before with her parents and friends, but with this stranger there was something different. Holiness. Yes, holiness. She had been raised in the Catholic Church, and she did have some misgivings about what she was doing. But it was a job. And it paid well. "I should turn around now and go inside," she thought. But there was something holding her, keeping her attention on this stranger. Something about her was different than the others who had tried to tell her that what she was doing was wrong.

"Do you know what I do?"

"Yes. God told me that you're one of the dancers here. He also told me that you have a little girl at home whom you love dearly," answered Leah.

A look of surprise and wonder came to Crystal's face. "God told you about me?" The team could hear a slight tremble in her voice as she spoke.

"Yes. You're a single mom, and you need a good job to be able to take care of your daughter. We're here to tell you that Jesus loves you and has a plan for your life to take care of you."

"Jesus has a plan for my life?" asked Crystal.

"He would say to you, '*For I know the thoughts that I think toward you…thoughts of peace and not of evil, to give you a future and a hope. Then you will call upon Me and go and pray to me, and I will listen to you. And you will seek Me and find Me, when you search for Me with all your heart.*' Jesus will help you find a good job, Crystal. But even more than that, He'll help you in every area of your life."

"You even know my name?"

"Yes. God revealed to me your name just now. He wants you to know Him." Taking her hands, Leah asked, "Don't you want to know Him?"

Crystal could feel the Presence of God, and when Leah took her hands in her own, there was a tingle, almost like a small shock, but not painful. She had never heard about anything like this in the Catholic Church that she was raised in, but she couldn't ignore this Presence. She could feel the love of God. Tears started to water her eyes as she made her decision. "Yes! I want to know Jesus! How do I?"

"It's easy. Just repeat after me. Heavenly Father, I believe in Your Son Jesus…that He died on the cross for my sins…and I ask for Your forgiveness for all of my sins…thank you, Lord, for Your mercy…and I ask for a new life in You…in Jesus' name I pray."

They could all see the transformation on Crystal's face as she was born again by the Spirit of God, her tears falling freely. Leah began to pray in another language, with Joe and Peggy also joining in. All three of them placed their hands on Crystal's shoulders, and as the Spirit of God baptized her, she began to praise Him with her spirit, speaking in another language.

Crystal wrapped her arms around Leah and embraced her tightly. Peggy reached into her purse for a Kleenex and handed it to Crystal, pulling out some more for herself and Leah, who was also crying.

Pulling back from Crystal, after wiping her eyes, Leah began to explain about the baptism of the Spirit, speaking in tongues, and her continued use of it as her prayer language.

"I've got some friends in my church that own their own businesses, and I'll talk to them first thing in the morning to see if they can give you a job. It wouldn't pay as much as you're probably making here, but God will be with you," said Leah.

"Thank you so much. You know, I don't even know your name," said Crystal.

Leah, beginning to laugh, said, "I'm sorry about that. My name's Leah, and this is Peggy and her husband, Joe."

Peggy stepped up and hugged her as she said, "I'm so glad to meet you, Crystal."

Joe held out his hand to her and added, "I'm glad to meet you, too, and that you've met my best friend, Jesus."

"So am I, Joe. I never knew that it would be like this. I feel so clean and good, even after what I've been doing here. I always thought that it was just religion, but now I know that Jesus is real. Thank you so much for being here."

"The blood of Jesus has washed away all of the sins of your past and will always be there to cleanse you in the future. Your life will never be the same," explained Peggy.

"Crystal! What are you doing?" a gruff voice called out. They all turned to see a man standing by the back door of the club. "If you don't get in here right away, you're going to be late."

"Mr. Layton, I'm not coming in tonight. I'm quitting," called back Crystal.

Mr. Layton came hurrying over to see what the problem was. He couldn't afford to lose one of his best dancers, especially tonight. There were too many people already in the club, waiting for her performance. He didn't stop until he was almost in her face but he began very gently to try to coax her inside.

"Crystal, you can't quit tonight. There are a lot of people here to see you. You're one of my best dancers, and I'm counting on you." Taking her gently by the arm, he turned to lead her inside, saying, "Come on, Crystal."

Crystal planted her feet and pulled her arm free of his grasp. "I said, I quit! Nothing you can say will change my mind."

Mr. Layton's look of surprise quickly turned nasty and vicious. "You're going in, Crystal. I'm not going to be stood up like this. I gave you this job against my better judgment, and now you owe me. I've got too many customers in there waiting for you and I'll lose a lot of money if you don't come in."

Leah stepped up beside Crystal and put her arm around her. Joe stepped up on the other side of Crystal to give his support, while Peggy stayed back and continued to pray in tongues.

"She's not going in, Mr. Layton. She quit, and now we're leaving," said Leah.

"And who are you?" asked Mr. Layton, a vicious snarl in his voice.

"I'm Crystal's sister. And if you don't like it, you'll have to take it up with our big Brother and our Father."

Turning a nasty stare upon Joe, he asked, "Is this him? He don't look like much to me. If he gives me any lip, I'll bust him in the chops."

Crystal was starting to get a little nervous. She didn't want her new friends to get into trouble, especially a fist fight. She'd heard some stories about Mr. Layton's temper and didn't want anyone to get hurt.

Joe looked back at him, listening to the Spirit of God. There was no fear in Joe, whether it came to physical fighting or not. Throughout his years as an alcoholic, he had learned to fight in the school of hard knocks and had learned well. But he knew that it wasn't going to come to that, for he was about to end the conversation.

"Crystal, I'm only telling you one last time. Get inside, and start dancing!" His anger was starting to manifest, and as Crystal stood there, not moving or saying anything, he began to curse them. His rage began to take over, and he stepped up to Joe to grab him.

"Stop in the name of Jesus! You foul spirit, shut your mouth." Instantly the man fell back from Joe and cowered to the ground, whimpering.

"Don't hurt me. Just go away and leave me alone," he begged. He started crawling away, and as soon as he was a few feet away, he stood up and ran back into the building.

The following week, at the youth group, Clare and Dan Shelton showed up with their daughter, Alice. Daren and Leah met them, and after introductions, they were taken on a tour through the building.

"So, Daren, how many kids do you have in the youth group?" asked Dan.

"Normally we have about thirty-five to forty, but these last two weeks there's been between fifty and sixty, and it looks like it's on the increase," answered Daren.

"Our first meeting after the church's first miracle service, we had about fifty kids, and then last week we had almost sixty. The Spirit of God has touched all the kids, and now they can't stay quiet about it at school. They're all telling their testimonies to their friends and acquaintances at school, and some of them are starting to show up," added Leah.

"The new kids from even the first week haven't missed a meeting yet. Once they've come, the Holy Spirit touches them, and they're changed. Now they're so excited about God that they can't stay away," said Daren.

"I can see why," responded Dan. "After Clare's healing, nothing has been the same for us. We're seeking God all the time in prayer and Bible study, and a lot of things that we used to do before, now we don't. Our perspective on a lot of things has drastically changed now that we really know God."

"It really seems strange now, looking back on what we thought was a relationship with Jesus. It was so shallow. We knew about Him, but we didn't really know Him at all. If only all of the people who confess to being Christians would come to know Jesus the way we are starting to know Him, the world would be a much better place," added Clare.

"Don't fret over it too much, Clare. We've all gone through the same thing. It's just one of Satan's schemes to keep people from being effective for the Kingdom of God, and it seems to have worked pretty well for him. But in these last days, God's Kingdom is going to overcome all of his tactics and win billions to Jesus," explained Leah.

Looking at Leah, Clare could feel a witness in her spirit that she was right. "I think you're right, Leah. The only question is how many billions will come to the truth before the end. This move of God is going to be so powerful, it's hard to understand how anyone will continue to deny Him."

"I know what you mean. Well, it's about time we got started. It's good to see you. Feel free to hang around if you like. Alice, I'll take you around and introduce you to some of our kids."

"Okay, that'd be great. About what time should my parents be back to pick me up?" asked Alice.

"We're usually all wrapped up by 9:30, so you could show up about 9:15 or so," answered Daren.

"Okay, guys. Alice, we'll see you later, and have fun."

"All right, Dad." Alice stepped up to her dad, gave him a hug, and then hugged her mom. "See you later."

Leah took Alice by the hand and led her around, introducing her to the other kids before things got under way. Lisa, Tina, Tracy, Kelly, Pete, and Lee were kids she met that were her own age. Two of them attended the Christian high school, and the other four attended her own school. So, she was looking forward to being able to hang around some strong Christian friends while at school.

While meeting the kids, Alice could see there were several people warming up with instruments to have a song service. She'd never been in a youth group that had its own band, so she was already getting excited about being there. Before long, Daren called everyone over to the band and opened the service with prayer. As the band started to play, hands were raised to heaven, and Alice began to feel the Presence of God once again. Alice was moved to tears to see kids her own age worshipping the Lord, pouring out their hearts before His Presence. Two weeks ago, she never would have pictured herself participating in something like this, but she was glad that God had revealed Himself to her in such a powerful way. She went to her knees and worshipped the Lord Jesus.

CHAPTER NINETEEN

The group from Victory Fellowship walked off the plane at the John Wayne Airport and went looking for their luggage. As they walked through the airport to the luggage area, there was a crowd of people all around them heading in the same direction. Joe and Peggy's gaze was drawn to a small boy in a wheelchair who was ahead of them, being pushed by a woman who they assumed was his mother. They began to pray and ask God if there was something that they could do for him, their hearts being moved with compassion.

The Spirit of God began to talk to them, telling them that the child had muscular dystrophy and that He was with them to heal him. They stepped up closer to Pastor John and told him of their leading.

"We'll back you up. Do what you know to do," answered Pastor John.

When they finally arrived at the luggage pickup area, the two of them were praying softly in tongues, waiting on the

Spirit to lead them. The mother had stopped the wheelchair, about twenty feet back from the luggage carousel, and as the luggage started to come around, she left her son to move closer to the belt to watch for her suitcases. Joe and Peggy moved up beside the boy and looked down at him.

"Josh?" Joe asked.

The boy looked up at Joe, a question in his eyes, looking to see if he knew this stranger who had said his name. "Do I know you?" asked Josh.

"No, but the Lord Jesus wanted me to talk to you."

Peggy, kneeling beside the chair, took him by the hand and asked, "Josh, do you want to be healed and to get out of your wheelchair?"

At first, Josh started to feel a little nervous with the two strangers, looking toward his mother to see if she was watching, but there was something about them that was trustworthy and reassuring. He looked at the woman, thinking about her question.

"Yes! I want to be like everyone else and be able to play with my friends," answered Josh.

Looking into his face, Peggy's eyes started to water. "Then you shall."

The mother turned to look at her son just in time to see Joe place a hand on his shoulder and watched as Peggy stood to her feet, holding on to her son's hand. She started to quickly move toward them, calling out her son's name. She thought that she could hear the man say, "Spirit of infirmity, leave him in the name of Jesus," but there were many voices talking all around her. Before she had taken three steps toward them, she saw her son stand up out of his wheelchair and then start jumping up and down, excitement on his face as he turned to look at her. When he saw her approaching him, he ran toward her, saying, "Mom, look! I can walk and run." He flew into her arms as she was starting to cry.

As Pastor John and the group stood watching, they all began to praise the Lord. Joe and Peggy continued to stand by the wheelchair, watching Josh and his mother, tears in their eyes and praises on their lips. The mother, looking through her tears at Joe and Peggy, smiled at them with appreciation on her face. After a long moment of holding onto her son, the mother released him and hurried over to them to find out how they healed her son.

As she neared them, she could feel the Presence of God, her tears starting anew. She was a believer, but had never in her wildest imaginings thought that she would see her son walking and running again this side of heaven. When she reached Peggy, she was enfolded in loving arms, her tears falling freely. After a moment, she stepped back from Peggy and looked in her eyes.

"Thank you, so much," she said with deep emotion, as she was wiping her eyes with the back of her hand. Joe handed her his handkerchief, and when her tears were under control, she then continued. "How did you do that?" she asked. "I haven't heard of anything like that happening in these days."

"Jesus healed your son. We're only the tools that He used to do it. Doesn't what you've seen fit in with what you see Jesus doing in the New Testament?" asked Peggy.

"We're as much disciples of Jesus as the apostles were, and we're just following His commandments to lay our hands on the sick," explained Joe.

By that time, there were several people overhearing what was being said, and it wasn't long before one of them had to interrupt their conversation.

"You're saying that you heal people?" asked a middle-aged man who was wearing a suit and tie.

Joe and Peggy both turned to look at the man and quickly noticed that there were several people waiting to hear their answer. "It's not by our own power that we can heal anybody, but it is by the name of Jesus and faith in His name that this boy was healed," answered Joe.

"Oh, you're one of those conservative right wing Christian fanatics. That explains it. Let me out of here." The man had a sneer on his face, and his voice was dripping with sarcasm and hatred. He immediately turned and walked away, pushing his way through the crowd. The mother stood there, dumbfounded at what the man said, feeling a need to say something back to him.

"They just healed my son! Is that a bad thing?" she called out to him, but she was only talking to his back. Most of the others scattered as fast as they could get their luggage, thinking that possibly it was a hoax or just a sick prank by right wing fundamentalists, not realizing that what they saw was for real.

But there was one older couple, around fifty years old, that stepped up to Joe and Peggy. The man wasn't quite bald, but most of his hair was missing, and even his eyebrows were very thin.

"We saw what you did. We were watching you before you stepped up to that boy, and we know you really healed him. I've been getting treatments for cancer, and we're not sure that it's going to work." His voice was starting to break, and there were tears starting to run down his cheeks as he finished speaking. The whole group moved closer and circled him, softly praying in tongues. "Would Jesus heal me, too?" he asked as he was wiping the tears from his cheeks. He was feeling the Presence of God as he looked around at the group.

Pastor John stepped up to speak to him. "Of course Jesus will heal you. He loves you and wants to see you well."

The man's heart rate was increasing in the Presence of the Lord; it felt the way it does when you're in a near accident.

Pastor John turned to Joe. "Joe, lay your hands on him."

Joe reached out his hands, placed them on the man's shoulders, and began to pray. "Lord God, we come before You to ask for total healing for this man. Reveal Your mercy to him, in the name of Jesus. Cancer, in the name of Jesus, leave his body!"

The man's body started to shake violently and then began to topple backwards. Jay and Kyle, who were standing behind him, quickly reached forward to catch him and lower him to the floor.

"Oh! What's happened to him?" his wife asked worriedly.

"He's fine. God's Holy Spirit touched him with healing power, and he's just fainted," explained Peggy.

A security guard hurriedly walked up and started to split the group open, trying to see why there was a man lying on the floor.

"What's going on here? Does this man need medical attention?" asked the guard.

"No, he's all right," answered Pastor John. "He just fell over for a moment."

Joe reached down and took him by the hands, and with Jay helping, they lifted him to his feet. "How do you feel? Are you okay?" the guard asked, looking into the face of the man who was healed.

"I'm fine, officer. As a matter of fact, I don't remember when I've ever felt better."

Joe looked at the man and asked, "Do you want to receive Jesus as your Lord and Savior?"

The man and his wife looked at each other, and then both of them said, "Yes, we do."

The security guard was listening to everything that was said, and when the name of Jesus came up, he turned around and strolled off, not wanting to hear any more of what was going on.

With Josh and his mother standing close by, watching the encounter, Joe led the couple through the salvation prayer, tears falling to the floor.

Meeting up with a local minister that was heading up the street ministry, they were given a ride to their hotel to check in and were then taken to the ministry headquarters to prepare for the afternoon witnessing. Several groups had already arrived, and after some introductions, they all entered into prayer, seeking God's will and direction for the day. The Presence of God became a tangible thing in the room, and for a few of the people in the other groups it was something new that they had never experienced before. Soon the prayer time turned into a worship service, all of them loving their God and King. With all of them on their knees, God began to reveal His plan for the week, sharing with them His desire to preach the Good News to the poor, to heal the brokenhearted, to proclaim liberty to the captives and recovery of sight to the blind, to set at liberty those who are oppressed and to proclaim the acceptable year of the Lord.

As they were filing onto the buses, many of them were still wiping the tears from their eyes, the anointing of His Spirit still upon them. All the way to their destination, praises and thanksgivings were rising to the throne of God, ministering to the Lord of Glory.

Arriving on Santa Monica Boulevard, all the teams went in their designated directions in groups of three or four persons. The Gay Pride parade was about to start, and there were thousands of people on the street, most of them unsaved. As the groups were walking the streets witnessing about the love of Jesus, they were being ignored for the most part. Many of the tracts they were handing out were received, because most of the people were at least courteous to the ministry teams. Every now and then, there were some crude or vulgar remarks made about Christianity, but as the teams were courteous themselves and walking in a loving and caring attitude, they at least received back the same courtesy.

The farther down the street they walked, the more remarks they began to hear about other Christians, farther down the street, who were trying to witness to the gay community.

"You guys are a lot nicer than those guys down the street. They're yelling and screaming at us and telling us that we're all going to burn in hell. If that's the love of Jesus, then I don't want anything to do with Him," explained one guy, who had stopped and received a tract.

"If I was you, hearing that, I wouldn't want to believe in Jesus either," replied Mac. "I'm not sure that those people even have a relationship with Jesus. None of the teachings of Jesus were screamed at the listeners with hatred and anger. There was only one group that Jesus was hard on with His words and that was the religious crowd who thought they were better than everyone else."

"So the Jesus you believe in isn't behind the kind of behavior that those guys are showing?" he asked.

"No, He's not. Jesus taught the people about God and the Scriptures, and then they decided whether to believe in what He told them and to act on it. Jesus also said that His disciples were to love one another and to always walk in love toward other people. You know, the golden rule: Do unto others as you would have them do unto you," explained Mac.

The young man could feel something different with Mac than he had with anyone else who had ever told him about Jesus. He realized that his heart rate was increasing just being in Mac's presence, and he couldn't understand why that was so.

"I was told that Jesus loves everybody. Isn't that true?" asked the man.

"Yes. He loves everyone. But you still have to ask Him to be your Lord and Savior to escape the punishment that's coming on all the unrighteous. Jesus died on the cross in our place so that our sins would be forgiven as we accept His sacrifice. If we don't believe in Him, then our sin is not forgiven. We must come to Him by faith, and asking Him to forgive us, we will be forgiven of all of our sin. And as we continue to seek Him and to know Him, we begin to confess His name before others because we have tasted of His wonderful grace. He said that if we confess His name before men then He will confess our name before His Father. But if we deny His name before men, then He will deny our name before His Father."

"But I'm gay. Does He still love me?"

"Yes, He loves you even now. Jesus said that He was anointed with the Holy Spirit to preach the Good News to the poor, that He was sent to heal the brokenhearted, to proclaim liberty to the captives and recovery of sight to the blind, to set at liberty those who are oppressed and to proclaim the acceptable year of the Lord. Right now, you are captive to your gay lifestyle. He is here to set you free. That's the Good News. You can be free of all of the bondage that your lifestyle has gotten you into."

"How will He set me free?"

"The same way that He sets anyone else free. It's not just the gay lifestyle that He sets people free from. People can be in bondage to many different sins: idolatry, adultery, sex out of wedlock, stealing, drug and alcohol addictions, hatred, envy, and pride. All of these things will prevent people from inheriting the Kingdom of God, and that is why Jesus wants to set you free, so that you can and will inherit the Kingdom of God. He wants us to be free from all unrighteousness, so that we can live for Him whole-heartedly and help advance the Kingdom of God." As the Presence of God was growing stronger, Mac could see tears starting to form in the man's eyes. "In the Bible, the Apostle Paul said to the people in one of the churches he started these same things that I'm telling you. He also said that some of them had been involved in those things in the past, including the gay lifestyle, but that they had been washed, set apart, and justified in the name of the Lord Jesus and by the Spirit of our God. Do you want to be set free and to live your life for Jesus?"

This was the most important moment, and Mac sensed that the man was ready to receive salvation. Looking at him intently, with love and care in his eyes, Mac waited for his answer.

"Yes, I do! I want to be able to hold my head up around my family again and to know that they love me." The tears started flowing freely as he was speaking, and Mac wrapped his arms around him in a fatherly embrace for a long moment.

"Hey, you queers! You're going to burn in hell if you don't repent and get right with God." Mac could hear several crude remarks and laughter as several guys stood by watching them. He could also feel the young man tightening up and pulling away.

At arm's length, Mac looked at him and said, "Don't be afraid, and don't leave. I'm going to settle this problem right now." Turning around to face them, he had Jay and Sandy beside him. Stepping up to the men, he could feel the Spirit of God rising up within him.

"Are you guys Christians?" he asked, his voice calm and confident. As soon as he had faced them, they began to sense something different, but they were totally unfamiliar with the Presence of God. As Mac asked his question, there were many gay men walking by, and as they heard him speaking, they all stopped to witness the altercation, supposing that Mac was also gay and was tired of taking crap from the Christians.

"Yes, we are. And if you don't change your ways, you're gonna go straight to hell," replied the leader of the group.

Mac, filled with the Holy Spirit, looking intently at them said, "Don't you know that I was about to lead that man to Jesus? He has already decided that he wants to accept Jesus, and now that you have butted in—rather rudely, I might add—he might change his mind. And if he does change his mind, I want you all to know this: if he ends up in hell, all of you will be accountable to Almighty God for it. The way you guys are acting, you are more the sons of the devil than you are God's. You are full of deceit and fraud and are enemies to all righteousness. Will you not cease perverting the straight ways of the Lord? Now indeed the hand of the Lord is upon you, and you shall be blind, not seeing the sun for a time. And when you repent for your actions here today, God will restore your sight."

The bystanders, hearing Mac's words, realized that Mac was also a Christian, and in their eyes, there were now two groups of Christians arguing with one another. Most of them began to smile at the scenario playing out before them. One thing that none of them could understand was why the five guys were almost cowering before the one who was speaking, but they could sense that Mac had some kind of authority that the others did not.

Immediately a dark mist fell on the five guys, and they started to cry out for help and grope about with their hands, for they were now totally blind. Excited talk began to circulate as the bystanders witnessed the miracle, and it was one that even they wished they could have done, to get back at the Christians who were, just moments earlier, condemning all of them.

Mac turned back to the man he had been witnessing to, and seeing the look of astonishment on his face, he stepped up to him and asked, "Are you ready to accept Jesus as your Lord and Savior?"

"Yes! I now believe that Jesus is real, and I want to give my life to Him!" There was an excitement in his voice as he spoke, and all of the bystanders were paying attention to every word that was spoken. Before Mac had a chance to respond, there were many voices joining in with their own desire to know Jesus, asking to be saved. Mac turned to the crowd and looked at all the faces that were now looking to him to lead them to Jesus.

"Please let me pray with this man first, and then I'll take care of the rest of you." Turning back to the first man, he said, "I'll lead you in a prayer to ask God for salvation, and so just repeat after me." Jay and Sandy moved into position behind the man to catch him if he fell and then began to pray softly in tongues.

"Okay."

"Lord God, I believe in Your Son Jesus…and that He died on the cross for my sins…and that You raised Him from the tomb…Lord, I come to You today and ask for Your forgiveness…and to set me free from the lifestyle I've been living…and to help me live my life for You…Jesus, I thank You for Your sacrifice…and I ask You to receive me now…in Jesus' name I pray, amen." The further into the prayer that he got, the more the tears began to fall. As he finished speaking, his countenance changed in an instant, and all of them that could see his face witnessed the change.

Pastor John and his group came up beside Mac as he was finishing and were watching as Mac laid his hand on the man's forehead and began to speak.

"Be free in the name of Jesus!" Immediately the man fell into waiting arms and was laid gently on the sidewalk. As he lay there, with tears pooling on the cement, he began to speak in tongues, praising God in another language, to everyone's amazement.

Turning to Pastor John, Mac raised a hand to his shoulder and said, "This is Pastor John. He is the one who has taught me all I know about Jesus, and we'll both pray with all of you who want to be saved." Mac stepped up to the first guy and began to lead him in prayer while Pastor John stepped up to another one. They all could feel the Presence of God and could hardly wait to be prayed for to receive Jesus and to be filled with His Spirit.

Two associates of the five guys who had been blinded came along, wondering what had become of them. Someone had taken mercy on them and had been leading them back down the street toward where their friends were located. Before they had left the scene, they had listened to Mac leading the young gay man to Jesus. They had all breathed a collective sigh of relief when they heard him praying, no longer fearful for his outcome.

"Hey! Where you guys been? You're missing all the fun," said one of their cronies. When he noticed that they were all being led, holding on to each other's hands in single file, he became a little concerned for their welfare, wondering if they had been sprayed with pepper spray or something.

"Dick? Is that you?" one of them called out.

"Yeah, Jack, it's me. What's happened to you guys? Can't you see?" he asked in return.

"No! We're all blind! Will you take us to the hospital?"

"I guess so. Tell me what happened."

"I don't know for sure. There was a guy talking to us, telling us we were wrong in yelling at the gays, and then we couldn't see."

Dick led them all down the street and over a couple of blocks to his car and then took them to the closest hospital that he knew of. When they were all in the emergency room, two doctors that were on call were examining them, but they couldn't find anything wrong with them that would explain why they couldn't see.

"Tell me again what happened that caused all of you to be blinded at the same time," commanded one doctor. One guy, named Nick, who had been quiet ever since they were blinded, cleared his throat and began to talk. He had been thinking seriously about what the guy had said to them and what had come about.

"We were at the Gay Pride parade to witness about Jesus, but our witnessing consisted entirely of yelling at them and telling them that they were going to burn in hell. And then we had accidentally interrupted another Christian while He was leading a gay guy to Jesus. He turned around and came up to us and told us that what we were doing was wrong and then told us to stop perverting the ways of God. He then said that the hand of God was upon us and that we would be blind for a time. But he never touched us or anything."

"That's odd," said the doctor. "I'm a Christian too, and just this morning I was reading in the Book of Acts about Paul and Barnabas running into a sorcerer who was saying lies about them to the head government official, whom Paul was trying to witness to. And then, the Bible says that Paul was filled with the Spirit and told the sorcerer to stop perverting the straight ways of the Lord and that the hand of God was going to blind him for a little while. And then the official believed in Jesus, because he saw that the guy was indeed blinded. It sounds just like what's happened to you guys. What do you think?" asked the doctor.

All five of them were thinking deeply as the doctor was speaking, and as he related the Bible story, the Holy Spirit was witnessing to their hearts about the true reason that they had received judgment. Nick, who had been thinking the most about what happened, slid to his knees, and as the tears started to flow, he began to pray.

"Lord Jesus, I am so sorry for what I did today. Please forgive me for not walking in love and not revealing You as You truly are to the gay people. Help me, Jesus, to be a better witness of Your mercy and forgiveness." The others were listening to his prayer and by the sound of his voice, they could tell that he was crying. Only a moment had gone by when they heard Nick exclaim, "Thank You, Jesus, for restoring my sight! Thank You, Father, for Your mercy!"

As the rest of them realized that Nick could see again, they remembered the last thing that Mac had said. "And when you repent for your actions here today, God will restore your sight." Immediately they all began to cry out for forgiveness and mercy, asking for help to be better Christians, and before they knew it, they could all see again.

The doctors were amazed at their complete recovery and began to check them again to see if they could find any change, but the only thing that was different was that they couldn't shine their lights into their eyes anymore. They could definitely see now, whereas before they were as blind as bats.

"Maybe you guys need to go back down there and see if you can locate that guy, apologize to him, and see if you can learn anything else from him," encouraged the Christian doctor.

"I think that's really good advice, Doc. And thanks for all of your help."

CHAPTER TWENTY

On Tuesday, the group rode the subway to downtown Los Angeles. Splitting up into their four groups, they all headed into different directions, walking the streets and witnessing to all that they came to, or at least trying to. Many people that walked by them, even as they tried to say something, never even slowed down. They would glance at them and, not recognizing their faces, would even quicken their pace to escape from being solicited about something. Others, when they had stopped to listen out of courtesy, would take off again as soon as they heard the name of Jesus.

They all knew that sometimes it just takes the manifestation of God's power to get people's attention. Mac, with Jay and Sandy, was approached by a young man asking for money. They all could see his red and swollen eyes, and by his jittery actions and demeanor, they could tell that he was a junkie, just trying to scrape together enough money for his next hit. Mac, looking intently at him, began to speak.

"If it were possible, would you want to be set free from your addiction?"

The man was beginning to feel the Presence of God, although he didn't understand what it was. "I've tried to quit, lots of times, but I can't. And I don't have the money to go to detox. I know it's ruining my life, but there's nothing I can do."

"Unclean spirit, leave him now, in the name of Jesus!" commanded Mac.

"No! He wants us here. You can't make us leave," said the spirit, starting boldly but finishing with a whimper.

"I said, leave now!"

Immediately, the man slipped to the cement, drawing the attention of a few of the passersby. One man stepping up to inquire about the young man.

"What's the matter with him? Do you need to call an ambulance?"

Looking at the newcomers, Jay explained, "He's fine. Jesus has set him free from a drug addiction." As the young man's eyes opened and looked up, Mac reached down to grasp his hand and lifted him to his feet. The look of surprise and elation on the young man's face as he felt the freedom from the drugs was etched on the minds of all three of the team, bringing smiles to their faces.

The man who had come up to them to inquire about the welfare of the young man was also a Christian, and once he heard the name of Jesus, he decided to watch and listen to the outcome of the situation.

"Jesus has set you free! Do you want to know Him and ask Him to be your Lord and Savior?" asked Mac.

Through the tears that began to water his eyes, he answered, "Yes! I do."

Continuing to hold onto the man's hand, Mac led him through the prayer of salvation. When he was finished, Mac began to speak in tongues, praising God, and the Holy Spirit fell upon the young man, baptizing him with the evidence of speaking in another language.

Upon seeing and hearing the young man's conversion and baptism in the Spirit, the stranger turned to Mac to ask his questions.

"I was reading in the Book of Acts just this morning, and seeing how the new converts were baptized with the Spirit and began to speak in tongues, I asked the Lord about it. I don't see that happening in my own church, but what I just witnessed here is just like the accounts in the Bible. Can I be baptized with the Spirit, too?"

"Of course you can," replied Mac. "There's enough evidence in the Bible to show that the baptism in the Holy Spirit is for all of God's children, but because it wasn't written about or explained every single time there were new converts, a lot of denominations and Bible teachers today don't want to accept it as the operational standard of the Church. Repeat after me. Heavenly Father, I believe in Jesus...and Your Word says that Jesus would baptize us with Your Holy Spirit...and I ask now for that baptism...and to be endued with power from on high...Thank You, Father, for Your goodness, amen." Mac, raising his hand, placed it on the man's head, and began to pray in tongues, as Jay and Sandy were already doing.

The Holy Spirit fell on him, and he began to speak in tongues, magnifying God. With tears on his cheeks, the man went to his knees worshipping the Lord.

After a few moments, arising to his feet, the man stepped up to Mac and hugged him. "Thank you! I never knew that being saved and baptized in the Spirit would feel so good. I feel different now than I did just a few minutes ago," exclaimed the man.

"Isn't God good to His people?" asked Mac.

"Yes! This baptism with the Holy Spirit is such a blessing. I can't wait to tell my wife about it. That reminds me. I need to make a phone call to delay my appointment." He turned away to make his call and reschedule his appointment for the next day. They all heard him say that something came up that needed his immediate attention. When he was finished, he turned back to Mac and asked, "Would it be all right with you if I tagged along with you guys for a while? I'd like to learn how this is done."

With a smile spreading across his face, Mac said, "Sure. That would be wonderful. My name's Mac, and these two are Jay and Sandy."

The man stepped up and gave them both a hug, saying, "I'm so glad to meet both of you. My name's Josh McClaren."

Turning to the young man, Mac asked, "And what's your name? We seemed to have missed it."

"I'm Ron Turner, and I'm glad to meet all of you." Turning to Josh he asked, "May I use your phone? I'd like to call my mom and tell her what's happened and to see if she'll come pick me up and take me home." His eyes were starting to water again at the thought of talking to his mom.

"Here you go. Talk as long as you want," said Josh.

Hearing him talk to his mom and begin to cry, asking for her forgiveness, brought them all to tears. Turning away from him, they spread out and began to witness to more pedestrians.

Meanwhile, Leah, with Joe and Peggy, was witnessing to several people in front of a Starbucks coffee shop. Most of the people were white-collar executives who were on a break and came to the coffeehouse to spend a few minutes with their friends and colleagues. One guy in a suit, after hearing Leah's opening statement of salvation in Jesus, stepped up to reply.

"Why should we believe that Jesus is real or that the Christian religion is any better than any other?"

"Because it's true. And I want you to know that Jesus doesn't leave Himself without any witness in the earth. He has given to those who believe in Him His Holy Spirit to live within them as a guarantee of our future with Him."

"So how does that concern me? If I don't believe in Him, then how do I know that you have His Spirit?" he asked. Leah closed her eyes for just a moment, listening to the Spirit. "I guess that question is too tough for you? Should I make it a little easier for you?" taunted the man.

Opening her eyes, Leah looked straight at him, and being filled with the Spirit, said, "When you were eight years old, your older brother was hit and killed by a car as he was riding his bicycle home from school. At the age of twelve, your father divorced your mom for another woman. The man your mom married three years later was resentful of you and would abuse you whenever she wasn't around. The day after you graduated from high school, you got in a fight with your stepdad and beat him up. You left home, and with your scholarships and a part-time job, you put yourself through college. After two years of marriage, you began to have affairs with coworkers, and when your wife found out, she divorced you. You have now come to the realization that you messed up; you've lost a good woman who loved you dearly but don't know if you can ever get her back."

As Leah was speaking, a look of astonishment began to grow on the man's face, and when she paused, he asked, "Do you know my wife? Did she tell you all of that and put you up to this?"

"You know that I don't know your wife. My friends and I live in Oregon and are here on a trip to witness to people about Jesus. It is by Jesus' Spirit within me that I know these things about you. Remember? You wanted to know how to tell if God's Holy Spirit was in me, and now you do."

The man was beginning to believe that what Leah said about Jesus was true. "Well, that's my past. What's in my future?"

"If you repent and ask the Lord for His forgiveness, then the Kingdom of God is in your future. If you do not, then hardship and tribulation await you and eventually eternity in hell. Your future is now in your hands. It is your decision to make." The seriousness in Leah's voice was very thought provoking for the man and for his friends also.

"I haven't accepted Jesus yet, and my life seems to be pretty easy. So why the hardships in my future? Is God going to be mad at me?" asked the man, the sarcasm gone.

"It's not that exactly, but there is coming in our near future a time of tribulation and judgment on the earth to test all those that are still here." Leah's answer was something that they all could relate to, for they had heard things about the supposed end-times tribulation taught by the church. A couple of them had even read some of the Left Behind books and had talked about it with their friends, trying to get some feedback from people they knew and respected.

"Why is that going to happen?" one of them asked.

"Because God has a timetable all planned out, and it's now time for the ones who love Him to live for Him wholeheartedly. When the trouble starts, His faithful people will be taken out of the world so they won't have to suffer through it, and all of those who don't love Him will go through the tribulation. It's a time of final testing—will they repent in their suffering and turn to God with their whole heart, or will they continue to deny Him? Those who hate Jesus and all He stands for will put most of those who turn to Him in those days to death. And many of those who won't turn to God will die in the tribulations that are coming, and the rest of them will die at the end of that time and be sent to hell. I'm here to tell you that God doesn't want you to go through that time of testing and suffering, because He loves you. He is trying to save you from the coming wrath. Will you believe what I'm telling you and accept Jesus as your Lord and Savior?"

They were all beginning to feel the Presence of the Lord as Leah continued to speak, and when she asked the final question, they could feel the Holy Spirit tugging on their hearts.

One woman had tears starting to moisten her cheeks, and she was the first one to reply. "I believe in Jesus. What do I need to do?"

"If you believe that He is the Son of God and that He died for your sins, I'll lead you in a prayer," answered Leah.

"I do believe."

Two of the other six people that were with her started to chime in with their own desire to be saved. As they were confessing their belief in Jesus, Leah noticed two women approaching the coffeehouse, the younger one wearing a dark pair of sunglasses. She was holding the arm of the older woman and also had a cane in her hand. The woman being led stopped, causing the older woman to turn a little as she took one extra step before halting. The blind woman turned her face toward Leah, listening to the voices and hearing the name of Jesus. She started to move straight toward Leah, pulling the other woman with her.

"*She sees you. Heal her.*"

As the small crowd of people took notice of Leah's gaze, they also turned to look at what had drawn her attention, seeing the blind woman walking toward them with her cane extended, searching for obstructions.

"Where are you going, Joan? The coffee bar is over here." They all could hear the older woman's question and also see that the blind woman was now leading the way.

"I see a light," was her only reply.

"But Joan, you can't see. What do you mean you see a light?" asked her mom.

"Mom, I can see a light, and I'm going to find out what it is." The crowd had quieted and was listening to every word as the two women approached, making a bee-line straight for Leah. The blind woman raised a hand in front of her, reaching for the light that only she could see, and as she closed the gap between herself and Leah, the crowd of prospective believers could see teardrops appearing out from under the glasses and sliding down her cheeks. She wasn't going to stop walking until her hand touched the light. Leah reached out her own hand, and when the woman was close, she grasped her hand and pulled it toward her.

"Who are you?" whispered the blind woman. "The light I see is coming from you."

"I'm Leah. The light you see is the light of God within me. He has revealed Himself to you. Do you believe in Jesus?" asked Leah.

"Yes. Almost my whole life," she answered. "I can feel His Presence here with you. Can you help me?" The tears started to flow freely, and she took off her glasses to wipe away her tears.

"Yes. Jesus brought you here to me to heal you." Leah reached up to her face, and as the woman felt her hands touch her, she closed her eyes, more tears running down her cheeks. With a hand on each side of her face, Leah placed her thumbs over the closed eyelids and began to pray.

"Thank You, Jesus, for complete healing in these eyes." With firmness in her voice she commanded, "Be opened in the name of Jesus!" Moving her thumbs away but still cradling her face with her hands, Leah looked into her face, waiting for her to open her eyes. The woman's eyes opened, and as she began to see Leah, she let out a screech of joy, throwing her arms around her in a tight embrace. After a long moment, the crowd listening to her sobbing with joy and thankfulness, she spun around to look at her mom.

"Mom! I can see you!" she exclaimed. With a squeal of delight, she threw her arms around her mother, both of them shedding tears of joy.

Turning to the crowd, which had grown by about eight more people who had witnessed the blind woman's healing, Leah asked her question.

"Now do you believe that Jesus is real?"

All of them began to nod their heads or voice their affirmation.

"If you want to receive Jesus as your Lord and Savior, repeat after me." Leah led them all in the prayer of salvation, and as the Holy Spirit fell upon them they began to speak in other tongues.

At a quarter to five, the teams started to make their way back to the subway entrance. As the last group came around the corner of the opposite street, they could see people were coming and going, many of them heading down the stairway into the subway. The other teams were witnessing to a few people as they were waiting for others to show up, and as Pastor John, Kyle, and Katie approached the area, an older man in a wheelchair rolled into view. As he entered the crowded area, he began panhandling, hoping to collect a few dollars as people were heading home. What really helped him out with the crowd was the fact that he didn't have any legs, only stubs to about mid-thigh.

Pastor John, moved with compassion, asked the Lord for the grace to minister healing to the man.

"*Yes.*"

He turned toward Mac and caught his attention, and they made their way up to the man as he was talking to two women, asking for money. The women were just handing him a couple of dollars as the two stepped up beside them. As soon as he thanked them, the women turned away, glad to be getting away with only losing a couple of dollars to the man. When the man had placed his money in a shirt pocket, he looked up at Pastor John and then turned his glance to Mac.

"How you guys doin'? Could you help me out with some spare change?" the man asked, his glance going to a couple of well-dressed younger men who were approaching. Hoping to get money from Pastor John quickly so he could hit on two guys that looked like an easy mark for more money, he spoke too quickly, and his attention was divided.

"Look at us!" commanded Pastor John. "Wouldn't you rather have your legs back than to panhandle for money all the time?"

Looking up at Pastor John, he began to feel the Presence

of the Lord, but being totally unfamiliar with spiritual things he didn't know what was happening.

"Of course, I'd like my legs back, but that's impossible. Unless you're talking about prosthetics," replied the man.

"I'm talking about your real legs. Jesus is here to give them to you."

The man looked at Pastor John, his heart rate climbing, feeling the Presence of God's Spirit. "Are you serious? God would do that for me?"

"Yes, He will! Stand up and walk in the name of Jesus!"

The man was almost ready to try it, but he just couldn't get past the fear of falling out of his chair in front of everybody. For a long moment they all thought that he would do it, but as the seconds rolled by, he didn't move, and tears started to fall on his lap. He slowly turned his chair away and began to roll down the sidewalk, the whole group watching him, praying softly in tongues. A few pedestrians who had listened to the conversation were also watching, and when the man was about fifty feet away, they started to walk off, thinking how cruel it was to talk to that man about God giving him back his legs.

One of them turned back to Pastor John to tell him what he thought of it. "I don't think that was a Christian thing to do—" he began, but Pastor John raised his hand to quiet him.

"Wait and see."

The guy in the wheelchair, as he started to roll away, could feel the Presence of God. He had never felt it before, but he knew that it was God. "*Stand up and walk! Stand up and walk! Stand up and walk!*" kept ringing in his ears. He started to slow, and when he had come to a stop, he turned the chair around and looked back at Pastor John. He saw that they were all watching him, and as he reached up to wipe his tears away, he could see Pastor John raising his hand up in the air palm up, motioning for him to rise.

Closing his eyes, he grabbed both sides of his chair and began to lift himself up, sliding his hips forward. *"Stand up and walk! Stand up and walk! Stand up and walk!"* When he was at the very edge of the seat, he pointed the stubs of his legs down, and with tears falling freely from his face; he gave one final nudge forward and let go of the chair.

Pedestrians were wondering what was going on, seeing this crippled guy crying and trying to get out of his chair. They couldn't understand what he was doing and were thinking, "That's gonna hurt." People going both ways were stopping to watch, even the guy who was going to chew out Pastor John for being so cruel.

When the man let go of his chair, with everyone watching, he felt himself starting to slide straight down. He knew that it was going to hurt, but he couldn't deny the voice in his head; he was going to walk, even if it was on his stubs. Before the eyes of all, something appeared at the bottom of his stubs and quickly began to expand, and as they all stood dumbfounded at what they were seeing, the man began to rise up above his chair until he stood a full and straight six feet tall. Barefooted, he began to jump up and down, yelling praises to Jesus, his tears falling to the sidewalk. The people who had stopped to watch were so astonished they didn't know what to do, and as the man ran to Pastor John to hug him, they began to close in and surround them.

"Jesus has healed you, and He loves you and cares for you. Do you want to ask Him to be your Lord and Savior?" asked Pastor John.

"Yes! I give my life to him!" he answered.

Turning his attention to the crowd, Pastor John looked around at all of them.

"All of you have seen a great miracle today. Jesus, who is the Son of God, has healed this man in front of you all. Give your heart to Jesus now, and you will be saved and live with God for all eternity."

"I believe in Jesus and want to be saved!" shouted one voice from the crowd.

"Me too," said another and then forty or so other people joined in with their decision for Jesus.

"If you want to ask Jesus to be your Lord and Savior, repeat after me." He led them all in the salvation prayer, and as he finished, the Holy Spirit fell on all those present, and they began to speak in tongues and to magnify God.

On Wednesday night, witnessing on Santa Monica Boulevard, the group was busy with people at several different locations when a young black girl, about twenty years old, came walking up. When she was close enough to Leah to see her face, she began to scream and shout with joy. Instantly, Leah recognized her as a girl that she had led to the Lord the previous year on that very same street. The girl ran to Leah, grabbed her arms, and began to jump up and down, excited squeals escaping from her lips. Several members of the group moved closer to see what was going on, because of all the excitement of two exuberant women.

"I can't believe it's you! I've looked and looked for you, hoping to see you again so I could thank you. I prayed to God that I would meet you again to tell you how much my life has changed because of you," the girl said, pulling Leah into her arms in a tight embrace.

"You look so good, Latisha. I hardly recognize you," replied Leah.

"Isn't God great? He's been so good to me ever since you led me to Jesus." Tears were flowing down her cheeks as she was speaking; her heart was full to overflowing with love and thankfulness.

"So, tell me what God's been doing with you," requested Leah.

"Do you remember last year when you and your friends prayed for me?"

"Yes, I do. I remember that you were addicted to meth, and your boyfriend was prostituting you for his drug money," answered Leah.

"That's right. God delivered me from the drugs that same day, and my boyfriend was arrested on drug charges right after that and is still in prison. Do you remember when you and your friends put your hands on my stomach and prayed in tongues?" Latisha was so excited to tell Leah everything that had happened to her that she could hardly contain herself; joy and excitement were bubbling out of her like a wellspring.

"Yes. I felt the leading of God's Spirit to do that, but we never did know why."

"Three weeks after you prayed for me I found out that I was pregnant! I've got a little boy who's almost four months old, and he's so adorable. He doesn't have any side effects from my drug use." The tears began to flow again as she told about her precious son whom God had protected from her sinful lifestyle.

"Praise God. His mercy is so wonderful," said Leah.

"Yes! He's been so good to me. When my boyfriend was arrested, I moved into a church outreach home for unwed mothers. They helped me to get on my feet and also taught me more about my Savior and to worship Him. I have a good job now, and I moved into my own apartment. My mom watches little Daniel for me, and she just loves him so much. I also help out at an outreach two nights a week, and at least one night a week I go out on the street to witness to others that are in the same shape I was in."

"Praise Jesus! I'm so glad for you. Your story really humbles me. I've led a lot of people to the Lord whom I've never seen or heard from again, not knowing how things turned out for them. But now, to hear how your life has changed so drastically for the better, I realize that God is able to take care of things after I've done my part. It really blesses my heart to know that I had a helping hand in bringing you to Jesus." Leah pulled her close, wrapping her arms around her as she whispered, "Thank you, Latisha."

As the ministry team was flying back to Oregon, Pastor John was going over in his mind all of the salvations, miracles, healings, and deliverances that the team had seen and participated in. After the first two days, when the other teams listened to their testimonies of healings and all the salvations that the Spirit of God had wrought at their hands, they realized that there was more to the Holy Spirit than they had been taught.

So, during one chapel service, Pastor John had been asked to give the message, and at the end of it, everyone in attendance had received the baptism of the Spirit with the evidence of speaking in tongues. From that time there was a new fire in all of them, and by the end of the week, everyone had testimonies of the power of God working to save and to heal the lost, delivering them from the bondages of the enemy. Over a thousand salvations had been recorded; almost two hundred people had received healing of one kind or another; numerous demons had been cast out; and many others were strengthened in their faith as they watched the ministry teams winning the lost. A couple of actors had even received the Lord when the group was witnessing on Hollywood Boulevard.

Thinking of how the goodness of God leads to repentance, he was reminded of an instance one night as they were walking the street back to the outreach center. They had come upon a woman who was bowed over, just coming out of a small market on the corner. Leah began to talk to her and found out that she had woken up one morning to find out that she couldn't straighten up. She had been in that condition for about nine months, and the doctors couldn't determine what was wrong with her. The Spirit of God revealed to them that it was a spirit of infirmity that had latched onto her. She had been struggling with a heroin addiction at the onset of the disability. Immediately, Leah took authority over the spirit and cast it out, the woman receiving complete healing while the Korean store owners stood by and watched, concern in their hearts, for they had known the woman as a regular customer. After the healing, the woman and both of the store owners received Jesus as their Lord and Savior, shedding many tears at His Presence. Pastor John was thinking that it was no wonder that God designed healing to go along with salvation.

As the group returned to their hometown, there was much rejoicing and praise, and on Sunday they all gave their testimonies before the church, causing thanksgiving and praises to rise to the throne of God.

CHAPTER
TWENTY-ONE

Two weeks after their return from Hollywood, the pastor of a local denominational church called Pastor John to set up a meeting to talk about the healing miracles that he had been hearing about. He was willing to listen to anything that Pastor John wanted to tell him, any doctrine, teaching, or biblical principle, for he knew that God was working in Pastor John's congregation and wanted to find out why and how and to get it started in his own church. He had a true heart for God and was willing to go the distance to see Him move among his own people.

That very afternoon Pastor John and Mac drove over to meet with Pastor Robert Wilson and his wife JoAnn in their own church, hoping that they would feel less defensive in their own office. When they arrived, they were pleasantly surprised to find not only the pastor and his wife but also their associate pastor and two other pastors from other churches in their denomination. As soon as the cordial greetings were over, they moved to the conference room, where they all sat down in chairs arranged in a circle.

Pastor Wilson cleared his throat as he turned his eyes to Pastor John. "Would you open this meeting for us with a prayer, Pastor?"

"Certainly. Lord God, we come before You today to seek Your face and Your wisdom and to ask for spiritual understanding of Your Word and Your ways. In all humbleness, Lord, I ask for all those present here for You to reveal Yourself as You are. I ask, Lord, for Your Presence to come into the room and touch the hearts of Your servants, in the name of Jesus." As Pastor John finished, God's Presence began to be felt, slowly at first, but as the seconds went by it became stronger and stronger until the others began to weep. Both Pastor John and Mac whispered praises to God as they slid to their knees, their eyes watering as they saw the effect of His Presence on the other leaders.

Within mere moments, all of them were on their knees, weeping before the Lord, asking forgiveness for the resentment and unbelief that they had been harboring within their hearts. The Spirit of the Lord was touching their hearts, ministering to their deepest hurts and needs, cleansing and refreshing them. They began to raise their hands to the Lord and to worship Him, finding His grace and mercy as they had never known it but had always hoped it would be. For over a half hour they worshipped the Lord, finding His Presence to be so much more than they had ever dreamed.

Pastor John stood up and stepped before Pastor Wilson, took him by the hand, and pulled him to his feet. Mac also stood, and after pulling several chairs out of the way, he took his place behind Pastor Wilson. Placing one hand on his shoulder, Pastor John began to speak.

"'*My son, you have belonged to Me for many years and have known me as Lord, Savior, and Redeemer. You have been faithful to Me through hardship and trial and have continued to teach others to know Me as you have known Me. But now I say to you that you will know Me as the Healer. You will know that I abound in goodness and grace, that kindness and compassion are part of Me, that My mercy will accomplish the impossible. Remember that My Son was anointed with My Spirit and with My power and went about doing good and healing all who were oppressed of the devil, for I was with Him. My Son was faithful to reveal My will for My people and then to go to the cross to completely destroy the works of the devil. I sent My Son that My people may have life, and life more abundant. Go therefore and continue in His works, trusting in Me to fulfill My promise, for I love you,*' says your God."*

"*Take his hand and restore his fingers.*"

Taking his hand and looking at two fingers that had the ends missing at the last knuckle, he said, "When you lost these fingertips to the lawnmower, it deprived you of the perfect function that God designed, but you adapted to the loss. In the same way, the Church has adapted to the loss of His gifts that He designed and placed in the body. But now, He is restoring what was lost, both in His Church and in you. Be whole, in the name of Jesus." Instantly, his fingers grew out to their full length before the eyes of all. There was an intake of breath as they all witnessed their first miracle, but the only word spoken was from Pastor Wilson.

"Jesus." As the name of his Lord fell from his lips, he began to sob, his body wracked with uncontrollable shaking.

As the others watched, themselves also crying, Pastor John lifted his hand to Pastor Wilson's head, and as the power of God surged into him, he fell back into Mac's arms, who laid him on the floor. Pastor John then stepped over to JoAnn, helped her to her feet, and began to prophesy over her in the same manner. After her, he went through the rest of them, all in the same manner, and when he was finished, they had all fallen to the floor under the divine touch of the Spirit of God. For the first time in their lives, they all experienced God's manifested Presence and power.

When the ministering was done, they all took their seats, and Pastor John began to answer their questions. Pastor Wilson was the first to ask the most important question, the one that was on all their hearts. "If, then, physical healing was included in the atonement, what was Paul's thorn?"

"Trials and persecutions that were instigated by the messenger of Satan. You remember that Paul, in chapter eleven of 2 Corinthians, recounted all of the beatings, whippings, shipwrecks, and trials that he had undergone in preaching the Good News of Jesus?" At the nodding of heads, he continued. "Paul never mentioned any sickness or disease in his long list of trials, and he finished his narrative with the statement that he would boast about those things that showed his infirmity. The cross-reference for that word is weakness. The Greek word for that word 'weakness' means 'want of strength, weakness, indicating inability to produce results.'[1]

"Clearly, the context shows that this word does not mean a disease. Paul had an inability to keep the beatings, whippings, shipwrecks, and the other trials he listed from taking place. He had no control over them. That was his weakness. The reason why he was going to boast about his weaknesses is found in the very next chapter, in verse 9. He says, 'Therefore most gladly I will rather boast in my infirmities, that the power of Christ may rest upon me.' It is in our weakness, or inability, that the dunamis (miracle working power of God) can and will be manifested on our behalf. Take for instance the episode where the viper attached itself to Paul's hand after the shipwreck on his journey to Rome. Paul couldn't stop the shipwreck any more than he could stop the poisonous snake from biting him. But in both of these instances, the power of Christ rested upon him, saving his life in both cases, and because of that, the islanders believed the word of Paul's preaching and opened the door for his healing ministry to touch every sick and diseased person on the island and heal them. It was Jesus' power that raised Paul after he had been stoned and left for dead; it was Jesus' power that released him and Silas from prison during the night with an earthquake that caused all the chains and cell doors to open; it was Jesus' power that kept Paul moving forward and fulfilling his ministry even in the face of severe persecution; and it was Jesus' power that delivered Paul from two other shipwrecks and all the other trials that were brought by the agent of Satan.

"Are you understanding this?" asked Pastor John.

"Yes, it's very clear," came several replies.

"Let's go to where Paul talks about being caught up to the third heaven. He said that he heard inexpressible words, which are not lawful for man to utter. Who knows what Paul might have seen and heard, but does it really matter? The thing is, Paul had an abundance of revelations from this experience. Would you agree that the revelations had something to do with the Kingdom of God?"

"Yes."

Pastor John swept his gaze over all of them to see their heads nodding in the affirmative. "Okay. Paul says that the abundance of revelations had the ability to exalt him above measure, and to prevent his exaltation, a thorn in the flesh was given to him, a messenger of Satan was sent to buffet him. If the word 'exalted' should have been translated out of the Greek as 'prideful, puffed up, or arrogant,' then Satan, according to what we know about him, would have been the last one to try to stop Paul. Pride goes before a fall, so Satan would have loved it if Paul had become prideful, even to the point of trying to help it along to its fruition, and Paul's ministry would have failed. Besides that, there are other Greek words that are used elsewhere to convey the thought of pride or arrogance, but they are not used in this text. But rather, the words 'exalted above measure' mean 'to raise over' 'above' 'excessively.'[2] The revelations would cause Paul to be 'raised over, above, excessively.' What is the thing that Paul would be raised over excessively because of the abundance of revelations that he received while he was caught up to the third heaven?" Mac could sense the intense interest that all of them had for Pastor John's teaching about Paul's thorn, and at that moment he could see them perking up to listen and even leaning in to the pastor to hear him better, not wanting to miss a single word.

"The Greek word for 'exalt' is used in the middle voice, which carries the meaning of 'exalting oneself exceedingly,' so either way you look at it, Paul will be raised over something to an excessive degree because of the revelations, whether it be by God or by himself, walking in and dispensing the power of God. If Satan felt threatened by Paul because he received the revelations and so sent the messenger to be a thorn in his flesh to buffet him, or to rap with the fist in a repeated fashion, then probably the thing that Paul would be raised up over was the kingdom of darkness, or Satan's kingdom. Does this make sense to you?"

"Yes. In all my years of ministry, I've never heard Paul's

thorn taught like this, so please continue." The others were all nodding their heads in agreement.

"The messenger was sent by Satan to try to stop Paul, to keep him from spreading the Good News about Jesus. He knew that because of the revelations that Paul received, he had to kill him or face losing a lot of ground that he had gained over the centuries. Time and time again, that same messenger stirred up the Jews against Paul and his ministry, to drive him out of their towns, to keep him from his mission, even to the point of causing them to follow Paul from town to town. On his first missionary journey, Paul was stoned by the Jews that followed him and was dragged out of the city and left for dead. The Jews were the ones that persecuted him the worst, in every town, and had him whipped with the forty lashes, minus one, five times. What Paul went through was way beyond the normal. There was a spiritual hand directing all of his persecutions and hardships, constantly on his heels, trying always to kill him and when that wouldn't succeed, trying to slow him down and make his ministry ineffective.

"Even the forces of nature were seemingly against him, with the storms at sea and the shipwrecks and even the poisonous viper that bit him. All of it was directed by the messenger of Satan, following direct orders from Satan himself to stop Paul at all costs. Now, I want your attention on this one. Do you realize that not one time did Paul mention sickness or disease in his list of hardships? Sickness and disease was the one thing that would not work on Paul, because physical healing is included in the atonement of Jesus and Paul was explicitly aware of that fact. Paul, who dispensed healing on a regular occurrence to those he ministered to, had the faith and power within him, by the Holy Spirit, to overcome any such attack on his own body. Do you remember the quote Paul used about not putting a muzzle on the ox as it treads out the grain? Paul asked if this was written because God was concerned about the ox or was it written for our sakes. He says it was written for us. Using this principle alone, would God, who was working through Paul to heal many hundreds of people and possibly thousands, put a muzzle on Paul when he needed or wanted to partake of the power that he dispensed? Absolutely not! If Paul needed healing, there would be no reason whatsoever that he would not receive it. Proverbs 3:27 says, 'Do not withhold good from those to whom it is due, When it is in the power of your hand to do so.' For God to withhold healing from Paul, *if* he needed it, would go against all that we know of God and Jesus' own teachings. Do you think that Jesus, if any of His disciples became sick while He was here with them, would have denied them healing? Not at all.

"Now, since we see that Paul's thorn wasn't a disease but rather a messenger of Satan constantly attacking him with trials, we can understand fully Jesus' reply to Paul when asked to remove it. Jesus said, 'My grace is sufficient for you, for My strength is made perfect in weakness.' No matter what trial or hardship Paul was going through, the grace or favor of Jesus was with him to deliver him, to help him, and to bring him through the trial. Of course Paul suffered, even as Jesus said, 'If they persecuted Me, they will persecute you,' but the bottom line is that no matter how many times the enemy knocked him down and damaged his body, Jesus picked him back up and restored him, thus revealing his miracle-working power in Paul's inabilities or weaknesses. Jesus' 'dunamis'—miracle working power or ability—was accomplished, made complete, or consummated in Paul's weakness. It was Jesus working through Paul's weakness that was a witness to those around him that God was on his side. Remember also, that people are not the only ones watching and witnessing God's work in His people, but even the principalities and powers in the heavenly places. It was as though Jesus said to Paul, 'Let Satan do his worst, and I will show My power in your deliverance and nullify his work against you.' This is the treasure that we have in jars of clay. Does this answer the question adequately?"

---

[1] *Vine's Expository Dictionary of New Testament Words,* 2 Corinthians 11:30 & 12:5, *weakness.*

[2] *Strong's Exhaustive Concordance of the Bible*, 2 Corinthians 12:7, *exalted*, #5229, *above*, #5228, *measure*, #5234.

CHAPTER TWENTY-TWO

Pastor Wilson cleared his throat before he answered. "Yes. I believe now that Paul's thorn wasn't any sickness or disease but exactly what you said: the persecution and trials. But I have another question that's also a tough one. We'd like to know about the spiritual gifts and how they operate, and also how come the church has been blind to their use."

"You're all familiar with Ephesians 4, so I'll start reading there, in verse 8. The Apostle Paul writes, 'When He ascended on high, He led captivity captive, And gave gifts to men.' And verse 11, 'And He Himself gave some to be apostles, some prophets, some evangelists, and some pastors and teachers, for the equipping of the saints for the work of ministry, for the edifying of the body of Christ, till we all come to the unity of the faith and of the knowledge of the Son of God, to a perfect man, to the measure of the stature of the fullness of Christ; that we should no longer be children, tossed to and fro and carried about with every wind of doctrine, by the trickery of men, in the cunning craftiness of deceitful plotting, but, speaking the truth in love, may grow up in all things into Him who is the head—Christ—from whom the whole body, joined and knit together by what every joint supplies, according to the effective working by which every part does its share, causes growth of the body for the edifying of itself in love.' Notice the way he describes the body and the parts, all the joints supplying what is needed to knit together the whole.

"In 1 Corinthians 12, Paul again alludes to the Church as a body that has parts. First of all, he is talking about the gifts of the Spirit that are given to the body, starting in verse 4, 'There are diversities of gifts, but the same Spirit. There are differences of ministries, but the same Lord. And there are diversities of activities, but it is the same God who works all in all. But the manifestation of the Spirit is given to each one for the profit of all: for to one is given the word of wisdom through the Spirit, to another the word of knowledge through the same Spirit, to another faith by the same Spirit, to another gifts of healings by the same Spirit, to another the working of miracles, to another prophecy, to another discerning of spirits, to another different kinds of tongues, to another the interpretation of tongues. But one and the same Spirit works all these things, distributing to each one individually as He wills. For as the body is one and has many members, but all the members of that one body, being many, are one body, so also is Christ.'

"Paul is showing that the different gifts of the Spirit are the members of the body, not just people themselves. Of course, the gifts don't operate outside of people working them, but in this context, Paul is clearly showing that each spiritual gift is an individual part of the body. He continues in verse 15, 'If the foot should say, "Because I am not a hand, I am not of the body," is it therefore not of the body? And if the ear should say, "Because I am not an eye, I am not of the body," is it therefore not of the body? If the whole body were an eye, where would be the hearing? If the whole were hearing, where would be the smelling?

'But now God has set the members, each one of them, in the body just as He pleased. And if they were all one member, where would the body be? But now indeed there are many members, yet one body. And the eye cannot say to the hand, "I have no need of you"; nor again the head to the feet, "I have no need of you."'

Lowering his Bible, Pastor John looked up at all of them and began to explain. "So you see, one spiritual gift can't say to another one, 'I don't need you,' nor can one gift say, 'I don't like what I am, so I don't belong to the body.' God designed each spiritual gift exactly the way He wanted it to operate and placed it where He wanted it. In His wisdom, He knows how best to edify and build up the Church, and in designing the spiritual gifts the way that He did, He set in motion the working and operation of the Church. So, who is man to say, 'I don't like that gift or how it operates, so I don't need it in my church'? Or, 'That gift it too volatile to be operated in my church and may cause a problem, so I don't want it'? Or even, 'I don't understand that gift, so I don't think it is necessary any more'? When people think in these terms, they are actually passing judgment on God's wisdom and intelligence. Nowhere has He said that any or all of these gifts shall stop operating in the church before Jesus comes again. Remember, in Ephesians it says 'for the equipping of the saints for the work of ministry, for the edifying [or the building up] of the body of Christ, till we all come to the unity of the faith and of the knowledge of the Son of God, to a perfect man, to the measure of the stature of the fullness of Christ.' Have we attained to the unity of the faith yet? How about unity in the knowledge of Jesus? Or has the Body of Christ, the Church, become a perfect man, to the measure of the stature of the fullness of Christ? These things have not yet come to pass, so it looks like the gifts should all still be in operation today until we are fully equipped for every good work. And since there will always be newcomers into the body of Christ until the day Jesus returns, we will need all of the functioning gifts until the day of the rapture. Is this clear?"

"Yes, it is."

"Very understandable, Pastor."

"It's so clear, I don't know how I missed it before."

"Praise the Lord! I'm so glad that all of you are receiving this. There is also one more text I'd like to address on this subject. In 1 Corinthians 13, Paul says, 'Love never fails. But whether there are prophecies, they will fail; whether there are tongues, they will cease; whether there is knowledge, it will vanish away. For we know in part and we prophesy in part. But when that which is perfect has come, then that which is in part will be done away. When I was a child, I spoke as a child, I understood as a child, I thought as a child; but when I became a man, I put away childish things. For now we see in a mirror, dimly, but then face to face. Now I know in part, but then I shall know just as I also am known.' All of these gifts will pass away, but only when certain conditions are met. Paul states the conditions in this very text, which are when that which is perfect has come, when we see face to face, and when we know fully, not just in part. Now, do any of you know of anything in the world or the church that is perfect?"

"No. Not anything."

"Anything that man is connected with, I know isn't perfect, because man isn't perfect."

"That's right," answered Pastor John. "Even our Bible isn't perfect. God's Word is perfect, but look at all of the different translations of the Bible. None of them were translated by perfect men, and that's why there are differences of opinions on what the Bible is saying. I'm not saying that the Bible can't be trusted, but rather that God must be helping the translator to accurately transfer the Bible from the original languages and also help the reader to understand what the Spirit was saying when He inspired its writing. The Bible is as close to perfect as possible and should be taken as such, but it cannot be taken as the perfection or completion that is coming that Paul is talking about here. That perfection is tied in with the next qualifier, which is seeing face to face. Face to face with whom? Our pastor? No! This is talking about being face to face with Jesus. And it is in that day that we shall know fully, just as we are known. The three qualifiers together will be when perfection comes, or when heaven arrives; then we will see face to face with Jesus, and we will know fully all things. But until that day arrives, we will know in part, we will prophesy in part, and we will see as in a mirror dimly, but also these three will continue to abide or remain, faith, hope, and love. And the greatest of these is love. So we are to pursue love and desire spiritual gifts.

"To answer the second part of your question is a lot easier. The spiritual gifts were lost to the church, because as the years went by, the new leaders that were elected or appointed to their positions by man, instead of God, didn't have a relationship with Jesus. Down through the ages, as time moved farther and farther from the early apostles and disciples, their authoritative teachings were watered down by the agents of Satan that had infiltrated the church. As this progressed, there wasn't anyone in authority that walked in the power of God, and since that was a noticeable thing, the teachings in the Word of God had to be explained in such a way that the people no longer questioned why it was so. That is why no one had a Bible in those days except the priests, so as to keep the people in the dark about what the Word of God actually had to say. And then the reformation came, little by little but as sure as the sun rises, and no one could stop it. Once again, God began to give insight into His Word, and revelation knowledge began to sprout in the hearts of God's people. But still there was a lot of tradition and false teaching handed down, even in the reformed churches, and God is still eradicating those things in His church today. Little by little, the truth of God's Word has been recovered and placed into the body of Christ, even which is what is happening right here, right now, between you and me.

"Think about this. All of the spiritual gifts are operated by our spirits in conjunction with God's Spirit. They all have a certain amount of the supernatural about them, although some are more so than others. Which spiritual gifts, the most evidently supernatural or the less supernatural, has it been taught were done away with?"

"The ones that are the most supernatural."

"Why do you think that is?" asked Pastor John.

"I don't know. I haven't spent any time thinking about it."

"The gifts that can operate without the supernatural aspect permeating them have been taught and embraced by the mainstream denominations because they are straightforward, easy to manifest, and even if your relationship with Jesus is lacking or deficient, you can still, to a certain degree, walk in or participate in those particular gifts. Some of them would be the gift of hospitality, ministry, teaching, exhortation, giving, and mercy. But the gifts that are very supernaturally oriented can only operate if your relationship with Jesus is very strong, close, and intimate. They operate by your faith, not by anyone else's, and so for people to escape the dilemma of not manifesting the power gifts, or the so-called sign gifts, it's been taught that they have been done away with, or that we no longer need them. It's nothing but a scapegoat to explain the absence of such powerful gifts and to relieve their own accountability. Do you remember the great commission in Mark 16?"

"Yes, I do," answered Pastor Wilson.

Pastor John turned his Bible to the Gospel of Mark and began to read. "'Go into all the world and preach the gospel to every creature. He who believes and is baptized will be saved; but he who does not believe will be condemned. And these signs will follow those who believe: In My name they will cast out demons; they will speak with new tongues; they will take up serpents; and if they drink anything deadly, it will by no means hurt them; they will lay hands on the sick, and they will recover.'

"So then, after the Lord had spoken to them, He was received up into heaven, and sat down at the right hand of God. And they went out and preached everywhere, the Lord working with them and confirming the word through the accompanying signs. Amen.'

"Jesus said, 'these signs will follow those who believe.' Do you believe?"

"Of course."

"Do any of these signs follow you in your ministry?"

"No. I've seen a few people get well after prayer but nothing of the miraculous that you're teaching about," answered Pastor Wilson.

"If a new believer came to you and, in all innocence, asked why these signs aren't manifesting in your ministry, would your answer be 'Because I don't believe in them' or 'Because the Bible says they were only for the early church'? The answer that removes responsibility from you is the second one, 'The Bible says they were only for the early church.' This answer keeps you from being accountable for your own level of belief. So, it is possible that this Scripture in Mark points to the fact that Jesus' followers must believe in the operation of the gifts and also believe that they can perform the miraculous by trusting in Him and imitating the Master in all that He taught them. It comes down to this: those who believe will lay their hands on the sick because they believe—what?"

"They believe that the sick will be healed by Jesus."

"Right. But Jesus is in heaven, so how does the healing come, and by whom?" Pastor John was trying to stimulate their thinking by causing them to come up with an answer.

"The power to heal comes from the Holy Spirit who is Jesus' stand-in," answered one of the other pastors.

"Yes, it does. When Jesus was here in the flesh, how did He heal, by what power?"

"The same. By the power of the Holy Spirit."

"At that time then, who was the Holy Spirit a stand-in for, if Jesus was already present?" asked Pastor John.

"What do you mean?"

"In other words, if the power to heal comes from and through the Holy Spirit, whether it is then or now, and yet

He is now a stand-in for Jesus, who is not here in the flesh, then according to what you've said, how could the Holy Spirit be a stand-in for Jesus when He was here in the flesh? That doesn't make sense. It would stand to reason that if the Holy Spirit is a stand-in now, then He was also a stand-in when Jesus was here. If that is correct, then who was the Holy Spirit standing in for, both then and now?"

"God the Father," exclaimed Pastor Wilson.

"Right. God sent the Holy Spirit to provide the power for His servant Jesus to walk in. In the same way, the Holy Spirit is given to all of God's servants to carry out His desires. Remember that after Jesus came out of the water at His baptism, the Holy Spirit came down and alighted upon Him. From that moment, Jesus began to exercise power and authority over creation. In the Book of Acts, chapter 2, the Holy Spirit entered the upper room as a mighty rushing wind, and became as divided tongues of fire, and rested upon each of those present in the room. And they were all filled with the Holy Spirit and began to speak with other tongues, or languages, as the Spirit gave them utterance. Jesus had told His disciples to wait in Jerusalem until they were endued with power from on high, which of course was the coming of the Holy Spirit, whom Jesus referred to as the Helper. If they were to receive power from the Holy Spirit, to be witnesses for Jesus, then wouldn't we also be endued with the same power to be witnesses for Jesus to our generation?"

"Yes. But back then they didn't have the completed Bible to teach from or to substantiate the accuracy or truthfulness of their doctrines."

"That's right. But what good does our Bible do us today if the people that we are witnessing to don't believe that it's true or that it's actually from God? We can quote to the

Jim Norman

unbeliever all the Scriptures we want, but that won't make
him believe that the Bible is true," said Pastor John.

"I see your point. We must have the power that Jesus
talked about to be an effective witness."

Pastor John, looking at all of them, was quick to add,
"Don't get me wrong on this point. As believers, we all
have the indwelling Spirit to help us witness about Jesus,
and when people are ready to believe in God, the Holy
Spirit is there to draw them into the Kingdom. The Lord
can still use us as His witnesses, but when we are endued
with the power that is described in the Book of Acts, we
become a much more effective witness. Think about this
statement: A student who is perfectly trained will be just
like his Master. Jesus said this to His disciples to reveal to
them that He wanted them to be just like Him. He trained
them for over three years to do everything that He was
doing, including the signs and miracles. The proof of that
is throughout the Book of Acts. Here's another thought:
Paul learned to walk by faith, to pray for the sick, and to
trust in the power of the Holy Spirit without walking with
Jesus in the flesh as all the other disciples had learned to
do. He learned it the same way that we have to learn it
today, by developing and growing in his relationship with
Jesus, studying His Word, and listening to His instructions
through the Holy Spirit. Everything that Paul had is available to us today, through the same Holy Spirit that supplied him and who also supplied Jesus."

"So, you can see that God is doing a mighty work, and
in these last days He is raising up and purifying His
Church so that He may present to Himself a glorious
Church, without spot or wrinkle. In Ephesians 3:8-11,
Paul says that God's intent is that His manifold wisdom

would now be made known by the Church to the principalities and powers in the heavenly places. As the principalities and powers have watched throughout the last two thousand years, they've seen the church start in power and Glory and also watched as Satan infiltrated the Church and introduced false doctrines and heresies, to lead the Church into chaos. But now they are watching as God is restoring His Church to its true design and function, overcoming all of Satan's schemes and deceptions, showing forth His wisdom and Glory within His people. The ultimate outcome of His wisdom will be that His Church will be full of His Glory, walking in all of His power at the last day, by faith overcoming all of the power of the enemy. This is where we are headed."

"All right, Pastor. I believe every word that you've spoken, and I think all of the others here also believe." Pastor Wilson paused to look at his friends and associates to see them nodding in affirmation. "Now, how do we get these things that you've told us about? Will you pray for us to be baptized with the Spirit as the early disciples were?"

"Yes, I will. Please stand up." Taking him by the hand and looking him in the eyes, Pastor John began. "Repeat after me. Lord God, I ask for You to baptize me with Your Spirit…to endue me with power to be a witness for Jesus…to lead me and guide me in all good works. In Jesus' name, amen." As Pastor Wilson finished speaking, the Holy Spirit came upon him and he began to speak in another language, and when he realized what he was doing, tears came to his eyes and began to cascade down his cheeks.

Pastor John stepped over to JoAnn, led her through the same prayer with the same outcome, and then did the same for the other three pastors. As they were all speaking in tongues as the Spirit gave utterance, Pastor John began to sing a song of worship to the Lord, also in another language. There was a beat and a tempo to the song that it caused it to sound beautiful. When he began, the Holy Spirit moved on Mac, prompting him to sing the interpretation of the song, and so, interrupting the pastor, he interpreted the first verse, and they then took turns singing, first the verse in tongues and then the interpretation.

"What a Holy Land; what a Holy Land; what a Holy Land there before you.

"A crown of thorns about His head, a wounded side, nail prints in His hands and feet, bearing sin for me.

"How could You give Your only Son? How could You give Your precious One? How could You love me so?

"But You had this plan long ago, ages and ages past. You saw this when mankind did fall; You knew Your own dear plan.

"And I celebrate, and I celebrate, and I celebrate in Your faithfulness, and I celebrate, and I celebrate, and I celebrate in the faithfulness of the Lamb.

"He could have called them; He could have called them; He could have called ten thousand angels. He could have called them; He could have called them; He could have called them, but He didn't for me.

"The joy was before Him; the cross was before Him; He knew the outcome of victory; He knew what would happen; He knew the Father's Glory would raise Him up from death's grave.

"And in my life, and in my life, there may be

things that look of death, but God's great Glory in the Lamb within me will bring resurrection power."

The others all remained quiet when they realized what was happening, listening intently to the beautiful song as it unfolded. They could feel the power operating in the gift of tongues and interpretation and quickly realized how those two gifts could edify the body in ways that preaching could never do.

As the meeting was drawing to a close, Pastor Wilson asked if Pastor John could come back to his church and teach his congregation about the Holy Spirit and His gifts.

"I will have to seek the Lord first, but if I can't, Mac here is my right-hand man and would certainly be able to. If you don't mind?" replied Pastor John.

"If you recommend him, we would be glad to have him," answered Pastor Wilson.

"Let us get back to you on that. Is there any certain date that you'd like this to happen?"

"I'd like it to be at a Sunday morning service so that the majority of my people can be here to receive it and also as soon as you can arrange it. What has happened here today has changed my entire outlook on God's will for His people and the importance of all of the gifts of the Spirit working in our midst, and I'd like my people to have the choice to receive this move of God as quickly as possible." Pastor Wilson was very frank with his reasons to enlist Pastor John's teaching abilities.

"Okay. I've got your number, and I'll give you a call as soon as I know something. I also want to thank you for this time that we've had together; Mac and I have both been so blessed by our time with you."

"I'm sure that our blessings have been greater," replied Pastor Wilson. With tears beginning to moisten his eyes and with a catch in his voice, he continued, "I'm sure that I speak for all of us when I say that our relationship with Jesus has now gone beyond our wildest hopes and dreams. What you have shared with us today has changed our entire walk with God and will bring us into a greater unity within the Body of Christ. Thank you, Pastor, for coming." He stepped up to Pastor John, and they embraced. Pulling back from him, he added, "I love you."

"I love you, too, Robert."

Afterwards, they all took their turns embracing one another and pledging their love for each other before parting.

CHAPTER
TWENTY-THREE

After talking things over with Mac and praying about ministering at Pastor Wilson's church, it was arranged for Mac to go and give the message on the following Sunday morning. Linda would also be there with him to help with the ministering after the Word was taught, and the Lord wanted Joe and Peggy to go with them, also. They were ready to begin stepping out to help with ministry to prepare them for going out on their own when the Lord called them.

The four of them were meeting with the prayer group every morning that week to prepare their hearts and to seek God in a corporate setting for His leading and instruction. The most important thing about the upcoming meeting was to have God's Presence in the service to touch the hearts and minds of the people who would be receiving teachings contrary to the ways that they'd been taught for many years. Only God would be able to pull it off and make it successful, so they had to be one with Him in Spirit to be able to follow all of His leadings.

Pastor Wilson's congregation had been notified of the special speaker from Victory Fellowship, and many of them were looking forward to the meeting, for they had all been hearing the magnificent stories about God's moving in the miraculous. Although they had always been taught against looking for signs and wonders, still, deep in their hearts, they wanted to believe that God would still move among His people as He did in the New Testament writings. There were still a few skeptics left, but they were willing to listen to what Mac had to say.

During the praise and worship, Mac, Linda, Joe, and Peggy sat in the front row next to Pastor Wilson and his wife JoAnn. As the worship progressed, the Spirit of the Lord began to be felt by the people, softly at first, but as the people began to respond to Him, His Presence began to grow and tears began to fall as hearts were melting before Him.

Pastor Wilson made his way up onto the stage and began to praise the Lord, tears streaming down his face. Most of his people had never seen him shed tears before and were moved to tears themselves as they watched his heartfelt worship before the Lord. When he had the tears under control, he raised his hands to quiet the people. With microphone in hand, he began to talk about his experience with Pastor John and Mac.

"Some of you have heard my testimony about my healing firsthand, and most of the rest of you have gotten the story from others. This morning, I'm going to relate to all of you what happened to me last week, and then I'm going to introduce our speaker to you for this morning's message." Pastor Wilson looked around at his people, the love of God in his heart as he told them of the healing of his fingers and being baptized by the Spirit of God.

"Pastor John Logan and Mac Henderson revealed to me the heart of God toward His people and also His plan for these last days to bring all of His people into the unity of the faith. I believe with all of my heart that what they shared with me is the absolute truth from the Word of God, and God's Spirit within me bears witness to it, also. This morning we have with us Mac and Linda Henderson and their friends Joe and Peggy Leland." Signaling for them to stand, he continued, "Mac is here to share with us the Word of the Lord. Please give them a warm welcome."

As the congregation began to clap, Mac walked up onto the stage and the two of them embraced. When they parted, Pastor Wilson spoke. "Mac, feel at liberty to share all that the Lord has instructed you."

"Thank you, Pastor Wilson. I want you to know that I'm very grateful to you for inviting us here."

Pastor Wilson nodded his head with a smile and then went to his seat.

"Good morning! It's good to be here. I believe that the Lord has already been touching your hearts during our worship time." There were several heads nodding in affirmation and also a couple of voices chiming in. "Let's open this in a word of prayer. Heavenly Father, we come before You this morning with sincere hearts, seeking Your face and Your Presence. I thank You, Lord, for visiting us as we worshipped, and we praise You for Your abundant goodness and mercy. We ask that You reveal Your Word and Your ways to Your people that we may know You in all of Your Glory. As we draw closer to You, draw closer to us, that we will be changed from Glory to Glory. In Jesus' name, we pray, amen.

"Many of you have heard stories from friends or acquaintances of what's been happening at my home church,

Victory Fellowship. There are several churches in the tri-county area that have been seeing God move among them with signs, wonders, and miracles. There have been many healing miracles of long-standing sicknesses and diseases, and even injuries to the body have been healed. I'm here to tell you that all the stories are true. I've seen them and have even participated in their operation. The Lord is good, and His mercy endures forever. His ways are so much higher than our ways, but now, in these last days, He is changing our old ways to line up with His ways. He wants us to lay down our old traditions, seeking His face and finding our answers in Him. The disciples of Jesus went through the same thing. They had to let go of religious thinking that was promoted and taught by the religious crowd of the day and allow Jesus to renew their thinking and their ways so that they could be effective in the advancement of the Kingdom of God.

"Over the centuries, leaders in the church lost their connection with the Spirit of God, and in so doing, they lost the Teacher and Counselor that Jesus sent. They also lost the power of God that the early disciples walked in. To explain the loss of the supernatural working of the Spirit of God, the leaders had to come up with explanations for why it was so. And so, the natural mind took over the operation of the church. In these last days, God is restoring to the church all of the Glory that she began with. All of the gifts of the Spirit are being renewed and walked in by those who are pressing in to God like never before. God, in His great wisdom and mercy, was the one that designed all of the spiritual gifts and their operation. He designed them for specific reasons, to mature the body of Christ and to equip the saints for work of ministry until we all come to the unity of the faith and of the knowledge of the Son of God, to a perfect man, to the measure of the stature of the fullness of Christ. You will find these things in Ephesians chapter 4 and 1 Corinthians chapter 12.

"The gifts of the Spirit are a teaching in themselves, so I'm going to take a look at the teachings of Jesus. In the fourteenth chapter of John, beginning at the seventh verse, Jesus says, '"If you had known Me, you would have known My Father also; and from now on you know Him and have seen Him." Philip said to Him, "Lord, show us the Father, and it is sufficient for us." Jesus said to him, "Have I been with you so long, and yet you have not known Me, Philip? He who has seen Me has seen the Father; so how can you say, 'Show us the Father'? Do you not believe that I am in the Father, and the Father in Me? The words that I speak to you I do not speak on My own authority; but the Father who dwells in Me does the works. Believe Me that I am in the Father and the Father in Me, or else believe Me for the sake of the works themselves. Most assuredly, I say to you, he who believes in Me, the works that I do he will do also; and greater works than these he will do, because I go to My Father. And whatever you ask in My name, that I will do, that the Father may be glorified in the Son. If you ask anything in My name, I will do it.'"

"If we ask Jesus today, 'What is the Father like?' He would say to us, 'Read about what I was like in the Gospels and you will see what God is truly like. For if you've seen Me, You've seen the Father.' God says of Himself, in Malachi chapter 3, verse 6, 'For I am the Lord, I do not change.' And in the book of Hebrews, the thirteenth chapter, verse 8, the writer tells us, 'Jesus Christ is the same yesterday, today, and forever.' Also, the fifteenth verse of the first chapter of Colossians says 'He is the image of the invisible God.' Did

Jesus show mercy and forgiveness? So does God. Did Jesus have compassion for the people? So does God. Did Jesus always do good? So does God. Did Jesus heal the lame, sick, and diseased? So does God. God has not changed, nor has Jesus. No matter how long it's been since Jesus walked the earth, He has not changed. He is still the Healer. He is still the Teacher. He is still the lover of our souls. He is still willing to heal the sick. 'If you can believe, all things are possible to him who believes.'"

Looking at the congregation, Mac's eyes were drawn to a young man in a wheelchair. Mac, observing him intently and seeing that he had faith to be healed, said in a loud voice, "Stand up straight on your feet!" And he leaped and walked and began praising Jesus for His goodness. As tears were falling, he ran to Mac and wrapped his arms around him in great joy. Others began to clap and cheer and many were crying as they witnessed God's great mercy and power for the first time in their lives. They all knew the young man that had received his healing, that he had been completely paralyzed from the waist down for two years, so it was a very emotional and profound healing.

Looking out at the people, Mac was moved with compassion. Turning to look at Pastor Wilson, Mac saw a huge grin and tears running down his cheeks. Looking back at the people, Mac began to pray for God's wisdom.

"If God is dealing with you on anything in your life, repent of it right now and believe that He will meet you with mercy and compassion, and when you feel Him drawing you to the altar, don't hesitate to come forward to receive your healing." At his last word, many people stood up and began to walk forward to go to their knees at the altar and begin to cry out to God for forgiveness and mercy. One older gentleman, also in a wheelchair, rolled down to the front, maneuvering the automated machine between those kneeling and standing, moving in as close to Mac as he could. Linda walked up to stand beside Mac; Joe and Peggy stepped up to stand behind the ones that were going to be ministered to. Pastor Wilson and his associate Ed Collins also moved up to help catch those who might fall over under the power of God.

Looking around at the people who were still at their seats, Mac could see that there were many that were still doubtful at what was taking place. He knew that it would be hard for some of them to look beyond their long held doctrines and beliefs and accept the fact that God was indeed moving among them with His Spirit. As he turned his attention back to the ones who were seeking a touch from God, he could feel the anointing of the Spirit within him growing beyond what he had ever experienced. Glancing at Linda, he could see that she also was feeling that same anointing, the excitement in her eyes shining forth out of a solemn face.

"Stop! You're not welcome here."

"Leave us alone." A second voice chimed in, and then a third voice from the back of the sanctuary could be heard.

"What have you to do with us?"

Mac turned to look at the man that was yelling at them to stop. Immediately, he heard the voice of the Spirit say, "*He has a demon. Joe will handle it.*" As the Spirit of God finished speaking, Mac watched as Joe and Peggy turned to look at the man and began walking toward him. As the gap between them closed, the man began to cower and murmur, speaking unintelligibly. Pastor Wilson was moving further back to the second speaker, recognizing the voice of one of his deacons of long-standing.

"In the name of Jesus, come out of him!" The authority in Joe's voice was unmistakable. Immediately, the man crumpled to the floor; quiet reigned within the sanctuary. As the spectators watched, Joe and Peggy knelt beside the man, took hold of his arms, and raised him to his feet. Tears began to fall from his face as he felt the freedom of the Spirit, his arms surrounding Joe in a tight embrace.

All eyes turned to follow Pastor Wilson as he approached Greg Landau, whom they all knew but few were close to. A few of them noticed the third speaker ducking out the door of the sanctuary before he could be addressed. The buzz of voices began to override the quiet, excitement and faith building in the air.

"No! No! Stay away from me! You have no right!" He also began to cower as Pastor Wilson moved up to him.

"*Cast out the religious spirit.*" Pastor Wilson heard the still small voice within him and looked at Greg for only a moment before speaking.

"I have all the right, and you have none. Go! In Jesus' name!"

Everyone was astonished to see the twisted hatred and malevolence on Greg's face as Pastor Wilson finished speaking and were equally surprised as they watched the transformation of his face from evil to innocence. Collapsing to the floor, he lay there for only a moment before stirring and raising a bewildered face to Pastor Wilson.

"What happened? Why am I on the floor?" asked Greg in a shaky voice.

Pastor Wilson, taking him by the hands, replied, "I don't know how to tell you this, other than that there was a religious spirit in you that seemed to be controlling you. The Spirit of the Lord told me to cast it out, and now you're free." They both turned and walked up to the front to stand before Mac and Linda.

As Greg stopped, he looked up at Mac and asked, "Could you pray for me the way you did for Pastor Wilson?"

Mac looked back at him with love and compassion. "Yes, Greg. I'd be glad to." Placing one hand on his shoulder and taking his hand with the other, Mac began to pray, "Repeat after Me. Heavenly Father, I thank You for Your goodness and mercy here today...and I ask, Father, to be baptized with Your Spirit...that I may know You to the depths of my being...to be endued with power to be a witness of Your goodness and grace...in Jesus' name. Amen." As Greg finished speaking, he could feel the Holy Spirit on him, infilling him with His Presence and as tears began to flow, the people could hear him speaking in another language. As soon as Mac placed his hand on Greg's head, he began to fall backwards, falling into the loving arms of his pastor, to be gently laid on the floor.

The Presence of God was almost overwhelming, something that most of them had never experienced. They all began to cry out for mercy and for the baptism of the Spirit. Mac turned to look at Joe and Peggy. "Start on that end and pray with them for the baptism." Nodding their heads, they immediately made their way to the other side of the crowd, and each began to lead someone in prayer, while Mac and Linda turned their attention to the ones at the front who had come forward for healing.

"*Start with Bob in the wheelchair. MS.*" Mac stepped up to Bob and put a hand on his arm that was resting on the chair. Linda placed a hand on his other arm.

"Bob, Jesus paid the price for your complete healing while He was on the cross. He has borne our griefs and carried our sorrows. He was wounded for our transgressions and bruised for our iniquities. The chastisement for our peace was upon Him, and by His stripes we are healed." Bob could feel the Holy Spirit on him. And then it felt like warm oil was being poured on his head and running down his face until his whole body was engulfed in the heat of it. Feeling was starting to come back to places that had been numb for a long time. Linda reached down to his feet and lifted them from the footrests, pushing them aside and placing his feet on the floor.

Looking intently at his face, Mac could see that he was receiving the Word. Stepping back a little, he spoke again. "Bob, Jesus has healed you. Rise up and walk!" Most of the congregation were watching and listening, with expectancy and hope that their friend would be healed of the sickness that had slowly destroyed his body before their very eyes. Bob leaned forward to gather his strength in preparation of pushing himself up with his hands on the arms of his wheelchair. A hush fell over the sanctuary as he began to rise, slowly at first, and as he moved higher and higher out of the chair, he began to gain speed until he was standing fully upright, completely free of the bondage of the chair that had become his home away from home.

Mac, stepping further back from Bob, held up his arms, saying, "Come!" With a smile, Mac waited as Bob took a slow step forward, then a faster step, and a faster one still, until Bob stepped into his arms. Laughing and crying, they embraced for a long moment as the congregation began to cry and to cheer at the same time, their hearts refreshed at the moving of the Holy Spirit in their midst. They were experiencing God's grace, mercy, and compassion in a way they had never seen before, the same way that Jesus ministered to the people.

Mac and Linda started down the line, laying hands on people, praying, prophesying, and healing all who came forward. Once the people accepted that the Spirit of the Lord was present and doing the work, they all received the baptism of the Spirit and spoke with other tongues. The joy of the Lord was in the sanctuary, people laughing as much as they were crying, giving thanks to God for a new and living faith stirring their hearts to new heights.

——Here ends part one of *Before the Trumpet Blows*——

ADDENDUM

1. PRAYING AND SPEAKING IN TONGUES

Praying in tongues, or other languages, which you have not learned is a gift or ability that God has given believers to use throughout their walk with Him. The Bible shows that all of the apostles received that ability when they were baptized with His Spirit on the day of Pentecost in the Book of Acts, chapter 2. But also note that there were about 120 people present that day who were all baptized with God's Spirit and spoke in other languages, not just the apostles but the laymen and helpers too. It was a widespread occurrence in the early church and throughout the Book of Acts, which may span up to about sixty years. There was never any directive that this gift or ability for all believers, upon their being baptized with the Holy Spirit, was to ever come to an end before Jesus comes for us. It is a supernatural gift to help us, teach us, and edify us. It is no wonder that the enemy hates it so much that he has caused division over it in the body of Christ. If anyone says otherwise, you should question their motive behind their opinion.

The big question is not what is tongues, or even if it was a spiritual gift in the New Testament writings, but rather, is it still in operation today? If you have a clear understanding of what it is and what it was for, then you will see that there would be no reason for its ending before Jesus comes for us.

The first occurrence of being baptized with the Spirit and speaking in tongues is found in Acts 2:1-4.

> *When the day of Pentecost had fully come, they were all with one accord in one place. And suddenly there came a sound from heaven, as of a rushing mighty wind, and it filled the whole house where they were sitting. Then there appeared to them divided tongues, as of fire, and one sat upon each of them. And they were all filled with the Holy Spirit and began to speak with other tongues, as the Spirit gave them utterance.*

Because of the sound of the rushing wind, within minutes a crowd had gathered, made up of Jews from all around the world from other nations who were in town for the feast. And as the disciples went outside, the crowd heard them all speaking in their own languages, declaring the wonders of God. So at its inception, speaking in tongues was used as an evangelistic tool. During Peter's evangelistic discourse with the crowds, he made these statements: *"This Jesus God has raised up, of which we are all witnesses. Therefore being exalted to the right hand of God, and having received from the Father the promise of the Holy Spirit, He poured out this which you now see and hear"* (Acts 2:32-33), and *"Repent, and let everyone of you be baptized in the name of Jesus Christ for the*

*remission of sins; and you shall receive the gift of the Holy
Spirit. For the promise is to you and to your children, and to
all who are afar off, as many as the Lord our God will call"*
(Acts 2:38-39). What they saw was a bunch of excited, on-
fire believers; what they heard was everyone speaking in
other languages in a supernatural manner. Peter says this
same gift shall be given to all who believe, the speaking in
tongues included.

The next instance, Acts 8:14-18, says,

> *Now when the apostles who were at Jerusalem heard
> that Samaria had received the word of God, they sent
> Peter and John to them, who, when they had come
> down, prayed for them that they might receive the Holy
> Spirit. For as yet He had fallen upon none of them.
> They had only been baptized in the name of the Lord
> Jesus. Then they laid hands on them, and they received
> the Holy Spirit. And when Simon saw that through the
> laying on of the apostles' hands the Holy Spirit was
> given, he offered them money.*

When the believers were baptized with the Holy Spirit,
something happened in the physical realm that Simon could
see. The only thing that would have brought him to that
conclusion was to see them speaking in tongues. Notice also
that there are two different baptisms spoken of: being baptized in the name of Jesus, in water, and being baptized with
the Holy Spirit. Water baptism is performed by people, but
Jesus is the one who baptizes with the Holy Spirit. John the
Baptist says in Matthew 3:11, *"I indeed baptize you with
water unto repentance, but He who is coming after me is
mightier than I, whose sandals I am not worthy to carry. He
will baptize you with the Holy Spirit and fire."*

In the next account, the apostle Paul is baptized with the Spirit in Acts 9:17-18.

> *And Ananias went his way and entered the house; and laying his hands on him he said, 'Brother Saul, the Lord Jesus, who appeared to you on the road as you came, has sent me that you may receive your sight and be filled with the Holy Spirit.' Immediately there fell from his eyes something like scales, and he received his sight at once; and he arose and was baptized.*

To be filled with the Holy Spirit is to be baptized with the Spirit. The word *baptize* in the Greek means *to make whelmed,* according to *Strong's Exhaustive Concordance of the Bible,* # 907. And we all know that Paul said in 1 Corinthians 14:18, "*I thank my God I speak with tongues more than you all.*" According to all other evidence, Paul began his speaking in tongues when he was filled with the Holy Spirit.

Next in line is the account of Cornelius and his household in Acts 10:44-48.

> *While Peter was still speaking these words, the Holy Spirit fell upon all those who heard the word. And those of the circumcision who believed were astonished, as many as came with Peter, because the gift of the Holy Spirit had been poured out on the Gentiles also. For they heard them speak with tongues and magnify God. Then Peter answered, "Can anyone forbid water, that these should not be baptized who have received the Holy Spirit just as we have?" And he commanded them to be baptized in the name of the Lord.*

Again, two different baptisms. The converts were baptized with the Holy Spirit, with the outward manifestation of speaking in tongues, and then were baptized in water in the name of Jesus.

The Jewish believers with Peter were astonished that the Holy Spirit had been poured out on the Gentiles (people other than Jews), that they had received the same gift as themselves. They knew it was the same gift because they heard them speaking in tongues and magnifying God. Peter also made this statement in Acts 11:15-17,

> *And as I began to speak, the Holy Spirit fell upon them, as upon us at the beginning. Then I remembered the word of the Lord, how He said, "John indeed baptized with water, but you shall be baptized with the Holy Spirit." If therefore God gave them the same gift as He gave us when we believed on the Lord Jesus Christ, who was I that I could withstand God?*

Speaking in tongues, or other languages, was the outward manifestation of the baptism of the Holy Spirit that confirmed to the Jews that the Gentiles had indeed received the same gift as them.

Then, in Acts chapter 19, when Paul entered Ephesus, he ran into some disciples that had believed in Jesus but had not been baptized in the name of Jesus but only with the baptism of John the Baptist. They had listened to Apollos teach about the Lord, but for some reason, at that time, Apollos didn't have the complete story about salvation. Apollos was mighty in the Scriptures and taught about the Lord accurately, but he only knew of John's baptism of repentance (Acts 18:25), not the baptism of the Holy Spirit. But when Paul's companions, Aquila and Priscilla, heard Apollos teaching about Jesus in the synagogue, they pulled him aside and explained to him the way of the Lord more accurately.

And soon after his meeting with Aquila and Priscilla, he left Ephesus and sailed to Achaia and Corinth to preach about Jesus with a new boldness.

But apparently the disciples that Paul found in Ephesus had previously been instructed by Apollos before he had learned the fullness of the Good News from Aquila and Priscilla, which is why they had no knowledge of the Holy Spirit or even that there was one.

What was it that Paul may have noticed about them that he was led to ask them if they had received the Holy Spirit? Possibly, that he had not heard them praying or speaking in tongues? But he did know that they believed in Jesus, for the Bible says that he found some disciples, after which he asked them if they had received the Holy Spirit when they had believed, indicating that somehow he knew by their actions or talk that they were already Christians.

When he explained to them about Jesus, they were baptized in the name of Jesus; then he laid his hands on them; the Holy Spirit came on them; and they began to speak in tongues and to prophesy. It was as if Paul was saying, "Being baptized in water is right and good, but there is also the baptism in the Spirit that you shouldn't miss out on. So here it is." Paul believed it was of the utmost importance to the believer to receive it, for after finding out that these disciples were indeed believing in Jesus, his first thought and question for them was about the Holy Spirit.

Speaking in tongues is a supernatural, divine gift of God for believers. To say that it is not is to say that God didn't know what He was doing, or that you have more wisdom on the matter, or that you believe that God made a mistake. Apparently, God didn't think to consult with any man before He made His plans.

But it is God who designed the gift, not man, and it is His wisdom that placed it in the body of Christ to help His children to succeed in their walk with Him. Just because it can be abused does not mean that we do away with it completely. In the twelfth chapter of 1 Corinthians, it says that God placed all the parts or members in the body. All the parts have a function to make the body work properly. And the parts are not just the person individually but the spiritual gift that God has called him to walk in. Just because one part doesn't want another part in the body doesn't mean we cut off that part. That's like the working of miracles part saying to the speaking in tongues part, "We don't need or want you because you sound goofy." God designed the parts by His wisdom to enable the body to function the way He wants it. If there are people who don't like the way God designed His body, with all the functioning gifts, then they are passing judgment on God's wisdom and His will. They are walking on dangerous ground.

There are several uses for speaking or praying in tongues that are listed in 1 Corinthians 14. In verses 2 through 5 it says,

> *For he who speaks in a tongue does not speak to men but to God, for no one understands him; however, in the spirit he speaks mysteries. But he who prophesies speaks edification and exhortation and comfort to men. He who speaks in a tongue edifies himself, but he who prophesies edifies the church. I wish you all spoke with tongues, but even more that you prophesied; for he who prophesies is greater than he who speaks in tongues, unless indeed he interprets, that the church may receive edification.*

In these verses it shows that speaking in tongues is speaking to God, speaking mysteries in the spirit, edifying oneself, and if there is an interpretation, it can be edifying to the church. Kenneth Hagin used to say that prophesying was equal to a dime and speaking in tongues was equal to a nickel. But the interpretation of tongues was also equal to a nickel. Either tongues or the interpretation of tongues by itself would never amount to prophesying, but the two together would be equal to prophesying. Paul is saying in this last verse that prophesying is no longer greater than tongues if there is an interpretation.

Also, in verse 6 it goes on, "*But now, brethren, if I come to you speaking with tongues, what shall I profit you unless I speak to you either by revelation, by knowledge, by prophesying, or by teaching?*" So, if there is an interpretation, speaking in tongues can bring revelation, knowledge, prophecy, and teaching. In verse 13, Paul says, "*Therefore let him who speaks in a tongue pray that he may interpret.*" In this way is the church edified.

Paul also says, in verses 14 through 17,

> *For if I pray in a tongue, my spirit prays, but my understanding is unfruitful. What is the conclusion then? I will pray with the spirit, and I will also pray with the understanding. I will sing with the spirit, and I will also sing with the understanding. Otherwise, if you bless with the spirit, how will he who occupies the place of the uninformed say "Amen" at your giving of thanks, since he does not understand what you say? For you indeed give thanks well, but the other is not edified.*

God made a way for our spirits to pray! Imagine that. We can pray in tongues, and we can also sing in tongues. We can give thanks to God in tongues. So, you see, there are many uses of speaking or praying in tongues.

Speaking in tongues in the church service, which Paul is mostly talking about in this chapter, is a ministry gift that not everyone is called to do, just like not all are called to be apostles, prophets, or teachers. Not everyone is called to be an evangelist, but everyone is called to evangelize. Some gifts you can walk in occasionally although you aren't called to that ministry gift full-time. But all believers, who have been baptized in the Holy Spirit, have the ability to pray in tongues. Remember also, that he who speaks or prays in a tongue edifies himself. The Greek word for *edify* means *to build up*. We build up our spirits when we pray in tongues. And in Jude verse 20, *"But you, beloved, building yourselves up on your most holy faith, praying in the Holy Spirit."* If praying in tongues is something that God designed for His people to use to edify themselves, then shouldn't we, today, be able to participate in that same function? Do we need edification any less than the early disciples did?

Remember, the apostle Paul said, *"Do not forbid to speak with tongues"* (1 Corinthians 14:39). He said this to the believers in the Corinthian church whom he had just corrected on its use. So, although there was some abuse of the speaking in tongues, Paul ended his rebuke and correction with *"Do not forbid to speak with tongues."* This means that the gift is important enough to keep around. That was and is the way God wants it.

Of course, there are some Bible teachers of today who think that they know God's ways and His Word better than anyone else, and since they don't speak in tongues, and maybe because they don't see any reason for speaking in tongues now, they have decided that speaking in tongues in today's church is the working of the devil. They are trying to understand a spiritual working with their carnal mind, and

295

since they can't, they try to explain it away. As it says in 1 Corinthians 2:14-16:

> *But the natural man does not receive the things of the Spirit of God, for they are foolishness to him; nor can he know them, because they are spiritually discerned. But he who is spiritual judges all things, yet he himself is rightly judged by no one. For "who has known the mind of the Lord that he may instruct Him?" But we have the mind of Christ.*

The Bible teachers that say speaking in tongues is of Satan are so far from the truth. Isn't that like the Pharisees saying to Jesus, "You cast out demons by the power of Satan"? If speaking in tongues is a gift of God and they are ascribing it to Satan, then do those people who teach against it even know our God?

We all need to start seeking our God with our whole heart with complete sincerity so that we know His voice and His ways. We need to put aside pride and be willing to accept God totally on His terms, not according to the way we think He ought to be. We need to begin to pull together as the one body that He designed us to be so that we can begin to accomplish the task that He has assigned to us. We will not fulfill that task without walking in His divine power. He said that we would be endued with power from on high when the Holy Spirit came. Well, He is already here now, so let's take our places in the final battle.

2. Satan's Schemes to Prevent Our Victory

As we've seen earlier, God is a God of goodness and grace; He does not desire to hold back any good thing from

His people (Psalm 84:11). He revealed this fact in the ministry of Jesus. If you want to know what God is like, study the life and actions of Jesus. He said, "If you've seen me, you've seen the Father." He is the exact representation of God the Father.

If we have not been receiving the blessing of God in our lives, it's not because God doesn't want to bless us. The Word of God is abundantly clear on that. Psalm 84:11 says *"For the LORD God is a sun and shield; The LORD will give grace and glory; no good thing will he withhold From those who walk uprightly."* The enemy knows the ways and the means that God Himself has ordained, in which we will obtain our victory, and he will try to do everything that he can to prevent us from receiving God's goodness; to lead us astray in our doctrines and our thinking. If he can get us to think that God doesn't bless His people in our physical bodies or in our finances, then we will have no basis for believing by faith for God's intervention. And again the enemy has won the battle.

When Abraham talked with God and found out that he would have his own child to leave an inheritance to, it took him many years to finally be *fully persuaded* that God was able to accomplish the impossible in his life. Until the time that he was *fully persuaded*, he had his eyes and thinking on the fact of his and Sarah's ages and the fact that Sarah had a barren womb even during her childbearing years. Once he got past the doubt and unbelief and became fully persuaded that God was able to perform what He had promised, no matter what the circumstances, Sarah became pregnant and bore to Abraham a son, whom they named Isaac. In the same way, we must get our eyes and thinking off of our impossibility and onto God's ability.

Before Abraham became fully convinced of God's ability to accomplish His promise, nothing happened. The promise still stood, but there wasn't any evidence for its fulfillment. But when he got to the point of truly believing the promise of God, then it came to pass.

It is the same way for us today. We must be fully convinced that God is able and willing to fulfill all the promises that He has made to His people. But the tactic of the enemy is to raise doubts that God has even made a promise to us, whether it be a promise of healing or health, or financial provision, or even a promise of salvation. How can we believe for His fulfillment of a promise if we don't know about the promise or we don't know if the promise is for us? Many Bible teachers today will say, "That promise is not for us today," or "That promise only applies to the Israelites," or "That's not what that promise means." When we hear about a particular promise and we want to believe it because it is a good promise, and then we hear from a prominent Bible teacher, "That promise wasn't made to us today," then the enemy has caused enough doubt about the promise that we cannot receive it by faith. We have to be fully persuaded that the promise is for us and God is able to fulfill it, before we will actually receive it. If we are not, then the enemy has won the battle. But remember this: 2 Corinthians 1:20 says, *"For all the promises of God in Him are Yes, and in Him Amen, to the glory of God through us."* This means all the promises that God has made to His people throughout the Bible are Yes! and Amen! to us that are in Him (Jesus). Are we not God's people, grafted into the vine of His chosen, no longer strangers and foreigners to the covenants, and fellow citizens with the saints and members of the household of God?

In the account of the sower and the seed, Jesus makes it clear that the enemy comes right away when the Word of God is preached, to steal the seeds of truth that have been planted in the heart of the hearers. Many times, even though the Word is received with rejoicing, Satan is able to steal the Word before it has a chance to send down any roots into the heart. It doesn't matter if the Word spoken was about believing in Jesus for our initial salvation or any subsequent teaching on how to live for God; he tries to steal it all, every time.

When he is unable to steal the Word, he goes to stage two. The hearer receives the Word with rejoicing but endures only for a short time because the Word found no place for its roots. When *tribulation and persecution arises for the Word's sake*, immediately they stumble.

If Satan cannot drive out the Word with tribulation and persecution, he goes to stage three. When the Word has found root in the heart of the hearer, Satan tries to choke its fruitfulness and productivity with the cares of the world and the deceitfulness of riches. In other words, if he can keep us so busy trying to survive, striving for success, raising a family, and all the other things of life so that we can't spend the time with God that we need, then we *will not* be productive for the Kingdom of God. We may start out good and even have some productiveness for God, but we will come to the place that we aren't producing anything for God. Just like a plant in the garden surrounded by weeds, most of the nutrients and water will be sucked up by the weeds and very little will be left for the fruit of the plant. What nutrients and water the plant does get will keep the plant alive, but little else. In the same way, we will be saved, but we won't have any fruit for the Kingdom of God.

Jim Norman

When Satan has completely failed to steal, kill, or destroy the Word of God implanted in us, then that seed of the Word will produce a mighty harvest. Of course, that comes about through the cultivation and watering of that seed. The cultivation and watering is based in perseverance, continuing to do what you know to do, in spite of all the tactics of the enemy. That is what keeps the seed alive and growing until it's ready for the harvest. First the blade; then the head; after that the full grain in the head.

This principle applies to every teaching of the Bible. You can be saved for years, living your life for God, and one day you hear a teaching of God that you've never heard before, some aspect of God or His Word that had not been taught in your church, for whatever reason. You hear the teaching, accept it for the truth that it is, start to put it into practice, and the enemy will fight you on it. The more helpful the teaching is to your Christian walk, the greater the effort of the enemy to steal the teaching before it takes root. If it does take root, the greater the tribulation and persecution to drive it out of you or to choke it before it becomes fruitful. If you're not careful, you will begin to think you were misled and completely lose that particular teaching. That is why the Word of God says that you will be tried and tested, not by God but by the enemy, for he is trying to make that particular teaching null and void in your life. But if you hold onto that teaching, even through the testing, that is when you have attained maturity regarding that teaching.

So, fight the good fight of faith, believing God for His promises, not letting anyone or anything talk you out of God's goodness. As it says in Romans 8:32, "*He who did not spare His own Son, but delivered Him up for us all, how shall He not with Him also freely give us all things?*"

Read Deuteronomy 28, Jeremiah 29:11-13; 31:12-14; 32:38-41, and Psalm 91. These will get you started. The early disciples and apostles taught the goodness of God exclusively out of the Old Testament and Jesus' life and actions. Study and pray, building an intimacy with the Spirit of God so that you can know Him and trust Him to bless you.